THE MANAGER

The Manager

Robert A. Crampsey

HODDER AND STOUGHTON

LONDON SYDNEY AUCKLAND TORONTO

For V.R.C. — a very good manager.

British Library Cataloguing in Publication Data

Crampsey, Robert A.
 The Manager
 I. Title
 823′.914 [F]   PR6053.R3/

 ISBN 0 340 27569 3

1

Vi Black, plain of face and delectable of figure, bent low over the bottom drawer of the filing cabinet in the manager's office and, not for the first time, the manager wished either that she wouldn't or that skirts were longer. Face to face with the recently-married, twenty-year-old Vi, he had no difficulty concentrating upon keeping Barford Albion in the Fourth Division and thus in the Football League. The rear view was more disturbing.

He had to think of his own eighteen-year-old, Phyllis, to fight himself back to a chaste sense of responsibility. Despite his moral strivings he was relieved when Vi asked if she could pop out to the shops to collect, amongst other things, the club's electric kettle.

The small, wood-panelled office in the Jubilee ground smelt stale even at eleven o'clock in the morning. Not a typical morning admittedly, for Arsenal had been there the previous evening in an FA Cup-tie postponed from the Saturday. Fourteen thousand had come through the turnstiles and in the crisp sunlight of the late January morning the terraces were awash with toilet rolls, crisp bags and cigarette packets. Within the office the heavy tobacco smell and two rings left by glasses on the window-sill testified to last night's crush.

'Can I get you anything when I'm out, Mr Calderwood?'

Bob Calderwood looked lost briefly. Then, finding himself, he said pleasantly, 'Thanks, Vi, nothing. I've to see Les Frith in ten minutes or so. It'll do if you're back for twelve. There's a letter for the League that won't wait. Don't forget the kettle now.'

The high heels clacked away down the wooden passage then tapped briefly on the tiled floor of the main entrance. Wearily he stood up, looked round the office, then in the mirror. It was

5

hard to say which depressed him more. The office conveyed an air of desperation and failure. The chipped desk of aircraft carrier proportions was bare save for an old-fashioned black telephone and some letters. The manager's chair was incongruously expensive, black leather and swivelling chrome. There was only one other chair in the room, kitchen, nondescript, as a Services inventory would certainly have described it. On the wall behind the desk was a glassed photograph of an Albion side from the thirties, arms folded fiercely as they glowered out from beneath centre partings. The shin-guards inside their stockings gave them a square-legged appearance, while the string ties at the necks of their jerseys suggested the orphanage.

Above the photograph two pennants presented by Guernsey football teams were crossed in a vague way. A small open trophy cupboard contained one large, silver-plated cup of an astonishing ugliness.

Spare of figure, his dark hair grey-dusted, Bob Calderwood surveyed his reflection ruefully. At least he hadn't run to fat since he stopped playing, despite a twice-broken leg, at least some of the time he was his own boss. If he hadn't realised the high hopes of his early football mentors at Lanark, he had worked in the lower reaches of the Football League as player, coach and manager for twenty-six years. It wasn't too negligible a record.

He'd had his moments. Last night would have been counted one of them by most people. For an hour his boys, Fourth Division Albion, had worried Arsenal sick, before experience and superior fitness told their almost inevitable tale. His head told him it was a fine performance, his stomach that if they could have hung on twenty minutes longer . . .

Which brought him to Les Frith or, more exactly, would shortly bring Les to him. Well, if Frith was punctual he would be breaking the habit of a lifetime. He could save a few minutes by having a word with Joe Staples on the state of the goal area at the river end. The groundsman was on the far side, tramping in the divots missed under last night's lights. Even one missed was dicey in January, when a sudden frost could leave a pitch rutted and ridged. Calderwood walked out of the tunnel, his back to the gaunt main stand with its fretted face. The enclosure, 'Belle

Vue' as the locals called it in oblique compliment to Manchester's Zoo, stood smartly in its fresh paint.

On his way back across the field, Bob Calderwood became aware of a rhythmic tapping coming from his office. A glance through his window was enough to tell him that his visitor had arrived and was improving the shining hour.

With his back to the window, oblivious of Calderwood, of the world, the little forward was juggling with a dingily-white football as with total assurance he flicked it from toe to knee to thigh to head to shoulder then all the way back. The manager watched him for some time, half indulgent, half annoyed, then ostentatiously opened the door. With an admirable smoothness Les Frith tapped the disciplined ball neatly into the wicker wastepaper basket alongside the desk. His black and white track suit showed him to be stocky but masked the depth of his chest and the power of his shoulders.

Calderwood walked deliberately round the desk, sat down and tilted his chair backwards. His brusque manner sat ill with his open, pleasant face and brown eyes which, warm when he smiled, were now coldly remote.

'You're here then? Two-goal Les Frith in person?'

The young player, cocky, confident, smiled pleasantly. He had a better smile off-field than on, ever since he had left three front teeth behind in Hartlepool the previous March.

'Like the *Examiner* says, Boss, "Les Frith in the first half ran the mighty Arsenal defence ragged. A glancing header and a fierce right-foot shot put Barford two ahead and made a major Cup upset highly probable." '

Frith's habit of collecting all his press cuttings and quoting them verbatim was normally a source of amusement at Jubilee Park. Calderwood was unamused, but he kept his voice smooth as he said, 'Aye, that first half was as good a forty-five minute spell as you've ever played, Les.'

The youngster ducked his head, but accepted the compliment as his just due. 'Thanks, Boss. I . . .'

He was stopped dead by the ferocity of Calderwood's onslaught.

'But the bloody game lasts ninety minutes, Les. We'd have been as well with old Joe Staples out there in the second half and he's sixty.'

Les Frith reddened. Deny, agree or bluff? He opted for two and three.

'Yeah, that were funny, Boss. Ah can't explain it. Seemed to lose it all after half-time, y'know.'

Calderwood thrust his face across the desk as he came down in his chair. His voice was brutal, offensive. 'You lost it all the night before, two-goal Frith. With a four-letter word. E-N-I-D Schofield. Between midnight and 2 a.m. approximately.'

Frith continued to redden slowly.

'Who says that?' The question was belligerent.

Calderwood shook his head angrily. His voice, with its hard ch's and stressed r's bore down the lighter South Yorkshire tones of the player.

'Half the bloody town. Do you put your brains in pawn when the whistle goes for time up? You ought to know what this place is like. Sneeze in the shower after training and someone'll say "God Bless You" at the Town Hall. But our Leslie takes the chairman's niece to Lowmoor Dene two miles from here in his secondhand yellow Porsche — with a red diagonal stripe. It's like something out of bloody *Room at the Top*.' He paused exasperatedly, 'A book, Les. Surely you saw the bloody film?'

Frith shifted to the defensive.

'We weren't doing anything, Boss.'

'Then she's as thick as you are. Not a manjack'll believe you anyway. Half the crowd here any Saturday afternoon were *conceived* in Lowmoor Dene.' He got up abruptly, speaking with his back to Frith as he looked out of the window. 'Anyway I don't give a . . .' he deliberately hesitated on the word . . . 'damn what you and Enid were or weren't doing. You were out till all hours the night before an FA Cup-tie and now we're out of the Cup. We'll sit around till May now contemplating our navels.'

Conciliation was Frith's next tack.

'Aw, c'mon, Boss, be reasonable. It was Arsenal. They'd have tanked us any road . . .'

' 'Appen they might. 'Appen they might not.' Calderwood's seething rage led him to attempt a bad burlesque of the local accent. 'The thing is, we could have beaten that lot. Do you

8

know what that could have done for you, for me, for the town? I'll tell you. We could have drawn a non-League club, Burton, or Mansfield or Chester at home. Win that and we were four matches away from Wembley. Don't forget I was with Port Vale when we reached the semi in 1954.'

Frith perked up momentarily, like a ball bobbing to the surface.

'None of the lads is likely to forget that, Boss, you tell us often enough.' Then, his thoughts reverting to last night's game, he said with sullen doggedness, 'Anyway, I still scored two.'

'And missed how many? We led 2-1, half an hour to go. You were five yards clear of their number five twice, after that. He caught you twice and he's thirty-three bloody years of age. You don't give Arsenal chances like that, that's why they've won the Cup six times and we never have.' He resumed his seat and slowing his voice to emphasise the insult, drawled, 'You were knackered, Les, worn out with demonstrating your thrusts through the middle to Enid Tuesday night.'

'You've no call to make allegations like that.'

'Allegations? Our vocabulary is looking up! But of course, the *Guardian* and the other heavies would be here for Arsenal. Did one of the other lads read their report out for you?'

He tired of baiting the player and said rapidly, 'You sold your mates, the support and the club down the river. You're a non-trier, Frith, and you're on the bench come Saturday. I'm not having ten other characters running their guts out for you.'

Frith started, furious, for the door. Halfway there he turned back and yelled at Calderwood across the manager's desk. 'You know what you can do with your bench, Mr Godalmighty Calderwood, splinter by splinter. I want away from this dump. I'm putting in to go on the list. I can do a bloody sight better than this fleapit. I know that Burnley and Everton watched me last night.'

'And told me nothing doing, last night.' Seeing the player flinch, Calderwood pressed home. 'There's not much of a market for one-footed, forty-five-minute centres in the English First Division, Les. And what you do best isn't a spectator sport — yet. You're a non-professional, Les, and that's the worst word in my mouth. You couldn't first-time a ball left-footed when you came here two years ago, and despite all the work Steve and I have done with you, you still can't.'

The youngster, glancing warily at the irate manager, felt his reputation at stake.

'The *Guardian* said I'm a dangerous leader. And when we played Hibernian at the beginning of the season, the *Edinburgh Evening News* said I was energetic.'

'Enid was in London that weekend.'

Calderwood suddenly decided he'd made his point and there was a weary tone as he added, 'You're a passable player, but the world's full of passable players. Most of 'em work a damn sight harder than you do. You'll get your transfer all right.'

Frith's smile was ready and honest. 'Aw, heat of the moment stuff, Boss. I'll sit on the damned bench if you want to show your muscle.'

Calderwood smiled thinly. 'I don't think it'll be that easy, Leslie. The chairman's bound to get to hear about Tuesday night, and I fancy he'll want something more for his niece than a morning-glory centre. Meanwhile, you're twelfth man on Saturday. I'm glad you've seen it my way for two reasons.' He ticked them off on his fingers. 'One, you'd be in breach of contract if you didn't. Two, nobody's going to come for you if you're sitting in the stand.' The telephone on his desk rang. He picked it up, and motioned to Frith to remain.

'Hello, Jubilee Park, manager here. That's right, Saturday's kick-off three o'clock . . . Well, with the lights, there's no reason to be earlier . . . No, the ground's fine, hard but flat and we'll sand . . . Well, short of a blizzard . . . Right . . .'

Frith was obviously keen to be gone, but hanging around as if there was something final to be said.

'Well, Boss, seems you have me by the short and curlies.'

'I have. Out with it, what're you hanging on for?'

'Your honest opinion, Boss, since I want away and you say they'll let me go, how far could I go in the game?'

Calderwood looked consideringly at him. He rated his own ability as a talent-spotter highly, and therefore believed he had a moral obligation to be fair and candid when his judgment was sought. He took his time now, reflected.

'On the line for you, Les, a struggling Second Division club, not more. You'll probably do it too, there are always fools of managers who think they can handle basket cases like you. Not too bad a level, Second Division, and you'll knock a couple of seasons out of them before they find out. It's Enid here, it'll be Doreen or Nancy there.'

'The fans won't like the transfer, Boss.'

'Then they'll have to do the other thing, won't they? The stones are worn smooth from here to the station with all the players this lot have let go over the years.' He crossed to the filing cabinet and extracted a file, a sign that the interview was ended. 'Well, put your request to the Board in writing. I'll pass it on.'

'I haven't made life easier for you, Boss, have I?'

Calderwood grimaced. 'Easy for a Fourth Division manager is when he doesn't have a broken leg. Or when his players don't keep him off his work. Off you go, and keep your mouth shut about being sub. Oh, just one thing more, don't be too surprised about the nice things I'll be telling the *Examiner* about you. We've got to bump your price up. I suppose we really should transfer you to Derby County.'

'Derby County?'

'Well, they're the Rams, aren't they?'

As Frith stood uncomprehending, he barked at him, 'Oh, get the sports editor to explain it to you.'

'Yeah, Boss,' and crab-like, the player was gone. He was brushed in the doorway by Vi, returning with the kettle and, as it turned out, news.

'You're back, Vi, thank God for that, my tongue's hanging out. Let's have a cup of coffee then.'

Vi bustled about making the coffee — it was always a slight sorrow to her that in no way could the manager be persuaded to eat at what he called lunch-time.

'What's the news down town then, Vi?'

'I was hardly as far down the hill as that, Mr Calderwood. Just the electrician's, the butcher's and I popped in to Dr Armitage.'

'Been off colour, have you?'

'Only in the mornings.' She giggled happily. 'Afraid you'll be

11

looking for a new secretary before the end of the season.'

'My God, you didn't waste much time, did you?'

'It's just over ten months since we stood in Holy Trinity. No time wasted, but quite legal.'

'Hell!' Calderwood thought, another upset to an already disordered routine. He thought of Vi's husband, Gary, an apprentice draughtsman, even more of a kid than Vi was, more in need of mothering than his own fathering. Damned young fools, to lumber themselves with an infant without taking the chance to enjoy each other. Aloud he said, 'That's great news, Vi. Does Gary know?'

She nodded. 'I phoned him at work. He told me to watch myself. How corny can you get? I told him I've at least another three months left, probably more.' She changed tack disconcertingly. 'Les looked a bit whipped as he went out.'

'Did he?' Calderwood's tone was discouraging. As a player he had always resented his performances being picked over by people with little skill and less knowledge. As a manager he made it a rule not to discuss players except with a handful of intimates, never with women under any circumstances.

'Did you chew him up then?'

'Not especially.'

Suddenly Calderwood found the kittenishness of this plain lass irritating. He rose and shrugged himself into his car coat. 'I've just remembered, I told Joan I'd look home at lunch-time today.'

Vi, on the point of remarking that this was an unusual event, refrained from so doing. Obviously the boss wasn't in a chatty mood, and already her own far-off event was pushing out less important, that is, all other matters. She contented herself by saying, 'When'll you be back then if anyone should be asking for you?'

'About half two.'

Vi thought this a quaint and great Scotticism. 'Two thirty, then?'

'That's what I said,' Calderwood grunted, with a faint smile. 'If prenatal influence means anything, your infant may well grow up to speak with a thick Scottish accent. That'd give you some explaining to do to Gary. Well, I'm off. Don't phone me at home unless Real Madrid comes on looking for a manager.' He stopped as he remembered something. 'You'd a letter to remind me about, hadn't you? It's the same return as we sent in October. Type it from the file copy and I'll sign it when I come back.'

On the way out he poked his head into the cubby-hole where Joe Staples was sitting drinking tea from a flask and devouring doorstep sandwiches. He reminded him of the colour clash with Darlington on the coming Saturday. Then he walked quickly and springily to the car park.

He had always liked big cars, and because players and managers even at a modest level could usually get favourable deals, he had been able to indulge himself, even if occasionally he had had to purchase from the secondhand stands. Now he switched on the radio of his Toyota Corona, stopped at the gate to sign an autograph for three small boys, checked that there was nothing of importance on the lunch-time sports news, then drove home.

2

Home for Bob Calderwood was Tarkington, two miles northwest out of Barford, and on the road that led across the top of the Pennines towards Lancashire and back to Scotland. As recently as ten years ago Tarkington had retained all the stone-built gravity of a northern village, neatly functional and Quakerish as a Kent or Sussex counterpart would not have been. Now, it was a fairly anonymous but pleasant adjunct of Barford, with a good golf course and air which bereft you of breath in the icy winters.

He and Joan had been under some pressure to live in a club house but he had taken advantage of his honeymoon period with Albion to persuade the Board that instead they should recommend other suitable properties. The Owlies, a gaunt,

13

two-storeyed building next to the War Memorial, was the result. The previous owner had been the last manager of a bank in Tarkington, a branch rationalised out of existence four years earlier. The front garden, virtually all gravel paths with but one vigorous plane tree, was grimly in keeping with the house. Joan complained that the rooms were high and difficult to heat, but Bob had fixed views on buildings. He had declared vehemently that he wouldn't for choice live in a house built after 1914 and certainly not in one built after 1945.

They ate in the kitchen, a warm sunny room which somehow conveyed the independence of the days when the two-mile distance from Barford had meant something. Joan often baked her own bread and would have gone to town on a vegetable garden but for the gnawing thought of the impermanence of football managers.

She was still, in her mid-forties, a very pretty woman, small, slim, copper-haired. When sixteen, she had played Puck in her girls' school Shakespeare play. Two children and thirty years later, she would not have been physically disqualified from the part. Joan's eyes, blue when by all the rules they should have been green, were friendly as they watched her husband eat his way through gammon steak and poached eggs. An observer would have marked them down as a couple for whom the gloss of marriage had long gone but who were, in the words of the old poem, 'Tightly keeping hold of Nurse, for fear of finding something worse.'

They had married in the romantic haze of the Coronation summer. Joan's father, recently dead, had been a well-doing butcher in Wellingborough. Bob was then with Northampton Town, and in the August of 1952 the football club had come over to Wellingborough to play a charity cricket match with the twin objectives of raising money for families left fatherless by a colliery explosion and of relieving the monotony of intensive close-season training.

After the cricket, in which the fine-featured, quiet young Scot had not distinguished himself, there had been a dance at the Hind. Before returning to Northampton on the team coach, Bob Calderwood had Joan's address and telephone number. She came to the next home match, and within six months they were engaged. Her father, who liked Bob but liked security better, was partially reassured by the constant paragraphs in the local press which told of the tremendous interest taken in his prospective son-in-law by such as Wolves, Everton and Sheffield United.

A year to the day from the drawing of stumps they were married and a month later, against Gateshead, with Joan and an Arsenal scout looking on, he fractured his left leg in two places. He missed most of the season, then made a full physical recovery. But something indefinable was gone; never again did he show the flashes which made him a better than ordinary prospect. The big clubs looked elsewhere.

His career as a player could by no means be considered a failure. He put in nine workmanlike years with Northampton, interrupted by three years with Port Vale in their Cup heyday and then four with Chesterfield. He had left the Midlands for a spell as player-coach with Maidstone and on the strength of a good Cup run there, had been offered his present job at Barford.

Joan poured a cup of coffee for him and he moved into the dining room, the winter sun shining red and cold on the hills above the houses opposite.

'Will you have to go back in again today?'

He swallowed and nodded. 'For a couple of hours or so. The part-timers'll be in pretty well straight from work at five. I should be finished about eight if you want to go out.'

'Phyllis and I are going to Sally Ogden's show of presents.' She sat down and lit a cigarette, which she placed in a holder as long as a flute. Her smoking irritated Bob who had that peculiar asceticism which certain athletes wear like a hair shirt. 'The Ogdens are coming here Friday night, you'll remember, Bob.' Her voice was calm, as if anticipating an objection.

'Can't be done, love. I'm off to Scotland Friday midday with Joe to look at the Albion Rovers goalkeeper. We've got to have cover for that position. Arnold Dearson's at the end of the road, I'm afraid.'

Joan's mouth tightened in annoyance. 'We made the arrangement with the Ogdens weeks ago.'

'Tim Ogden'll understand. Dammit, he's a season-ticket holder. Ask if Sunday'll do. Or if not Sunday, next Saturday

15

night. We'll have no game that day since Halifax are still in the Cup.'

'Why must *you* go to Albion anyway?'

Calderwood looked up at her wearily. Joan really was fairly good at understanding what a manager's life involved, but he wished now and then she could remember more about other clubs.

'Not Albion, Joan, Coatbridge. It's a town about fifteen miles this side of Glasgow. If this boy's good we can maybe sign him before the big clubs get too interested. That's why I'll take Joe. Goalkeeping's a specialist position and he was a damned good one.'

'I still think they should be Coatbridge Rovers,' Joan said mutinously.

'Sure,' Bob agreed good-humouredly, 'and Arsenal should be Highbury and Crystal Palace should be South Norwood. To say nothing of Hearts being Edinburgh City. Ah, there goes the wee smile.'

If Joan Calderwood had been asked in a matrimonial quiz game for her husband's most irritating habit, she would almost certainly have cited his ability to make her laugh when she herself was annoyed. Possibly it might just have been his predictable phrases, like the one he used now.

'Come to bed . . . and possess me utterly.'

Joan decided to astonish him. 'All right.' In response to his semi-startled look she said, 'I mean it. I'd like to have you undress me in daylight.'

He caught her hand and bustled her upstairs. 'With one bound, Jack was free.'

They stripped each other slowly and stirringly and finally with a rush. Once in bed, Bob took his time and it was, by their standards, a very good lovemaking. In twenty-two years he had struck from Joan no word or groan of sensual delight. A fierce little nod of the head was her ultimate in appreciation and today it came. Afterwards they lay relaxed, watching the light go slowly, and hearing the uninhibited yelling and running which meant that school was out.

'That was very nice, Joan. I like your breasts.' He added force to his testimony by cupping them gently in his lifting

16

hands.

'There was a letter from Fraser today. I meant to tell you.'

Bob fought down a wild surge of irritation. This wasn't 'Sam, the ceiling needs painted,' the classic put-down. He knew Joan well enough to know that, by her lights, the bedding had been enjoyable. It was simply her Midlands practicality; he, the dour Lowland Scot, had to supply the romance for both. It was the way things were, something to be accepted.

'How's he doing?'

'Fine, mid-term's week after next. He's got a match against Lancaster University today. He seems to think he might make the UAU team against the Wallabies.'

Fraser was an engineering student at Salford, and a lock forward, not necessarily in that order, Calderwood reflected ruefully. But who was he to talk? His own university place at Glasgow had been assured, his teachers were nudging him towards pharmacy, when the lure of professional football had proved too strong.

Fraser played both kinds of football. His father inevitably had groomed him at soccer from an early age, but at grammar schools in Chesterfield and Maidstone the boy had revelled in the competitive rugby of South Yorkshire and the more sociable version of the game purveyed in Kent. He was twitted sometimes by his father for having opted for the less skilful game, but Calderwood had the sense and the magnanimity to recognise the virtues of the other sport.

He warmed at the thought of his powerful, earnest son, and rolled towards that son's mother.

'A good first half, Joan, but that's only forty-five minutes. Let's have an even better performance.'

Joan was out of bed in a blur, standing naked and trim on the rug.

'It's full-time for you, m'lad, you're scarcely young Lochinvar.' Her tone was snappish but there was a sense of having been complimented.

Calderwood got out of bed, surveying her and himself complacently in a mirror. 'Not bad for a forty-five year old,' he murmured, looking at the spare figure which he had never stopped training.

17

'Forty-six,' Joan said quickly, 'there was the matter of your birthday last month.' She was actually three months older than he was and slightly resented that part of the year in which she was numerically his senior.

'All right, have it your way, forty-six.' He looked gratefully across the room to where she stood in her underwear, pondering the selection of a dress. 'And thanks for just now.'

'It was nice,' she said matter of factly. 'I think I'll come back into town with you; they've asked me to go full-time at the shop and I said I'd let them know before the end of the week. I did mention it to you.'

Calderwood frowned. His wife worked mornings at Naughton's, a large newsagents. She had started with two days per week, ten till one, and now went in every day except Thursday. Derek Naughton who owned the business was in his mid-fifties, Calderwood guessed, compact, brisk, just below middle height with a fine head of greying, wavy hair and a particularly florid face. There was a wife, Evie, somewhere, but nobody remembered seeing her for some years. His sister, Elsie, looked after the house and shared in the supervision of the shop.

Bob had always found Derek Naughton perfectly affable and, for a layman, remarkably sensible on the subject of football, but he didn't like him. The older man had a predatory reputation with women and while he didn't for a moment imagine Joan was interested, the news displeased him and his wife was quick to realise it.

'Any reason why I shouldn't say yes? I'd only mooch around all afternoon. Today was in every sense an exception.'

Bob shook his head, put out. He had been on the point of saying that he'd try to make sure he was free in the afternoons more often, but his basic fairness prevented him. There was nothing to tie Joan to The Owlies, she could do in an hour any housework that needed doing. His only argument would be the masculine, 'Because I don't want you to.'

'If you want it, go ahead.' He looked at his watch. 'Time we were heading for Barford. I'll put the kettle on for a quick cup of tea.'

In the kitchen Joan looked at him. 'Derek Naughton says you'd be very welcome to come in some Sunday morning and

18

have a look at how things are run.'

'That's decent of him. Against my impending retirement? Doesn't he know that seedy ex-pros like me are supposed to take over seedy pubs?'

Joan refused the gauntlet. 'It's a perfectly straightforward invitation, you either come or you don't. It might be useful one day to have some idea how a shop like ours works.'

'Well, if I ever have the time and the inclination together. Keeping this lot in the Fourth Division's a full-time occupation. You know that more than most.'

Joan made a face. 'Did you sugar my tea? I thought not.' She looked at him searchingly. 'What if you finish bottom?'

'If we finish in the bottom four it means we have to apply to the Football League for re-election. There was a time when that was a formality. But not in the last ten years. Gateshead, Barrow, Bradford, they've all been voted out. And God knows we're vulnerable, this would be our fourth application for re-election in twenty-two years. With home gates averaging around the two thousand mark we're no great catch at the gate either.' He repeated slowly, 'We'd be vulnerable, God knows.' In a brisker tone he said, 'Jack Schofield, "dynamic chairman of Barford Albion" — last Tuesday's *Mercury* — wouldn't be at all delighted. There'd very possibly be a Scottish manager, domiciled in The Owlies, who'd be honestly seeking work. Fortunately, I'm pretty sure we'll survive.'

His wife's question was hesitant. 'I suppose a club chairman would be very keen to stay in the Football League?'

'Of course. That's where it all happens. A non-League club only comes alive once a year for the FA Cup. You know how it was at Maidstone. A chairman who didn't want to stay in the League would be a loony.'

'Do you think that Jack Schofield's a loony?'

'I do not, he's a bright fellow, young Mister Jack.'

Joan finished buttoning her coat and checking windows. They drove into town amicably. As he dropped her off at the Lawnmarket, Bob asked Joan to collect his sports jacket, and to remember to switch the Ogdens to the Saturday or Sunday.

3

By the time that Bob had arrived at the Jubilee ground, a hard, fine sleet was falling, almost heavy enough to deter the early trainers, who had hurried straight from their daytime jobs to crowd in an hour's work in what remained of the daylight.

Of the first-team squad only Les Frith, who was bone-idle, thought Calderwood grimly, and Arnold Dearson, the long-serving goalkeeper who had never known any other trade, were full-timers. The rest were apprentice mechanics, local government workers, foundrymen, with a teacher, a bank junior and a couple of students to give intellectual ballast to the side. One of the students, Phil Gifford, was possibly the most talented player on the club's books, but Calderwood had written him off as a prospect at top level. Quite simply the boy didn't want it enough. No reason why he should, the manager thought ruefully. By all accounts here was a physicist of high promise, but to succeed in First Division football, ability was not in itself enough. There had to be a driving ambition, the merest tinge of ferocity.

Vic Slocombe, the young banker, had that all right. He was going to have to choose his road very soon — banks were still very sticky about members of their staff playing professional football. For midweek matches Slocombe was either not released or grudgingly allowed to go, with a warning sounding in his ears that a match against Chester was not going to do his long-term future at the bank much good. Calderwood frowned as he stood at the tunnel mouth gazing out at the pitch. While he watched, Slocombe killed an awkward cross perfectly on his chest, pivoted and stroked the ball deliberately away from Arnold Dearson in goal. Dearson — there was another headache.

He turned irritably on a shout from the groundsman, the Planet. The Planet had a name, Joe Staples as a matter of fact, but he was invariably addressed by his celestial title by friends and acquaintances of long standing.

'What is it, Planet?'

'Mr Adamson from the *Examiner* in your office.' There was the faintest ironical emphasis on the mister.

Calderwood sighed. He would have welcomed an hour on his own to sort out his thinking about Les. And, yes, about Joan and her job, which was deflecting him from his own in a niggling, unprofessional way. He put the thought aside and turned down the tunnel, his tan shoes flecked with red blaes-spots from the thawing track. As reporters went there were a lot worse than Dave Adamson, sportswriter of the *Barford Examiner*.

Adamson always dressed in a manner which hinted at gentle self-mockery. He was tall, rather pale, and a fine head of white, wavy hair curled from his neck over the collar of his suede jacket. He had thrown an Alpine hat and black boar-skin gloves with a careless assurance on top of Bob's desk. His face was youthful, and his direct gaze disconcerted men and attracted women. Joan had known him through her tennis in earlier days and entertained a high regard for him. Bob shared this view. If Adamson was a lad with the girls, he was also a man's man, and in professional matters Bob had never known him betray a trust. Occasionally indeed he had stopped the manager early in a story with the warning straddle-shot, 'I don't think I'd better hear any more of that unless you've a wish to see it in print.'

The relationship of local reporter-team manager is a fraught one at the best of times. The reporter is too close to the team, he lives in their pockets. It is almost impossible that he will not become either sycophantic or carping and he has a lot more space to fill than his national colleagues. But when he criticised, and he could be trenchant, he said nothing that he would not confront Calderwood with, and he notably refrained from stirring the fetid waters of dressing-room gossip. When Calderwood threw open his office door therefore, his opening salvo for the reporter was gruff but far from malevolent.

'You've a bloody nerve knocking my door after the rubbish you wrote this morning. "Frith's pre-lemon blitz rocks Gunners".' He spat out the cliché in mock disgust.

Adamson was unperturbed. 'I wrote that rubbish last night, Bob, and you've been around newspapermen long enough to know that we creative artists don't do our own headlines.

21

Complain to the desk, they're the villains.' He swung his legs, perched on the desk. 'You can't blame the subs too much. Les is the nearest thing to a personality you've got.'

The most selfless of managers finds it difficult to accept that any team of his is a one-man band. Displeasure caused his normal caution to waver as he growled, 'Well, we won't necessarily have him come Saturday. He's down as sub.'

Instinctively Adamson fished in his pocket for a rather smart notebook.

'He's not quite a hundred per cent fit then? Is it a carry-over from last night?'

'You could say that.'

'I notice you're not. It wouldn't be a matter of discipline, Bob?'

Calderwood's voice was stubborn. 'He was told he was substitute this morning, I'm saying no more than that, Dave.'

The reporter smiled quietly. In his mind he placed such remarks in his 'I don't know and don't quote me' managerial file. Aloud he said, 'How did Les take it?'

'How should he take it? We've an odd system at this club. He plays the football, sometimes, I pick the team, always. He sees it my way, now.'

Adamson changed the subject. 'I ran into Tim Ogden in the Lamb and Flag at lunch-time. He was saying that they're going out to see you tomorrow night.'

Bob made a face and shook his head. 'That was the idea, but it's going to have to wait. I'm off to Scotland tomorrow. Albion Rovers play Meadowbank in Edinburgh and I've great reports on their keeper. Arnold'll not go on for ever here.' Quickly he jerked at Adamson, 'I want this quiet for the moment, Dave. As soon as we look like doing business, I'll phone you direct.'

The tall reporter nodded. 'A bit of a sudden journey, isn't it?'

'We only found out at ten this morning the game is definitely on. He's a young lad name of McNally. The Planet's seen him and thinks he's a good 'un, and Joe Staples knows goalkeepers. He's available and we could get him cheap before the big Scottish clubs move in.'

'How cheap would he have to be?'

'For here, very cheap. Funny thing about Boards of Directors. Even a club like this would spend quite heavily on a has-been centre forward, sorry, striker, with a Second Division reputation, but they'll howl with anguish if you ask for £5,000 to buy a damned good keeper. It's a bit like buying a grand piano for a house where the roof leaks.'

Adamson made a gesture of mock protest. 'Here, I'm supposed to be the writer. That's rather good.'

'Then quote me as saying it. It'll help my shrewd, genial image. I know I should be genial, shrewd *and* pipe-smoking, but two out of three's not bad.'

'So the game plan is up North tomorrow, back down overnight, game here Saturday?'

'That's about it.'

Adamson's voice was wondering. 'It's never dull, is it?'

Calderwood smiled tightly. 'No-o-o, it's not dull. It must be easier for the Shanklys, the Dochertys, the Steins. Here it's a struggle to get money for the everyday things. We're still owing for the buses for the last two away matches, and our medical kit's a disgrace. The Planet had to use insulating tape for injuries at last week's reserve match.' Suddenly his bitterness overwhelmed restraint. 'How the hell the Board — well you know that Schofield *is* the Board — how the hell he expects us to win matches and stay in the Football League beats me.'

'You're assuming he *wants* the club to stay in the Football League.'

Calderwood's voice was scornfully dismissive. 'What the hell else would he want? A non-League club's a non-event. I know, I had some at Maidstone. We'll get clear too, given half a chance. We're fifth from bottom and even if we slip a place or two we'd be safe enough.' He broke off to look at the reporter, suddenly suspicious. 'Look here, Dave, do you *know* anything?'

Adamson lit a cigarette and studied it minutely. 'No, I don't . . . know . . . anything. But I met Emery, the Stalybridge chairman, in Manchester yesterday.'

The manager laughed shortly. 'Are that lot still trying to get into the League?'

'Fair's fair, Bob. Some of my colleagues, one or two pretty

23

influential fellows amongst them, think "that lot" should be in the League rather than our lot here in Barford. Anyway Tom Emery says they'll be in the League this time next season. He said something else too which I didn't like.'

'What?'

'He said, "You'll have to travel a bit further for your football next season, Mr Adamson," '

'That's a load of crap. We won't finish within three places of bottom, you can have a tenner on it now.'

Adamson waved aside the bet on offer. 'Supposing, Bob, the club didn't apply to continue in membership of the League?'

Calderwood stared angrily at him. 'What are you at, Dave? You *know* something.'

'It's only talk, you understand. One or two kites are being flown in town about the ground being sold for housing. It's very central now, the way the town's developed, and there's that new private estate down the road. This ground'd be worth a packet as building land.'

'If they got permission,' grunted Calderwood morosely.

'Not too hard, I'm afraid. Barford needs new industry. New industry needs middle management and middle management wants private housing. They'd get permission all right.'

'The shareholders would never stand for it,' but as he spoke Calderwood knew that he was not even persuading himself.

'There's not another shareholder with as many as two hundred shares. At the end of the day it's purely Schofield's decision.' He stood up suddenly, pulled on his gloves and checked in the glass-fronted cupboard that his hat had sufficient tilt. He punched Calderwood amiably on the shoulder. 'I'd forget it, Bob. Look at Halifax, Rochdale, Crewe. They've been shutting shop for fifty years according to the wiseacres, and they're still with us. Well, I must go. Give my love to Joan. I . . .'

He broke off as the phone rang. Calderwood picked it up. 'Jubilee Park — oh, good evening, Mr Schofield . . .'

Adamson semaphored farewell from the door, but the manager indicated that he should stay.

'Just a normal training night, Chairman. Yes, I'll be here for another hour or so. Fine, I'll expect you then. In about twenty minutes.'

He put the phone down and looked at Adamson. 'That's odd.'

'Doesn't he ever come down on training nights?'

'It's not unknown but it's very rare. Anyway, we'll find out what he's after soon enough. In the meantime the club won't run itself. See you Saturday.'

Calderwood used the time between the departure of the reporter and the arrival of the chairman to get an up-to-date report on the injury position from Steve Birkenshaw the trainer. The table was occupied by Les Frith, who appeared to enjoy massage not only in off-duty hours.

'Well, Steve, what's the tally?'

'I'm just going to work on Phil Gifford, he has a very slight groin strain, nothing to bother us. Arnold has a staved finger from last week, if he plots it constantly in hot and cold water he'll be OK, Boss.'

'What's the news on Ian Gregor?'

Gregor, a rangy Scot, had been a comparatively expensive buy by Barford standards as a central defender. His first four games had been abundantly promising, but a simple tackle in the next had led to an operation for the removal of cartilages. He was crucial to Calderwood's planning, and Birkenshaw knew it. It was with the smugness of one bringing acceptable tidings to his master that he said, 'I spoke to Dr O'Halloran at the County General today. Big Ian's doing well, Boss. He can start light training in a fortnight and we could have him back in five to six weeks.'

Calderwood nodded contentedly. This was the best injury position since the season started. He indulged himself in a playful swipe at Frith's nude backside.

'Get your fat arse out of there, Soldier. We need this bed for the wounded.'

'OK, Boss, a shower, change, a whiff of *Old Spice* and I'm set. I wonder do the Barford women realise their incredible luck?'

In football terms this was positive by-play. Calderwood went along with it, knowing that no player was ever offended by having his sexual appetite or prowess exaggerated.

He shook his head at the trainer in an affectation of sadness.

25

'You know his trouble, Steve,' he said, jerking a despairing thumb at Frith, 'it's what the doctors call satyriasis. He can't see a skirt but he wants to have it down. Better watch it, Les,' he turned to the player, 'it can make you go blind.'

The forward writhed around in an ecstasy of well-being. Only the assurance that he was the best striker in England could have pleased him more. Calderwood went out on to the field, testing the turf appraisingly. There was a bit of give in it, overnight frost did not seem to be a threat, and unlike several of the First Division grounds, the low stand and enclosure would not exclude the sun's rays come the morning.

He quickly wrote out Saturday's side and affixed it to the club noticeboard. From his own playing days he had always felt that the players had a right to see the manager's preference boldly stated rather than learn of their exclusion by word of mouth. Likewise, wherever possible, he gave his selection to the press in good time for publication. He held the old-fashioned view that the public had the right to know who they would see. You didn't go to the theatre to see *Hamlet* starring Albert Finney, but it just might be Fred Fazackerly. Besides it wasn't as if he had the choice of Kruyff or Pele to baffle and pulverise the opposition. His option was mediocrity A or mediocrity B. By heavens it was. Much of a manager's job is motivation, attributing to players qualities which they do not have. The idea appears to be that if complimentary phrases fly around a dressing room, then players may acquire these qualities by oral ingestion. Equally though, every manager in the Fourth Division has moments of candour when he realises that if any of his players were consistent possessors of exceptional qualities then by definition they would be playing elsewhere.

He was in the process of working out a rough timetable for the Edinburgh trip when the door opened without the preliminary of a knock and the Barford Albion chairman, Jack Schofield, came in. Six years at Denstone had given him the assurance which parents desperately hope will be the return on their capital. Arguably, it had simply confirmed an assurance he had always had. In his working life as owner of a large fleet of motor coaches and mini buses, he could switch from Denstonian to earthy northern businessman with the speed of thought.

26

He dressed very well, although he was far from a clothes-horse. He did well to be elegant, for his figure was chunky and compact — in his late thirties, he looked the scrum-half he had been at school. Not everyone would have worn a dark purple shirt with his light grey suit; on most other men the red, white and black tie might have appeared garish. Calderwood was always fascinated by the chairman's shoes. He bought shoes as others bought books.

'Good evening, Robert,' Schofield was practically the only man who ever awarded Calderwood his full baptismal title. Calderwood couldn't quite understand why he himself was irked by it rather than otherwise. 'Got over last night yet?'

'Beginning to, Chairman. It's always harder when you were in the game with a chance. Easier to take, funnily enough, if we'd got a real hiding. If Les Frith had taken one of those two chances in the second half we were there. We could have used the money too.'

'Well, that's football.' Schofield said with the aplomb of one uttering a novel sentiment. 'It was Frith I wanted to see you about as it happens.'

Calderwood frowned. 'Has he gone running to you about Saturday?'

'No, I haven't seen him. What about Saturday, Robert?'

'I bawled him out this morning for his second-half display against Arsenal. I told him he'd be substitute on Saturday and he didn't like it. He wants away.'

'Did you tell him to put it in writing?'

'Of course.'

'He'll be surprised how easily we grant his request. I know why he fell away in the second half. Do you?'

'Yes.'

Schofield scowled and drew his stylish square toe across the floor. 'Whole bloody town knows, I don't doubt.'

'How did you find out, Chairman?'

'One of my drivers saw them. It was Enid he spotted first. He thought she might be in a bit of bother. Then he realised she wasn't . . . yet.'

'There's always plenty of folk willing to pass on bad news.'

'Oh, I think Jim Farrimond, the driver, was genuinely disturbed about telling me. He did it, I really believe, out of loyalty to me. It hasn't totally disappeared, hasn't loyalty, in this part of the world.'

'Hasn't loyalty' — the switch to the local patois, Calderwood noted incidentally. The chairman said decisively, 'You did the right thing, Robert. Frith'll have to go. I don't blame him especially, Enid's man-mad.'

'I'm not so sure she is, Mr Schofield.'

'You hardly know her. You don't suggest there's anything lasting in this?'

'Not on his side maybe.'

'Well, he's got to be sent packing. A one-night stand's one thing but I'm damned if I'll have the *Examiner* quoted at me over Sunday lunch for the rest of my life. How much will he fetch?'

'Hard to say. It's a good time to sell with the transfer deadline coming up in six weeks. As against that, of course, he's Cup-tied with us. Portsmouth need a striker pretty badly. They might be prepared to go to fifty-five or sixty thousand.' Calderwood decided to take the flood tide. 'Look, Mr Schofield, we could perhaps do a player-swap with Portsmouth, they have a midfield man, Kirkpatrick, who wants back North. He's a good player — I'd a season with him at Maidstone. We'd get money too, of course, he'd only be a part-exchange.'

Almost too quickly, too jocularly, Schofield cut in, 'No, Robert, take the money, my son, praising Allah.'

Kipling, thought Calderwood grimly, a fragment of his Lanark education surfacing. He strove to keep the stridency of his anxiety from his voice. 'We're desperately weak in the midfield, Chairman. We've got nothing between the two penalty areas.'

'Not to worry, Robert, we'll be all right.'

What a bloody lunatic phrase, thought Calderwood. He refined his thought into words. 'We can probably stay up, but I was thinking towards next year.'

'That's next year.' Schofield changed the subject definitely and finally. 'Any other staff changes pending?'

'Not on the playing side.' Calderwood glanced despondently towards the filing cabinet and a thought struck him. 'But Mrs

28

Black will be going soon. She's pregnant, told me so this morning.'

'Daft young bitch,' Schofield muttered without malice. Then consideringly, 'So you'll need someone in the office?'

'Yes, but not immediately. Mid-April, I should think.'

Schofield shook his head impatiently. I've got an idea. We'll pay Mrs Black off at the end of the month and bring Enid in. She's done a couple of years at secretarial college.'

'But, Chairman, it's fairly specialised work.'

'Balls, a good office junior could pick it up in a month. I'll meet your objection partly by giving Vi a month's notice. At least I'll know where Enid is during the day.'

'You haven't forgotten Les'll be here too?'

'As long as you check out the trainer's couch every now and then there's not a lot they can do. You're the brains here, Robert. You're certainly the most literate manager in my experience. We're lucky to have you. I'll send Enid along first thing Monday.' For the first time he appeared less than fully in control of events. 'It'd have been a damn sight different if my brother had lived.'

Calderwood smiled in polite disagreement. 'I think you'll find, Chairman, they all gang their ain gait at that age.'

'Well, perhaps you're right.' He glanced at his watch. 'Good Lord, almost nine o'clock, I've a bridge date. See you Saturday, Robert. Oh, by the way, there'll be a camera crew down from BBC Manchester to take some film.'

'It's not *Match of the Day?*'

'No, no, it's not for their sports programme. Some documentary or other, I gather. Good night, Robert.'

'Just a minute, Mr Schofield. Planet was doing the check for Saturday and we don't have a new match ball.'

Schofield looked irritated. 'Must we have one?'

'Yes, it's a League requirement.'

'I know that. Must we have one?'

'Yes. And I'm away all day tomorrow. And I wouldn't trust Vi to remember it's Friday.'

Schofield frowned. 'Well, I suppose that's why God made directors — I'll see to it.' He broke off. 'Damn it, I've got that wedding Saturday.' Silently he calculated. 'Don't worry, I'll tell Enid. I'll see there's a ball there.'

'I'm depending on you, Chairman.'

'You are. You can. Good night, Robert.'

Calderwood checked with the Planet that everyone else had left, that the offices were lockfast, and the Alsatian given free run of the ground. He debated briefly whether to earn a credit tick from Joan by turning up, however briefly, at the show of presents, but the ethos of Barford was sufficiently strong on shows of presents being hen-parties as to allow him to turn the car to the Tarkington road without guilt or repining.

4

There were occasions, infrequent but searching, when Bob Calderwood regretted that he had ignored the advice given him by his form teacher at Lanark. That advice had been that he should proceed to a science course at Glasgow University. Had he taken it, he might not now have been crouching beside his car in driving, sleety rain, in a lay-by near Thirsk on the A1 in the early hours of a Saturday morning. Beside him the Planet, defying all commands to the contrary, shone a torch on the rear wheel that Calderwood was struggling to change.

He had never found that the safety-valve of swearing was easily available to him. He could have used it now, remembering that he had lent Joan the spider, without which it was almost impossible to loosen wheel nuts that had been machine-tightened. The pathetic effort that came with the tool kit was worse than useless. He should have remembered to ask Joan for it back, she should have remembered he'd need it. Well, he thought, glancing down grimly, she won't be too enchanted that I'm kneeling on her best travelling rug, instead of some old sacking.

Every time he got a new car, he resolved that he would check the position of the jack points, every time he failed to do so until a puncture arrived. This one hadn't been very sudden or remotely dangerous, just the realisation that cornering was becoming increasingly heavy, and when eventually they stopped, there was the back near-side tyre hanging limply. At least the spare was adequate for the occasion.

With icy rain running down his neck and flaying his trouser legs, he changed the wheel doggedly rather than skilfully. The Planet wordlessly clanked the tools together in their plastic container, and Calderwood tore a nail as he slung the defective wheel into the boot. Still in silence they drove on through the night until, cutting over to the M62, they stopped at the first service station. The early day staff were just beginning to come on duty, putting out the notices — 'No Football Coaches — Except By Appointment'.

The cafeteria was almost empty — a few gummy-eyed motorists obviously unused to such eccentric hours, two perky Scots lorry drivers who just as clearly were. The coffee was passable and the ham roll remarkably fresh. There was a lulling warmth in the place, and very shortly Calderwood noticed that his trouser legs were steaming damply. It was the Planet, chomping happily and noisily on his roll, who broke what was becoming an oppressive silence.

'Pity about the young lad, Boss.'

Calderwood nodded morosely. It had indeed been a pity about young McNally. The boy, even in the morgue-like atmosphere of a Scottish Second Division match, had looked a thoroughly good goalkeeper. 'His chairman would have let him go all right. And the lad's father was friendly enough. A fine big West of Ireland man.'

But the boy had heard that Celtic were watching him. That was all, just watching him, but it had finished Barford Albion. Calderwood tried to tell him that Celtic didn't have a great track record in picking keepers recently; that even if they signed him he'd only be one of four or five, but it did no good.

The Planet mumbled something amiable through a roll-filled mouth.

'What?'

'Not even these did much good, Boss.' He produced a pair

31

of rosary beads.

Calderwood shook his head irritably. 'There's not the auto-
matic connection and pull that there used to be. It's perhaps
because the father's first generation that the offer's so attractive. Or perhaps it's that we just can't compete at all. The King
Billy handkerchief of mine did us no good with that kid
Drysdale.'

'Why are they like that up your way, Boss?' asked the Planet,
his face creased in honest puzzlement.

'I'll tell you sometime, Planet, when we've a month or two to
spare. It'd take half the close season.'

'You don't really like the rosary and nose-rag, do you, Boss?'

'No, Planet, I don't. We've cheapened ourselves — even if
we'd got the player. Hell's teeth, if a Sikh came into this café
and he could keep goal I'd sign him and I wouldn't feel I'd need
to sacrifice a lamb to him or whatever the hell it is that they do.'
He swallowed the remains of his coffee and stood up decisively.
'Right then, with luck thee and me'll have just enough time to
get home.'

In another half hour, the day brightening from dark to
medium grey, they came to the Barford turn-off. Calderwood
drove along deserted streets until they came to the little enclave
of terrace houses where Planet lived, ten minutes from the
ground. The morning rain, a smirr, thought Calderwood from
his boyhood, glistened damply on the undistinguished row of
dismal, red-brown brick. Watching the Planet open his door at
the end of a three-yard path, Calderwood reflected that from
this very house the Planet had gone out in 1941 to acquire a
Military Medal in Italy, and that his brother Jeff, taking the
quick road to a commission by volunteering for air gunner, had
earned a DFC and bar. Moreover he'd survived the war and two
tours of ops to live with his brother ever since demob. Unlike
Joe he was totally uninterested in football, and not all the
complimentary tickets in the world could have got him within
shouting distance of the Jubilee ground.

It was just after 7.30 a.m. when Bob pulled up at his front
door. He came in quietly, threw off his wet things, telling Joan
to stay where she was, then went off for a quick bath. The hot
water — and Calderwood regarded no bath as satisfactory that

32

did not leave you lobster pink — was both gain and loss. It thawed out the rigid limbs beautifully, but induced a lassitude which had no part in the day's programme. Back in their bedroom, he resisted Joan's suggestion that he should grab a couple of hours' sleep.

'No thanks, love, it'd only leave me a mouth and a head.'

'But you've been up all night, Bob.'

'Don't I know it. I'll manage fine, though. The trick is to fix on 8 p.m. this evening and make it till then.' He waved an admonitory arm at her. 'Don't stir yourself, I'll get breakfast.'

He was an adequate cook of about seven dishes, his scrambled eggs being certainly his best. He pottered around quite happily, fixing the coffee, making toast, fetching the cherry-wood tray that he and Joan had bought in an old treen shop during an Edinburgh holiday. He was pleased to notice that the papers had arrived, *Yorkshire Post, Sun, Examiner* and *Telegraph*. Joan chided him about his expensive tastes in newspapers, and wasn't totally convinced by his half-jocular references to his homework.

He carried the tray carefully upstairs; it was nice to do something like this for Joan, even if very occasionally.

'Your scrambled eggs *are* good, Mr Calderwood,' she said, sitting up squarely in bed and reading the *Sun* with large-framed glasses she had needed only within the last year.

'Thank you, m'lady. As a young man I had no small-talk, couldn't dance, but the women were powerless against me scrambled eggs.' He perched on the bed, picked up the *Yorkshire Post* and began working through it, starting with the sports page. Joan looked up enquiringly as he made a clicking noise with his teeth.

'What's up, Bob?'

'Tim Lawrence's got the chop at Hull.'

Lawrence had been a clubmate of Bob's at Port Vale and had gone into management a couple of years earlier than he had.

'Was it on the cards?'

'We-ell. They're middle of Division Three and that's no use to Hull; they've a large population, big ground, their natural place in life is the Second Division. They've lost their last four games, three by the odd goal, I grant you; but they're still losses. Tim's been unlucky too, only two blokes score goals for him, Ken Swaddell and Ernie Ollerenshaw. Ken's been out since September with ligament trouble and Ernie's a right little toerag; he's been suspended twice already this season. Still, when did a Board of Directors ever take a hard-luck story?'

With deliberation he selected the smallest, most thinly-buttered piece of toast. From force of habit Joan observed, 'You've hardly eaten a thing.'

'I'd a roll in a motorway cafeteria. Seventy pence for a roll and coffee. Highway robbery.' He stopped, grinning, as he realised what he'd just said. 'Anyway, Joan, you know what I tell you, eat for need, not for society. Few of us are as lucky as you are. You can eat like a vulture and look like a wren.'

'Charming,' said Joan absent-mindedly. 'What'll Tim do, do you suppose?'

'See what turns up. Drop a division maybe, Crewe, Rochdale. Maybe assistant with a First or Second Division club. Perhaps non-League, though I don't think he'll do that.'

'He'll stay in football then?'

'You know Tim, a big, mad Irishman. A nice fellow, but not especially bright.'

Joan put her paper down, snapped her glasses off and looked determinedly at Bob. 'You're lucky to have options, Bob.'

He snorted, half in irritation, half in affection. 'Sure, I can either be Prime Minister when Jim goes, or perhaps put in for chairman of the CBI. Let me spell it out again, Joan, I have five Highers under the Scottish Certificate of Education. By English standards I'm probably a two 'A' level man. Not dumb, but it hardly makes me Einstein. I can't remember when I last read anything more demanding than the *Daily Telegraph*. Your old man's a football manager, overworked, not all that well paid. But just over ten years ago Bill Shankly at Huddersfield was basically doing the job I'm doing here. So, give us a kiss and make the most of it.'

They kissed, harder than either intended and held the kiss. Calderwood freed his left hand, loosened his dressing-gown cord and, having set the tray on a bedside chair, climbed on to the bed.

'It's only sleeping that'll set me back, Joan.'

34

Joan went through the motions of fighting him off, but allowed herself to be pushed back on the pillows. Calderwood, aroused, began to loosen the buttons of her nightdress, and to pull the quick-release belt which gathered the waist.

'You're a beautifully-built wren, Joan.'

They had begun their preliminary explorations very happily when the doorbell rang loudly.

'Post,' said Calderwood as his wife stiffened.

She remained tense for a moment then relaxed as Calderwood's right hand cupped her left breast high. 'Bills, no doubt.'

The bell rang a second time, then almost immediately a third. Calderwood, furious, got out of bed and stood for a moment, absurdly tumescent, in vest and pants. Then kicking his feet into slippers and wrestling with the sleeves of his dressing-gown, he stamped downstairs. Annoyance, relief, amusement, were commingled on Joan's face.

A tall figure appeared dimly on the other side of the glass door, but unmistakably Fraser.

'I didn't know you were coming up this week, Fraser,' Bob greeted his son and heir.

'And a Merry Christmas to you too.'

The young man, immensely tall, did his best not to appear too downcast by his less than cordial reception. Calderwood perceived his hurt.

'Didn't mean it to sound like that of course, son. Come on in. We're just finishing breakfast. I'll make some more scrambled eggs for you. Come on up, your mother'll be pleasantly surprised.'

'Nothing for me, Dad. Cup of tea perhaps. Watch me throw a fit into the old girl.' He bounded up the stairs in what seemed four strides at most and flung open the bedroom door. Joan looked up half-alarmed by this irruption. Her son stood smiling at the door.

'Fraser! How lovely to see you. It's not mid-term, is it?'

'No, Mum, something much more important. I'd like you to meet someone I'm sure you'll like, Mumtaz Soraya.' He put his head out into the hall. 'Come and meet my mother, darling.'

Dismay and hospitality contended for Joan's face in the few seconds before her son broke into roars of laughter. 'By

35

heavens, that had the old knickers in a twist, eh? Don't worry, little Joan, your big son is still unspoken for.'

'Fraser!' Joan struggled for speech and dignity. 'That's a terrible thing to do to anyone, let alone your mother. You know that I'd welcome anyone who was a friend of yours, or of Phyllis.'

'Yeah. Su-ure!' her son mocked her.

'And another thing,' Joan said indignantly, trying to regain the ascendancy from her man-mountain of a child, 'you really should knock before you come storming in. I might have been standing there in me nothings.'

'Great!' said Fraser, making a grab at her. 'I love older women, especially when they're assembled as well as you are. Let me take you away from him. He doesn't appreciate you.'

'Can I have that offer in writing?' said Calderwood, coming back with the tea.

They settled down happily enough in the bedroom once Joan had ascertained that Fraser didn't want anything to eat.

'He's not exactly like something you'd see on an Oxfam poster anyway,' Calderwood grunted. 'With that frame he'll be eighteen stone in ten years unless he watches his diet. How heavy are you anyway?'

'Fifteen stone four in the buff.'

'And did you come up with Eric on the bike?'

'That's it. Ninety-three miles in eighty-five minutes. Mostly motorway, of course. Who've you got this afternoon, Dad? Darlington?'

Calderwood nodded, pleased. 'Want to look in?'

'Thanks, I'd like to but Harry Wylie's called off from the OB's side and I can get a game at lock. We're playing Roundhay Seconds and if we run them close or better still really duff them up they might give us a midweek fixture against their Firsts next season. It's quite a big game for us.'

Again Calderwood nodded. He was well aware of the importance of improving a rugby club's fixture list.

Fraser stretched himself. 'Can I have a bath?'

'After your mother. She's due down town for ten o'clock.'

'Fine. Actually, I don't think I'll bother. I'll get a shower after the game and you often do better in the set scrums if you're

36

not nice to know. I'll just play a few records.'

Within minutes the music centre was giving out the mono-
tonous thump, thump, thump of the records approved by
Fraser. He took his father's jibes good-naturedly as he took life,
grinning tolerantly when the older man asked about the for-
tunes of such mythical groups as the Plastic Bed Socks and the
Septic Tanks.

Joan and Bob dressed quickly, he in club blazer and club tie.
The Barford tie was perhaps the most elegant thing about the
club. On a dark blue background the white rose of the county
was surmounted by a golden mitre. Below at an angle was a
bishop's crozier and, in gold on a white scroll, *'Dum spiro,
spero,'* (While I breathe, I hope).

Calderwood inclined to the traditional in his players' dress
and appearance. On match days, especially away matches, he
liked his players to wear the club livery as a matter of commitment. He himself set the example. For the duration of his
contract he was the club's man. This did not mean that he
became a zombie, unable to argue, unable to differ, but he was
very willing to assume the outward symbols of service.

Joan, increasingly and more frequently depressed, looked at
his trim, spare figure. With his short hair-cut there was something of the fifties about him. He could not quite impose his
own norms on the players, neither could he mask his distaste for
long hair and socks flapping around boot-tops. He was not
stupid enough to equate either of these fashions with vice, they
merely struck him as 'sloppy', to use the favourite word of his
National Service drill instructor.

A little before ten they left home, Joan pleased that she would
be amongst people for the rest of the day in the shop, Bob
unable to stay easy as kick-off time approached. In answer to
Joan's instructions on where the food was located, Fraser yelled
above his hellish din that he'd grab a snack at the clubhouse
before kick-off.

At the shop, Calderwood had a word with Derek Naughton.
As they talked he watched Joan go into the back shop and
emerge seconds later in overalls. She was a natural for shop
work, alert, pleasant, informed, firm. He was surprised to hear
Naughton say that he hoped to get along to the match.

'We don't often see you at Jubilee Park.'

'No, but Christmas and the sales are over, so is stock-taking. The girls and Joan will manage very nicely. I'll be back for the last two hours or so. Mind you, I've divided loyalties today, y'know, I used to watch Darlington as a boy.'

'I didn't know that,' Calderwood muttered politely.

'Oh yes, we lived at Barnard Castle, they were the nearest team to us. Quite good they were too, then. It was during the war, of course, and there were a lot of top players stationed at Catterick. I remember seeing them beat Newcastle once, about 1941.'

'Well, I hope you don't see a repeat today.' Calderwood tried to sound good-humoured but came out terse. 'I'll leave the car round the back if I may and walk.' He looked down at his tie with the mitre and rose. 'We could do with a bit of assistance from his lordship today. Let's hope he provides it.'

5

Shortly after one thirty Calderwood began to experience the sensation that had been inseparable from every Saturday afternoon of the season during his adult life. It was a physical thing, often pleasurable, like sex, sometimes hurting like an actual pain.

The gates had just opened, admitting the first knot of vigilant small boys. These were the handful of individualistic heroes who were prepared to take the jeers each school day for being Barford Albion supporters. The success-worshippers amongst their classmates, perhaps wiser in their generation, had already identified with Leeds United, Arsenal, Liverpool, Manchester United. Later, even smaller boys would come, escorted by their fathers, boys who had no choice as yet since they were too small to journey to the grounds of the big clubs.

From now till six o'clock he would have a thousand things to do, dozens of people to see. He'd already had a word with the turnstile-checkers, really a social call since they were essentially the responsibility of the club secretary, Leonard Steele, a local solicitor. He had scanned a copy of the club programme, which Dave Adamson edited. By Fourth Division standards it wasn't a bad publication, although he found the title, 'Jubilee Jottings', a bit much. Quickly he re-read his own contribution, 'From the Manager's Desk', automatically and belatedly checking it for errors of spelling and grammar. He scanned the pen-portraits of the visiting players in case Dave had included any nugget of information which he didn't know and ought to have. He noted the referee's name, Paul Poole of Tamworth. It meant nothing to him, but then there were so many rookies on the League list these days. He hoped to God that Schofield had remembered to tell Enid to buy the ball, more important, to bring the ball.

His door rattled for the first but certainly not for the last time that afternoon. It was the Planet, freshly-shaved, his wavy grey hair springing thick and wiry above a sweater of the same colour. He wore this over the dark blue track-suit trousers with yellow stripe which were standard issue for the home players. Calderwood looked up invitingly at him.

'Well, Joseph?' It was a mild pleasantry between the two men that the manager occasionally addressed the Planet by his full given name.

'That's Darlington arrived, Boss. They've just brought the hamper round to their dressing room.'

'Fine, I'll have a word with Ralph Marks in a few minutes. Everything OK?'

' 'Fraid not, Boss.'

'What's up, Planet? Quick with it, I'm not in the market for riddles.'

'I've just seen their gear in the dressing room. They're playing in their change strip and it's new to me, green with a broad black hoop.'

'What about it?'

'What about Arnold's sweater, that's all?'

Calderwood frowned, out of love with himself. The little

39

things missed . . . of course, there would be a clash of colours with his goalkeeper's jersey.

'Hell's teeth, I should have remembered they've changed their change strip. Sounds like a job lot they got from a Rugby League club. Can we dig up a yellow jersey for Arnold?'

'We've got one. It's a bit scruffy but it'd do.'

'Good. Fish it out then.' The Planet held fast.

'Arnold thinks yellow's unlucky. You remember, that Cup-tie at Chesterfield where he wore a yellow sweater and threw two in the back of the net.'

Calderwood blew up in exasperation. 'Then he can wear that dark blue sweater he turns up in every day for training. He probably sleeps in the bloody thing anyway. Find something for him, just so long as he's happy.' He made it clear that his annoyance was not fixed on the Planet. 'Good job you noticed it before the referee did, Joseph.'

'Aye, 'twas.' The Planet went off stolidly looking exactly like an ageing but still very fit baths instructor.

The pace increased after two o'clock. The trainer reported on Phil Gifford, who had passed a late fitness test. That would save any possibility of having to bring Frith into the side, thought Bob with grim satisfaction. The tannoy began to blare out pop tunes, mingled with information about the supporters' club. This information also appeared in the programme under the heading, 'Supporters' Snippets'. The compilers of the programme had a severe and permanent attack of alliteration. It was a well-produced publication though, much in demand by programme collectors. Even more in demand would it be if Albion lost League status. The programmes for the last matches of such vanished clubs as New Brighton and Accrington Stanley were now of great price, literally collectors' items.

He could hear the studs drumming on the dressing room floor in a nervous tattoo as he opened the office door. He almost collided with a brown-haired girl of medium height, carrying a large plastic bag in which was, quite obviously, the match ball. Her smile and voice were pleasant, her features good, the face broad, tending towards square-shaped, perhaps the jawline rather stronger than it might ideally have been. Her throat and neck were quite beautiful; she herself must have been fully

40

aware of this, for she had no scarf, despite the weather. Under a suede jacket, unbuttoned, she wore an oatmeal-coloured dress, above the vee neckline of which the creamy column of her neck appeared. She gave the impression of great health and vitality, rather than that of strict beauty.

'Hello, Mr Calderwood. Uncle Jack said I'd to buy a ball in Essendean's and charge it to the club. They were very nice about it, blew it up for me. Shall I take it from its bag?'

'Don't bother, thanks.' Bob's tone was disapproving, barely civil. 'Just leave it by the desk. Sorry you've been put out.'

'No trouble, please. I've been in Essendean's lots of times before.'

With that little tyke Frith, no doubt, was Bob's unspoken thought. What he did say was, 'I take it your uncle's coming on after his wedding?'

'To the match? Oh yes, he's nipping away after the toast to the newlyweds. He said he'll get here before kick-off time.'

'It's a pity to spoil the day for Mrs Schofield,' Calderwood murmured sardonically.

'Oh, Aunt Lucy won't mind, she'll stay and chat with the chums. They both do their own thing, that's why they've a happy marriage.'

Bob nodded, not really in agreement but anything was better than a prolonged conversation with this juvenile Evelyn Home. Even when her face was straight, she seemed to be mocking him, finding him absurdly staid. Looking directly at him, she said, 'Are the players in the dressing room yet?'

'This ten minutes. Did you want to see anybody?'

If he had expected any kind of evasion he got none. 'Yes, Les Frith. I hope he gets a couple more today.'

'He'll be pushed, he's sub,' said Calderwood and had his reward in the girl's look of disappointment. Quickly she recovered herself.

'Do you know I might be coming to work in the office, Mr Calderwood?'

'I do.'

'How do you feel about it?'

'I've got no opinions on the matter. The appointment of non-playing staff is properly for the chairman or his delegate to

41

do. All I'll say is that I'm fairly severe in the office.'

Enid gave the kind of giggle which Calderwood marked down as 'cute'. 'Yes, Vi told me. Imagine young Vi being preggers.'

'Indeed, Miss Schofield. I hate to appear to rush you, but you'll understand.'

'Of course. Good luck for this afternoon. And if the team's in trouble, don't hesitate to bring on Les. He'll show them what he's made of.'

As he has done you, Enid, I don't doubt, reflected Calderwood as he watched her principal-boy behind bounce away down the corridor. He gazed after her absently, his mind already on what he would say to his team in twenty minutes or so. This was always difficult. Was there any other sphere in which the manager had so little control over employees once the manufacturing process started? He often queried the validity of such talks, distrusting the gung-ho — 'I want players who will bleed for me' — approach of some of his managerial colleagues. The intelligent players simply refused to. The plodders might bleed, but the world was full of plodders, honest-to-God players who could frighten Arsenal for an hour or so, but thereafter, nothing. For real success, you needed the thoroughbreds, the Laws, the Di Stefanos, the Peles, and if you were lucky enough to have one of them, then there really was little need to explain what was required. They knew!

He went to the mouth of the tunnel and looked out. The ground was taking on a more populous look, quite respectable with half an hour to kick-off. The small boys spotted him and set up a discordant chant,

> Calder, Calder, Calderwood,
> Calder, Calderwood.

The loudspeaker drew attention to next week's rearranged game at Bournemouth, giving details of the special coaches leaving. For those going by car there were detailed instructions in the programme, 'Where It's At'. Nobody can accuse us of not trying, Chairman, we really care.

In the passage outside his office a tall, heavy man in a fairly

42

well-tailored coat, maroon scarf and round deerstalker pebbledash hat was waiting for him to return. Even had he not been carrying a bag, Calderwood would have marked him as the referee, for he had the healthy but oddly unathletic build that most whistlers have. Bob found him slightly older than he would have expected a newcomer to Football League refereeing to be.

The newcomer nodded rather diffidently to Bob and introduced himself. 'Mr Calderwood? Good afternoon. I'm Paul Poole from Tamworth, I'm in charge of today's match.'

'I hope you've more idea than the comedian we had at Southend last week,' Calderwood said heavily.

The portcullis came down straightaway. 'We try to referee impartially everywhere, Mr Calderwood,' Poole said stiffly.

'Indeed,' Calderwood murmured pacifically. No use in antagonising the fellow before the game started. 'I hope you enjoy today's match. It'll be your first visit here?'

Each knew that it was, but it was etiquette to be doubtful, thereby implying that the referee might be slightly more senior than was actually the case. They had gone into the office and stood talking together by the glass cupboard with its hideous trophy. A firm knock on the door preceded by seconds Adamson's good-humoured face.

'Got the line-up, Bob? Oh, sorry, didn't realise you'd got company. I'll pop along for the Darlington team.'

'Just a minute, Dave. Mr Poole, today's referee, this is Dave Adamson of the *Examiner*. The two men shook hands, appraisingly.

'I'll run along, ref, and get the Darlington side. I'll maybe have a word later on about your pigeons.' He turned to Bob. 'Can I look in for an after-the-match piece?'

'I suppose so. For God's sake go easy with those flowery adjectives or our lot'll be wanting another two quid per man.'

'You've got to go easy on the flowery adjectives at eight hundred words plus teams. See you later, ref.'

'How the hell did he know I'm a fancier?' the official inquired.

'Search me. He's a bright lad, our Dave. Not too much he doesn't know, or doesn't ferret out. Have you seen the pitch?'

43

Poole nodded. 'I walked over it on the way in. You've no problems there. Can I have your team lines?' Calderwood handed them over. Poole shifted his weight cautiously. Rather embarrassed he said, 'Actually, Mr Calderwood, the main purpose of my visit is to check the match ball. I've been asked specifically to see that there's a new one.'

It was Calderwood's turn to be less than comfortable. 'I know. We've been doing a bit of repainting in recent weeks.'

'I understand that the club has used the same ball for the last three games. The last team to play here complained officially.'

'We wouldn't have used it if I hadn't been away with the reserves that day. They had every right to complain. It must have been like kicking a bloody enamel po.'

The referee looked relieved at this reasonable view of things. 'I wouldn't press it, but I've found out there's a referee supervisor here today.'

'Don't give it a thought, Mr Poole, you have your job to do. No worries today, anyway, here's the little beauty.' He withdrew the ball from the plastic carrier bag. As he did so, the confidence drained from his face and his 'Christ!' was more a mark of desperation than of fury.

Poole had turned away to inspect the dust-gathering pennants. 'What's up, Mr Calderwood?' Silently Bob handed him the ball.

'This is a size four, Mr Calderwood.' Bob shrugged, nodded mutely. 'We can't use this as a match ball. If you'll excuse my asking, who would buy a size four for the club?'

'A good question. The chairman's niece is the answer. An even better question is who the hell in Essendean's would be silly enough to sell a size four? For God's sake, a bloody size four.'

'I don't suppose you could send somebody down now for a full-sized ball?'

There was a helpless weariness in Calderwood's look. 'Essendean's close at one o'clock. All their prospective customers are playing on Saturday afternoons.'

Poole remained silent, considering. At last he said, 'You realise I'll *have* to report this to the League, Mr Calderwood? On an ordinary day I might just have taken the chance, but with the supervisor there he'll gut me and it won't help you.'

The referee picked up the ball, rotated it between his hands, pressed it with his thumbs. He thought for a moment.

'You know, this ball's not fully inflated. I'll pump it up a bit and risk starting. After a minute or so I'll call for the ball and find some defect in it. Then we can carry on with another.' He stopped, speaking half to himself. 'We only have to *start* with a new match ball.'

'That's very good of you,' Calderwood stammered. Poole looked embarrassed. 'I know you've got troubles. I don't want to add to them. I take it my room's beyond the dressing rooms?'

'That's it. Last on the left.'

As the referee went out, the loudspeaker was blaring again. 'Here are today's teams.' Bob listened as the announcer droned through the visiting line-up. There was a cheer as the metallic voice said, 'Barford Albion . . .' Bob waited for the boos which would greet the announcement that Les Frith was substitute. They came right on cue. As the crowd's displeasure rang out, Schofield came in quickly, wearing a grey morning-suit and carrying a suit-bag.

'D'you mind if I change here in your office, Robert?' It was not really a question. With amazing deftness he changed from his wedding gear to a russet sports suit with a pronounced green check. Calderwood would have liked sufficient courage to wear it.

'I'd have used the boardroom, but the Darlington directors are already there. Leonard is entertaining them.' He grunted as he zipped up the trousers of his sports suit. He reached into the bag and from across the hanger-bar pulled a brown tie which had for motif two boxers in yellow, pummelling each other.

'Oh, the BBC people are there too. I think I mentioned them. Enid brought the ball, I hope?'

Something in the cavalier striptease, the airy tone, riled Calderwood. He made a point, normally, of speaking politely and respectfully to the chairman, not from servility but from a real attachment to order and duty. It was a measure of his anger that he departed from it now.

'Oh, she brought the ball all right, a size four. Bloody hell! I've enough on my plate on a match day without that.'

Schofield made an explicit sexual reference to his niece. Calderwood was taken aback. He never used the word of any woman and he was truly shocked at its application to a relative. If Schofield noticed his unease, he gave no sign of it. Outside, the announcer repeated the teams, the crowd booed again.

'They should boo that stupid bitch,' Schofield snarled. 'She's got eyes and ears for nothing but the terracing's hero.'

'We shouldn't have had to depend on her.'

'Well, we did, didn't we?' Schofield adopted his beating-down tone. 'About the ball then, I hear the League have been moaning?'

Calderwood was still extremely nettled. 'They'd be well within their rights. Anyway the ref says he'll start with it and kill it after a moment or so. Damned decent of him, I thought.'

Gratitude was not a Schofield long suit. 'I suppose he knows who writes the fitness reports on him,' he said offhandedly. 'Hell, she's a stupid . . . What was that?'

Through the open door, muffled but distinct, came a popping noise. For the second time in five minutes, Calderwood called on his Maker.

'Jesus!'

Schofield showed imminent signs of departure. 'If that's what I think it is, Robert, I'd better go up to our visitors. In case there's a delayed kick-off. Looks bad if the home chairman doesn't show up for a pre-match sherry. See what you can do for us with the ref on the old boy network.'

'I only met him thirty minutes ago.'

'But your credit's good. I'll bring the BBC people down after the match. Good luck.'

'Good luck,' echoed Calderwood unbelievingly to the confident, receding back. Poole came in, undaunted. He had changed for the game and was carrying a pump and the deflated ball.

'The last couple of strokes did it, Mr Calderwood.'

'Well, nice try, ref,' Bob managed gamely. Then he realised that Poole, poking about in the innards of the football, appeared anxious to continue to offer assistance, and even stranger, reasonably convinced that he could.

'Look, I don't think this hole's all that big. Have you had

your word with the team?'

Calderwood shook his head.

'Then be quick about it. After that I'll send both teams out. I'll go out without the match ball and toss. You pump this up like hell. When I signal, throw this one straight out to me, bypassing the linesman. That's important. As long as we kick off with the new ball, who's to say it wasn't an accident?'

'You're going to a hell of a lot of trouble for us,' Calderwood said worriedly.

Poole interrupted him. 'I haven't got time for the story of my life now. But when I was eight, my father was in Barford with the Customs and Excise. He brought me here every Saturday. I saw all the players you've only heard about; Legs Gillan, Joe Anderson, Porky Farrell. I suppose Barford were my first team.' He switched on his authoritarian look. 'Not that you can look for any favours out there once the whistle blows.' With a glance at his watch he said, '*And* you'll be fined for a late kick-off if you don't get a move on. A minute or so with it,' — gesturing towards the ball — 'that's all you'll need.'

He went out and Calderwood set to work with the speed of an actor in a silent film. He visited his side's dressing room and gave a sensible, brief, tactical talk which entertained Les Frith, was barely listened to by Gifford, the physics student, and minutely appraised by Slocombe, the banker. There was a clattering of studs in the stone corridor as the visitors took the field to a derisory scatter of applause and half-hearted booing. A few seconds' silence, the same exciting drumming noise, then the best in cheering that two thousand-odd spectators could provide, with a particularly affectionate reception for the ill-done-to Les Frith.

Back in his office Calderwood, manager of a club which was sweatily about to strive to preserve League status, pumped doggedly as he stuck to his task of inflation. The telephone rang. He ignored it, picked up the ball and carried it caressingly down the tunnel and out to the touch-line. For all the real influence he could exert now, he might just as well go home. A kick-about for some of his players, a shop-window for others, his bread and butter. In fact, just another Saturday.

6

The game had been over for almost an hour. The players had gone home, so had the crowd, the four reporters had phoned over their copy from the tiny hen-coop of a press-box. The floodlights dimmed, went out. Calderwood, drained of energy and emotion, sat back in his Habitat chair, looking at Adamson. He forced himself to rise slowly and go to the cupboard underneath the near-empty trophy case. He placed a bottle of whisky and two glasses on the desk top. He invariably had a whisky after each home match, but in his eighteen months with the club, no one had ever seen him take two.

He half-filled a glass and pushed it at Adamson; his own was fractionally more miserly.

'Here you are, Dave.' He drank his own, making a smacking, irritating sound. 'Bloody hell, I needed that.'

'It worked out all right, Bob. 3-0's not at all a bad old result.'

Calderwood exhaled through pursed lips. 'The game's often the easy bit. It's what goes before that ages you.' He put it all behind him. 'It was a pretty fair result. Young Slocombe had a good game, didn't he?'

'He's a good lad. I liked Gifford too.'

'He wasn't bad,' Calderwood said, almost slightingly. 'Not the greatest team man in the world, is Gifford. It worked out well with our Leslie too. He gets a goal after we bring him on for the last fifteen minutes when the game's been sewn up anyway. But it keeps the crowd happy, couldn't have been better.'

Adamson permitted himself a grin and a flourish of his notebook. 'Can I quote you as saying that you are quietly confident that better times are ahead?'

'I knew a Rangers manager once,' growled Calderwood, 'who used to tell the press boys, 'I don't know and don't quote me.' You can write what the hell you like so long as you put in the bit about shrewd, pipe-smoking Bob Calderwood. The fans have no respect for a non-pipe-smoking manager.'

The bantering tone disappeared as Adamson asked, 'What do you suppose that BBC chap's down here for?'

'I dunno,' Calderwood said dourly. 'Not for *Match of the Day*, that's a certainty. Ever see him before, Dave?'

The telephone shrilled, forestalling Adamson's reply. He shook his head over the ringing. Bob picked up the receiver.

'Hello, Jubilee Park. 3-0 for Barford. That's it, Barford Albion three, Darlington nil. How did we play? Why the hell don't you come down here and see how we play?'

He slammed the receiver back on the bar, and there was a honed edge to his voice. 'These people get on my wick. They sit on their arses every Saturday afternoon watching two great eunuchs of wrestlers and then phone up dripping interest and concern.' He dismissed the caller from his thoughts with the air of a batsman pulling a long-hop for six. 'Where were we? Oh yes, that BBC fellow. You haven't ever seen him?'

'No,' said Adamson consideringly, 'I don't think he's on the sports side. He's certainly not one of their northern people. He's possibly not a football man at all.'

'What makes you think their sports commentators are?' Calderwood jibed maliciously. The reporter could see that the impending visit both irritated and worried the manager. 'Well, I suppose we'll find out soon enough. You going?'

Adamson had drained his glass and was assembling hat, gloves, paper and notebook. He nodded. 'I'll look back into the office for half an hour to check out a reference on our microfilm. Bloody murder on the eyes is that. I'd far rather have the stacks, but we've so many back numbers we'd have had to move to Huddersfield by now. See you then, Bob. Crewe going down at home was a bit of a bonus.'

'Not for the poor sod in this office at Crewe it's not,' Calderwood said grimly. He sighed. 'Still, I'm short on sympathy these days. Are you coming to Exeter next week?'

'Unless I get a better offer. Dear God, Workington, Gillingham, Hartlepool and Chester since Christmas, and now Exeter. It's like being in the grip of a demented travel agent. Never mind, eight hundred thoughtful and analytical words for Monday and I can put my feet up with John Wayne and *Match of the Day*.'

'Exeter doesn't seem so bad suddenly,' Calderwood said with a sourish smile. 'Good night, Dave.'

49

'Good night, Bob.' He stopped at the door almost shyly. 'Nice one. Give my regards to Joan.'

'Who's Joan?'

There were still sounds of conviviality drifting down from the boardroom, but shouted farewells began to be heard and he could make out the noise of the Darlington bus revving up outside. Schofield would be down in a few minutes. He turned to his reports.

It was Calderwood's practice to make two assessments of his players' performances, one immediately after the game, the other on the following morning. He completed his second set of reports without reference to the first before comparing them. He made some rough jottings then turned to his referee's report, which he compiled on the same principle before submitting it to the Board of Directors. This week it would scarcely need revision on Monday morning. It had been a quiet game, well controlled by Poole. Barford's superiority had been so marked from the word go that the game had never threatened to boil over. He was therefore less irked than he might have been when the phone rang yet again, and positively expansive on realising it was Ron Akenshaw of Doncaster.

'How's Ronnie then? 2-2, eh? That's not a bad one against Portsmouth. Yeah, 3-0 for us, very comfortable.' In response to a query from the other end of the line, he riffled through the pages of his desk diary. 'Just a minute. I think . . . yes, we could probably play off our reserve match with you on Thursday night. We'd like to crack on too, we're a couple of games behind . . . I'll have to check with Steve Birkenshaw on the injury position, but we could always shove in a couple of trialists. Better than that, I'll give Les Frith a run in the stiffs, might put a few dozen on your gate . . . Yeah, he was on the bench today, came on and scored . . . No, there's damn all up with him. He's there to make him start chasing the ball and stop chasing skirts . . . Well, he was always a bit of a head-banger. Ronnie, do you think your lot can run to a 7.15 p.m. kick-off on Thursday? That'll let our lads get the last train from here to Leeds when the coach brings them back to the ground. Otherwise we'd have to put them up at the Plough and we lose enough on reserve games as it is . . . About three hundred pounds

every match, chairman says. Thanks, that'll be a big help . . .
Oh sure, I'll almost certainly be over with them. Right,
Ronnie.'

He put the phone down with a happy expression on his face.
There were a few villains in managership, but not many. There
was in fact the close camaraderie which came from the knowledge that every season, approximately one in three of the
ninety-two Football League club managers would be fired. It
was physically impossible for more than ten of them to achieve
actual success in any one season. There were of course different
yardsticks of success. If Revie or Shankly came third in the
League and went out in the Cup semi-finals, that might be
comparative failure. If he, Bob Calderwood, only just managed
to keep Barford Albion in the Football League at all, that would
be comparative success. He hoped that Schofield would see it
that way.

As if he had conjured a spirit, Schofield's shape darkened
the door. He was accompanied by two other people. The man
was very tall, very heavy, with a black, stained fisherman's knit
sweater, green corduroys and, astonishingly, open-toed san-
dals. He looked like an unimaginative stock actor's conception
of a television producer, was Calderwood's first impression.
This couldn't possibly be?

'We're not disturbing you, I trust, Robert?' Schofield ques-
tioned with totally unconvincing distress.

'Not especially, Mr Schofield.' He motioned towards the
desk. 'I was just tidying up the odds and ends.'

'Good. Excellent performance from the boys today, Robert.
You must have had them well motivated.'

('Oh, I did, Chairman. Like, lose this bloody game and we're
for the chute. I'm looking for a job and you lot are back to
playing in the public parks.') He contented himself with nod-
ding.

'Allow me to introduce our visitors from the BBC. Miss Pam
Correll and Mr Oliver Dampenay.'

It was true then, this great thirtyish capon was the producer!
The capon spoke in a light, brittle voice, his eyes flickering all
around him.

'How do you do, Mr Calderwood. This *is* an atmospheric

51

room. I'm with *Sidelight*, the features programme, and Pam's my PA . . . Programme Assistant,' he expanded graciously.

Calderwood nodded at the small, slim girl in the sheepskin jacket and long, expensive boots. Even in that unpromising garb, he detected that her figure was quite exceptional. Oliver was prosing on.

'Your chairman, Mr Schofield here, has kindly allowed us to look over your patch for a feature we want to do. You know our subtitle, "The World's Our Beat".'

'What sort of feature?' Calderwood emphasised the last word as if it was an oath.

'Well, a mini-documentary really, perhaps half of our forty-five minutes' running time.'

Pam Correll butted in with an oddly ingenuous keenness. 'We thought of getting Tom Fleming to do the commentary. He's a Scot too, isn't he?'

Calderwood ignored this attempt to foist kinship on him. 'What's he know about football?'

'He's got a glorious dark voice and he's very professional,' the girl said.

Oliver, who gave the impression of wearing a spiritual kaftan, cut in with daunting news. 'I'm afraid we can't have Tom, Pam love. I quite forgot to tell you. In Manchester this morning I was having breakfast in the Midland at the next table to the Controller and I heard him say — actually he's *such* a Bull of Bashan, it's hard not to catch his little *entre nous* — that HRH is going to open the new hospital at Salford next Tuesday and Tom'll have to be up there for rehearsal and transmission.'

Schofield was unable to maintain his pose of detached amusement. With a real interest he asked, 'Is he the only one who could do the Salford piece?'

'I should say so,' said Oliver with a lofty professionalism. 'No one else can do the reverential hush bit half as well. "And now His Royal Highness, who must have happy memories of opening the Labour Exchange here four years ago, cuts the ribbon." And Tom's great on trees. "HRH, with the skill of the accomplished woodman, plants this sapling that with the passage of years will soar skywards as a noble tree." ' The massive man was almost genuinely involved in what he was saying, but his eyes danced with mocking malice as he went on, 'I suppose Canterbury might be as good but he *could* come a touch expensive for the Beeb these days. Tom's never short of a few thousand well-chosen words. Doesn't matter a hoot which of the Royals performs the ceremony, but you must have Tom.'

Calderwood was uneasy in the face of Dampenay's quasi-feminine gestures and expressions. He turned belligerently to Schofield. 'I suppose you've okayed this, Chairman?'

Schofield adjusted the knot in his tie to bring his two boxers into more perfect alignment. 'Yes, Robert. It'll do us no harm for Jubilee Park to be given a screening.'

'That depends on the screening surely.' He swivelled to Oliver. 'When did you have in mind to come?'

'Let me see now.' He turned to Pam, who had sat down, uninvited, on the other office chair. 'Is that aqualung thing Thursday, love?'

Pam nodded. 'If they can get Dorothy Hibbet to do the piece. You know how keen they are upstairs on the woman's angle.'

'It'll probably be Tuesday then,' said Oliver querulously. 'Dear Dorothy, such a *severe* case of BO. And having to have her idiot questions held up on a board behind the interviewee.' He ceased to meditate on the malodorous Dorothy and snapped back to the present. 'Yes, Tuesday, Mr Calderwood.'

'Tuesday's a training day with us,' Bob reminded Schofield stubbornly.

'Doesn't matter all that much, Robert, does it? We'll only have the two or three full-timers in. I've given Mr Dampenay the run of the ground, he won't get in your way.' He turned to the television man. 'You can shoot anything you like, we've nothing to hide. By the way, how many of you will there be?'

Oliver just beat Pam in a rapid head count. 'Oh, two cameramen, sound man, PA, commentator, driver and myself. That should do it.'

Schofield beamed expansively. 'Fine. I'll have a word with Mrs Armitage and she'll lay on coffee and sandwiches in the boardroom.'

Pam flashed a smile of appreciation. 'Super. I must say that's more than the Forestry Commission did the other day when we went up to Northumberland.'

'Well, they didn't stint the creepy-crawlies, dear,' Oliver said roguishly. He became brisker as he spoke again to the manager. 'We'll come about ten, and with luck we'll clear just after three. Otherwise the crew's wage slip will look like a ransom demand. We would transmit probably about a month later, it's what we call a timeless piece.'

Schofield made a production of consulting his diary. 'That'll be around February 19?'

Oliver beamed on Pam. 'We've a viewer here, cherub. He knows we go on Friday nights.'

The chairman gave signs of departure. 'Well, do your best for us.' He forestalled a movement by the broadcasters to accompany him. 'Why don't you stay on for a few minutes and clue things up with Robert? Tell him some of the interesting angles you told me upstairs.' He switched to a social martyrdom look. 'I'd much rather hang on but there's a bit of a do at the bride's father's house for the antiques like Lucy and myself. The younger element, thank God, are going off to some disco. See you Wednesday, Robert. Well done.'

He was gone. For a few moments there was an unfriendly silence which Calderwood broke truculently and rather inconsequentially.

'Why do you need all that clamjamfry for a twenty-five minute documentary? It sounds more like *Gone With The Wind*.'

'Sound is trickier,' explained Oliver. 'We only shot silent this afternoon. Some lovely stuff though.'

It was possibly the fact that Oliver made no move to specify what the 'lovely stuff' was that angered Calderwood. He jerked a peremptory thumb towards the door in the direction of the departed chairman.

'Look, since he's given you the OK, I can't do a thing but, just to humour me, exactly what kind of programme is this going to be?'

This time Pam anticipated her master. 'We see the club as mirroring the town's decay . . . the driftwood of the Industrial Revolution, something washed up and stranded like . . . like a slagheap. Isn't that it, Oliver?'

'My word, yes! You know, shots of rusting cranes by the

canal wharves, shots of rusting rails in the sidings, shots of rusting iron bars here in the footie ground, you know, those iron things . . .'

'Crush barriers,' said Calderwood laconically.

'*Crush* barriers,' breathed Oliver, transported. 'What a chance for a splendid ironic comment, the crush barriers that contain a scattered handful. Do make a note of that, Pam.' She complied, busily, dutifully, prettily. 'Some shots too of the creaking of those disused turnstile things, cuts to the faces of the old boys in the crowd. Very few lusty youths today, did you notice that, Pam? And that marvellous John Betjeman grandstand, like an eight year old run amok with a fretwork set.'

'Isn't your programme about people at all?'

'Heaps of people!' said Pam smoothingly. 'Oliver . . . he's so observant . . . Oliver, you noticed that old man sweeping the corridor outside the boardroom.'

The big man snorted with commingled laughter and fervour. 'God, yes! The first collar-stud I've seen outside *The Forsyte Saga* in years. And that player, the little bald chap with the beefy thighs, we should get some good shots of him training and sweating and grunting.'

Calderwood's eyes were murderous. His rage was such that his tone was flat, breathless.

'You won't. He trains at night. Archie's a full-timer, but his wife's got sclerosis and he looks after her until her sister finishes work. I've given him permission to train in the evenings, so you'll have to use flashlights for your comic shots.'

Pam, a decent girl, stammered, 'We didn't know.'

'Of course not,' hammered Calderwood, the implacable tone at odds with the reassuring words. 'You couldn't, and Archie's the only hard-luck story. The rest are just drinkers, gamblers and bed-minded lads.'

'How sad!' murmured Oliver abstractedly. Calderwood felt that this disembodied response would have been forthcoming had he proclaimed his players to be all masochists or Seventh Day Adventists to a man. Then, visibly brightening, Dampenay said, 'But you'll come over well, very well, Mr Calderwood.'

'No, I won't,' Calderwood gritted quietly.

'Why do you think not, Mr Calderwood?' Pam was the questioner.

'Because I refuse to utter a bloody word to people who're out to cut my throat.' He stabbed a lean forefinger at Oliver. 'It's *his* ground, it's *his* club, if he wants you, I can't stop you. But I'm the club manager, not a bloody marionette or performing seal. My tongue's my own. You people have no interest in football.' He rounded ferociously on Pam. 'Do you ever see a match?'

Pam was half-defensive. 'Well, if we do a feature on the national side, or a European team. But I know more about rugby, I'm afraid. My boyfriend's the Waterloo stand-off.'

'Squash is my game,' Oliver volunteered.

Calderwood looked at his majestic gut in pointed and insulting disbelief. 'And you expect me,' he resumed his tone of quiet, cold disgust, 'to put a rope around my neck? Maybe your costume department could kit me out with a check suit, bowler hat and cigar to make me more in character?' He made a gesture in the general direction of his desk. 'If you don't mind, I'm not quite through here yet.' The dismissal lost a little in finality as the damned phone rang once again.

'Hello, Jubilee Park. I know, love, twenty minutes. Phyllis too? At the bus station? I see . . . Yes, a good enough day. Right, Joan.'

The other two were still hanging on indecisively. 'We've offended you, Mr Calderwood,' Pam ventured timidly.

'You haven't,' Calderwood said. 'Your organisation has. I get a bit short with commentators, too, who tell me exactly what my centre said in a goal-mouth punch-up.'

Oliver stopped twittering. 'Let's get back, Pam.' And to Calderwood, 'Our driver is inclined to punish the light ale if left too long. We promise to keep out of your road on Tuesday morning.'

'Do that,' said Calderwood, not giving an inch.

They went out, Pam uneasy, her boss unconcerned. Calderwood put on his coat and hat. He moved to the doorway to switch off the light and collided with a soft young body. Momentarily he assumed it was the programme assistant, but it proved to be Enid.

'Just a minute, Mr Calderwood, did I by any chance drop a

glove in here when I brought the ball?'

'If you did it'll be the wrong size.'

'Whatever do you mean?'

'Forget it. Could you possibly hurry up? I've had five hours here.'

'Of course.' She found the glove, to Calderwood's surprise under the desk, managing to display an interesting amount of leg in the process. Calderwood reacted despite himself and was annoyed when her level gaze caught him out.

'Look at that run in these tights,' she invited Calderwood. It was a long, graceful run.

'I have an appointment, Miss Schofield.' What a prissy, weary phrase that was, he thought, even as he said it.

'So have I. I must go.'

'With the scorer of our third goal?'

He was asking for it. It was no concern of his and he derogated his position by enquiring. Enid, however, seemed to take no offence.

'No, I wish I were. Les is in the final of his club snooker championship tonight. All beer and boys. I'm going with Peter March to the disco.'

Peter March was an inoffensive young man who, when his father — the biggest hotelier in the district — died, would be an inoffensive, wealthy young man. Bob felt he owed the girl a pleasantry.

'Well, it beats sitting at home with the knitting.'

She wrong-footed him once more by glancing at him with total composure. She had only just finished taking stock of her thigh. He switched off the light.

'When you know me better, Mr Calderwood, you'll discover that I'm not much of a girl for the knitting.'

7

Ten days after the Darlington match, Bob found himself standing in the large reception room of the Hat and Feathers, talking
to Gilbert Oldfield, secretary of the North Barford Rotary
Club. The two men golfed together some six or eight times a
year, and on their last outing of the previous summer, Oldfield
had asked Bob if he would come along to Rotary and give a 'my
job' talk. With all the euphoria of a fifteen-foot putt, last-green
victory behind him, he had affably agreed and was currently in
the position of wishing that he had not.

He liked the Rotarians, such of them as he knew, a cheerful,
friendly crowd who, in their demonstrative way, did a great
deal of charitable work. Nor did he deny — indeed he would
have insisted — that part of any manager's job was to become
involved in exactly such exercises in meeting the people. He
had resisted invitations to join Rotary however. For one thing,
he was away rather a lot, for another, his formal Scottish
upbringing inhibited him from throwing himself into compulsive first-naming.

All around was a babble of talk about Secretary Gilbert, Area
Officer Philip and Junior Vice-President Michael. Bob was at
the top table on the President's right, President Cyril. He was
an amiable, if rather lugubrious, optician with a beautifully
clipped, martial moustache which was somewhat at odds with
his generally unassertive face. He was not a football fan, he told
Bob regretfully, not really much of a sportsman at all, though of
course he played golf with Rotary socially. All the members, it
appeared, were looking forward to hearing Bob speak, and
indeed the attendance, at thirty-four, was markedly above their
usual.

On his right hand Bob had a fellow-Scot, David Geddes, who
had come originally from Falkirk to Leeds, but now ran a very
well-doing travel agency in Barford. Bob had always had the
notion to go to Iceland, and he quizzed David on ways and
means of getting there. The discussion took them through the
main course, cold beef, tongue and salad, which they fetched

for themselves from the buffet. Only the top table was conventionally laid out — the other Rotarians sat in little groups of five or six to encourage members to vary their table companions at each meeting.

Bob did not go back for the gateau, and momentarily paused in his coffee-drinking as the President proposed the Loyal Toast. Soon they moved to the business of the meeting. The President called on Secretary Gilbert, who reported on the success of the Winter Project, a twenty-mile sponsored cycle run for charity. Charlie Hiddle was mending nicely after his encounter with the wall (shouts of 'Charlie who?'), and it would be a good thing for the club if a few members could find time to visit him.

Details were requested of visits to other clubs. There hadn't been any, which slightly displeased President Cyril. He was happier to recognise officially from the Chair a visiting Rotarian from Finchley and one from Bordeaux, especially happy to greet the latter and 'charge' him to convey 'fraternal greetings' to the Rotarians back there in Bordeaux. There was to be an area conference at Harrogate soon and he hoped that it would be possible for some of the North Barford Rotarians to attend. Those who thought they might be able to manage should have a word with Secretary Gilbert.

Then at last he moved to introduce Bob who was, he ventured to say, one of the best-known figures in Barford, and one who had made an astonishing impact on the town in the comparatively brief time he'd been amongst them. Although Albion had been outgunned by the Gunners — he waited for the loyal laughter to die away — they'd given Darlington a thrashing and got an excellent point at Exeter. He himself, President Cyril, wanted to see the team do well, because when Albion did well the town perked up and business did likewise.

'. . . And so I have great pleasure in introducing to you Mr Bob Calderwood, manager of Barford Albion Football Club, who is going to address us on the topic "my job".'

There was a civil patter of applause as Bob got to his feet, took the lectern which was pushed along to him by President Cyril, and placed on it a single sheet of paper.

He had never found that speaking in public presented any

special difficulty. By no means was he a gifted performer, but he could structure a speech: he had the capacity for logical thought. Besides, he thought, glancing around the dining room, palely lit by the thin sunshine of late winter, he'd have to be very bad if he couldn't do a 'my job' talk. He was the expert.

'President Cyril, Rotarians,' he began, 'I'm very grateful that you asked me here today. You've concentrated my mind wonderfully on what I'm supposed to be doing. I suppose,' he continued thoughtfully, 'the main difference between my job and those of you gentlemen is this. If you do your job well, your business will flourish or you'll get promotion within your company. If you do it badly, you'll go bust or you'll get the sack. Now with me, it's different. If I do my job badly, I'll very soon be fired. If I do it well, then it'll take a little longer to be fired.'

The Rotarians smiled with relief. Today there might, then, be the occasional leavening.

'I have a strange job. There's no real qualification for it except having been a player. I have the FA coaching certificate from Bisham Manor, but I'd have a better chance of a job if I were somebody famous like Bobby Charlton or Charlie George, even supposing I had no certificate. With a small club like Barford, you have to do much more than, say, at Arsenal, where I'd have a general manager to do all the secretarial work, an assistant manager and three or four on the coaching staff.'

He broke off to frown slightly at the young waiter who was rattling coffee cups rather too loudly at the back of the room. The rattling stopped.

'Does a team need a manager? Does an orchestra need a conductor? I saw a TV programme once which suggested they didn't. It's true that once my players are on the park I can't control them. So, is it all just luck? I don't think so, because you can think of managers who have been consistently successful with clubs of different potential. Think of Herbert Chapman with Huddersfield and Arsenal. Brian Clough in our own time with Derby and Notts Forest, Jock Stein in Scotland with Dunfermline, Hibernian and Celtic. They must have had something . . .

'I've got to be a psychologist with my players, got to know who to coax, who to hammer. I've got to be a good judge of a player, an even better judge of a scout. If I managed a big club, I'd have to resist the temptation to think that I could control Stan Bowles or George Best when none of my fellow managers has managed it. I have to be a P.R.O. for the club — I suppose that's what I am at this minute. I have to try to attract people to the ground' — with a mock touch of exasperation he flashed — 'I don't seem to be doing too well with you lot.' The Rotarians, not noticeable in strength at Jubilee Park, tittered guiltily.

'I have to be able to get on with the press and the media. Even at the foot of the Fourth Division this can happen: the BBC paid us a visit week before last as you possibly know. It's difficult talking to the press; most of them are okay, but there are one or two stirrers.

'As far as money is concerned, I'm a salaried employee with an overriding responsibility to my chairman and the Board, but if, in the dressing room, they don't see me as a players' man, I'll not get the best from the lads . . .

'I like the job, I like the day-to-day involvement. It's not too clever for the family though — managers tend to be perfectionists. I know it's most unlikely we'll ever make the First Division, although my old club, Northampton, went from Fourth to First.'

'And from First to Fourth in successive seasons'. Gilbert Oldfield couldn't resist the interjection.

Bob smiled ruefully. 'Granted. But a really astute manager could have baled out at Division One or at worst Division Two level and I have to believe *we* can do a Northampton. Anyway, I was told to keep it short and I will. All that remains for me to say is that I like the challenge, even the uncertainty. I wouldn't really want to do anything else . . . I think.'

He made to sit down, then half-standing said rather awkwardly, 'Thank you for hearing me so patiently. If you've any questions, I'll be happy to answer them.'

There are never many post-talk questions at a Rotary lunch. The calls of business begin to sound insistently. Junior Vice-President Michael wondered if making a star a manager on the strength of his playing record wasn't like offering the conductorship of the London Symphony Orchestra to the most technically proficient musician. Bob answered that it seemed to him

61

exactly like that. President Cyril bridged an awkward gap by wondering whether a businessman could not manage the club. This time the answer was that this had happened in a few, a very few instances — George Allison at Arsenal, for example. The difficulty was that players were a bit snobbish in a strange way. They tended to despise anyone connected with the game who had not been exposed to the pressures of League football. It would be hard, Bob thought, for a modern manager who had never earned his living as a player to command the respect of his staff.

When Secretary Gilbert had proposed the vote of thanks — least he could do, Bob mused vengefully — and the toast of Rotary International had been drunk the members dispersed. Gilbert thanked Bob again for coming. Jocularly he suggested that Bob might have put a few dozen on the next home gate.

'I doubt it, Gibbie. These fellows are too comfortable for football now. The golf-club lounge is more in their line.'

A florid, expensively-suited man was hovering deferentially nearby. 'Could I have a word, Mr Calderwood?'

'Certainly.'

'I'll crack on then,' Oldfield cut in. 'I've got some samples to see. The light will be good enough in the afternoon for a few holes in a month or so.' He went his cheery, uncomplicated way.

'My name is Newton, John Newton. You won't know me. I'm in charge of production at Tunstall's' — he mentioned a large chemical factory — 'I was very taken with your speech, Mr Calderwood.'

'A few random thoughts, Mr Newton,' Bob said. 'It's easy when the subject's one you're bound to be the most knowledgeable about.'

'A few random thoughts are exactly what they were not,' Newton told the manager authoritatively. 'You've a definite capacity for structure, for getting from A to B.' He pulled out a card-case. 'Here's my card. If your love affair with football ever turns sour, I want to know. Schofield tells me you got Higher Science at that Scottish school of yours.'

Without pausing for a thank-you or a no-thank-you, he turned away abruptly, his burly figure nudging those sluggards in front of him in the direction of the door. Calderwood took leave of President Cyril, exchanged a few words with three or four rank-and-file Rotarians, and eventually found himself driving down the pitted avenue which linked the Hat and Feathers with the Barford-Otley road. The car bumped and lurched. Bob deduced that the game-plan was for the owners of the Hat and Feathers to allow the whole driveway to fall to the level of the potholes. As he turned on to the main road he shrugged off Rotary and turned his attention back to the problems of the Albion.

Or rather he tried to. That had been a worrying lunch because what he had said to Gibbie on leaving had been devastatingly correct. At table there had been thirty-four Rotarians, all of them, give or take one or two, men's men. And yet their involvement with the town football club was minimal, despite the brave words of President Cyril. If this group of potential spectators was lost permanently to the game — and in his gloomier, perhaps more perceptive moments Calderwood thought that it was — then did professional football have a future in England? Certainly it could not be sustained by Oliver Dampenay's old-timers and the young yobbos who were driving away the family men in thousands.

He sighed, whipped through the gears and jerked his attention from abstractions back to more immediate problems. Vi had gone at the end of the previous week. Clearly she had not relished sharing the office with Enid, even on a short-term arrangement, and she had touchily declined Schofield's offer to let her work out a fortnight's notice. Her father-in-law had a well-doing greengrocer's business and could always use an extra pair of hands until bringing forth would compel her to lay off.

Calderwood frowned in exasperation. Vi hadn't been a particularly good secretary, or even especially congenial to work with, but she knew where things were and how far she could go with Calderwood. Enid, potentially, was trouble. She was the chairman's niece, there was the danger of the carried tale, the retailing of his conversations with the Planet, the occasions when he had to bawl out his players for a less than acceptable performance. Again, he detected that Enid had set her cap at him, but that did not perturb him greatly. Joan had always said that if he went off the rails it would be with someone fair and fortyish, and this he considered slightly the less fantastic of two improbabilities.

Enid would find an older man attractive, especially one who had kept in shape. Anyone who had slept with Les Frith was bound to find even Jojo the Chimp intellectual by comparison. And she had very good legs.

Back at the office he skimmed through the mail. Notification of the referee against Crewe, a letter from the League calling upon the Planet to explain some derogatory remarks he had made about the referee at Exeter, a letter, badly written, from a man in the Barford Cleansing Department who recommended his son, a goalkeeper, for a trial. Bob frowned thoughtfully. Such amateur referrals hardly ever repaid investigation, not even once in a hundred times, but a goalkeeper? Might this be the once? Whether or not, it had brought Arnold Dearson to mind.

He said to Enid, 'Make a note that I'll want to see Arnold on Thursday.'

'Arnold Dearson?'

'Have we another one?' Bob snapped irritably, and felt pettish as he said it. 'Sorry,' he grunted as he turned back to his mail. There was an invitation or rather, an offer, from a Scottish First Division club to play a match at the Jubilee on their way down to Wembley. Patriotism fought a brief, losing struggle with economic common sense. Friendlies had lost all appeal. The Scots wanted a guaranteed sum rather than half-gate, and the locals equated all Scottish football with the Fourth Division anyway. True, Scotland occasionally managed to beat England in internationals, but only because they stacked their side astutely with players who had the benefit of Football League experience every Saturday. He sighed as he scrawled 'No thanks' across the top of the letter. The Wembley-bound Scots would be passing through, more accurately, passing by.

'Anyone ring while I was out?'

'Oh yes, there was one call.'

'Well, you tell me rather than I have to ask. Who was it?'

The girl flushed in the face of his directness. 'It was a Mr Peterson of the PFA.'

'What did he want?'

'He'd like to come out some evening next week to talk to the players. About freedom of contract that's coming in a couple of years or so. At least I think that's what it was about. Would that be right?'

Calderwood nodded. 'I'll have to get the chairman's OK on that one. Still, I'd rather he talked to them here than in some pub. And I can't imagine that Barcelona or Arsenal will be cutting each other's throats to snap up our lot.'

'Can I ask you a question about football, Mr Calderwood?'

'You can ask. I may answer.'

'Could Les be a top-class player?' Again she showed absolutely no trace of hesitation or embarrassment in the use of the name.

Bob looked consideringly at her then drawled, 'No.'

'Would you very much mind telling me why?'

'He doesn't quite have the ability. Good player, a little bit short. Not keen enough at the end of the day. On the things that matter for a professional footballer, that is.'

'Could you be wrong about him?'

'Of course,' Bob said, rather to her surprise. 'Most judgments in football are purely subjective— personal.' He changed the word for her and a momentary coldness in her look told him the change had been unnecessary and patronising. Damn it, why should he be considering the feelings of this chit who'd been foisted on him? It was time to set out guidelines.

'Look, Miss Schofield, since we'll be working together — '

'Since we will be, could you call me Enid?'

Bob considered the suggestion, as Enid swept on. 'What did you call Vi, Mrs Black?'

'All right, Enid it is then.'

'I'd like that much better. Can I call you Bob? Or do you prefer Robert?'

Calderwood glowered. 'I've a strong preference for Mr Calderwood. See that my preference is met.'

'Yes, Mr Calderwood,' the girl said demurely.

The afternoon passed. Calderwood caught her looking at the card on the inside of the dressing-room door. 'What you do here, what you say here, what you see here, let it stay here.'

'It's a good motto for anyone working around a football club,' he growled defensively.

'Yes,' said Enid. 'A bit simplistic, but then most sayings and writings about sport are.'

'You're an authority on them, are you?'

Her voice was convinced, matter-of-fact. 'I've seen enough of Les's cuttings to be pretty sure.' She quoted, semi-contemptuously, ' "Frith Bags A Brace", "Deadly Duo Rocks Rovers". And their nicknames — "Frithie"! There's a piece of imagination for you. They *are* overgrown boys.' From her greater maturity she dismissed the juvenile phrase-makers and players. 'Mr Calderwood?'

'Well?'

'My car's in for servicing at Harrison's, I've to pick it up at four thirty if I can. Might I go off a few minutes early?' She looked out of the office window to see heavy drops of rain pinging off the roof of the smaller of the two enclosures. 'Just my luck, it's raining.'

'I'll give you a lift.' Really, the tactics of this moppet were transparently guileless; he could afford to be detachedly magnanimous.

On the short drive to Harrison's, he bought an evening paper. He insisted on waiting while Enid checked that the car was ready and he flicked through the paper as her neat figure disappeared into reception. Many a day since a nubile young woman had occupied his front passenger seat.

On the back page, not too prominently, was a story that Peter Runciman, former Orient, Ipswich and England player (two caps against Finland and Mexico), had accepted the post of player-manager with Stalybridge. Calderwood's eyes narrowed. Runciman was totally untried as a manager, but he was a name of sorts, quite a name, to be honest. One would have thought that he could have found a player-manager's job at League level, Fourth or even Third Division. His mind went back uneasily to Adamson's remark, 'Some of us think they've as much right in the League . . .' Stalybridge! He stared absently at the paper. There had been a time when that Cheshire-Lancashire area had been bad news for the League — they had never forgotten the collapse of Wigan Boro' and

Nelson in the twenties or of New Brighton just after the war. But recently there had been signs of forgiving, if not forgetting. The tap of a key on the passenger window recalled him to his surroundings. It was Enid, emerged from reception.

'Car's ready, thanks, Mr Calderwood. Thanks for offering to drive me home. I'll see you tomorrow.'

He watched her cross the forecourt and settle in her car before he drove off in a prickle of doubt and irrational disappointment.

8

Of all the tasks which fall to the manager of a football club, Bob found hardest the letting go of old players whose time was up and young players whose time would never come. He had a puritanical regard for the game which allowed him to move on the wasters like Frith without troubling— indeed with a kind of high priest's pleasure. Now, however, he had to tell Arnold Dearson that the club was about, in the lingo of the game, to dispense with his services.

The really outstanding managers, like the great Prime Ministers, have been good butchers. They are not tormented, as they set to the task of firing, by a mental picture of the old, devoted horse Boxer being borne off by van from *Animal Farm*.

Arnold had come in early to train that day. What he did outside playing time had always been rather a mystery. Offers of odd jobs put his way by various club officials had invariably been politely but very definitely refused. Normally in football that would have meant that he could have been looked for, and probably found, in the billiard saloons and pubs of Barford, but he was not a frequenter of such places. He was very much the one-pint-of-lager man on Saturdays after the match. To the two thousand or so regulars who stood on the Jubilee terracings he was certainly the most popular player in the Albion side, Les Frith not excepted. His appearance radiated honesty, a desire to serve to the best of his ability. There was as yet little grey in his short black hair — it had remained short even when that of his team-mates had reached shoulder-length in the late sixties — but his face was seamed and lined. He was not specially tall for a goalkeeper, a little under six feet, but deep-chested and with very long arms. His hands, too, were long and broad, like the shovels of mechanical diggers, according to Les Frith.

Calderwood waited on him and fidgeted with some papers on his desk. At times like this he was visited with an irrational wish that he smoked. The fact that he was certain in heart and conscience that the course of action he was about to take was the correct one, the beneficial one, did not diminish his reluctance to play the executioner.

In other directions, things were going well. Wins against Peterborough and Lincoln and a draw with Gillingham could well be traded against a rather disastrous evening in Doncaster. Enid continued to exceed his gloomy expectations. Even the Planet had mellowed towards her after she had very much got off on the wrong foot by calling him Planet. Players could call him that, he informed her, players' floosies could not. Enid had giggled happily in recounting the incident to Calderwood. Bob had rocketed her and told her that, in any conflict of interest between Enid and the Planet, it would not be the Planet who was expendable. One had, however, to be careful not to tell Enid off too often. Her liking for Calderwood was going through a phase where abasement was eagerly sought, the wish to be dominated was strong.

'Afternoon, Boss.'

In his youth, and at quite a few Caledonian Society Burns suppers since he came south, Bob had made and renewed acquaintance with the works of Burns. What had seemed a tired, worn line acquired vigour and truth as he looked at Arnold. 'An honest man's the noblest work of God.'

He was wearing his inevitable sweater and heavy grey flannels of a rather antique cut. He was for all the world like a photo from the pre-war *Topical Times*, showing the Arsenal of Alec James and Cliff Bastin preparing at Bognor for some important

Cup-tie. Well, remember the man-management course Maidstone sent you on. In a situation such as this, knock the man down cold at the start of the interview. Make damned sure he knows what the outcome *must* be, then spend the rest of the interview seeing how, the inevitable accepted, matters may be mitigated.

'Sit down, Arnold. Thanks for coming in.' He looked at his senior player sombrely. 'I shan't wrap it up, Arnold, no pretty speeches. All of us who've ever played football know that for most of us there's a spring afternoon in the manager's office ahead of us.' He half-shrugged in apology. 'We're letting you go at the end of the season, Arnold.'

There was no immediate argument. Dearson looked at him with a puzzled calm. 'First week in March, Boss? It's a bit early, isn't it? End of April's usually sacking time in our line.'

'I'm telling you early so that you can look around, maybe get fixed up non-League or somewhere in Ireland.'

Arnold spoke, still with great placidity. 'I'm thirty-nine. You don't think I could go another season, Boss?'

Calderwood shook his head emphatically. 'You scared me stiff last Saturday, Arnold — twice. Start to come out, hesitate, and then down for the smother. It's becoming a habit, Arnold, the most dangerous a keeper can have. I don't want to be your manager when you get your head stoved in.'

Calderwood was slightly perturbed, slightly baffled. Normally by this stage of the parting interview the player about to be released was screaming injustice or lapsing into offended silence. Arnold simply continued to put up the mildest of defences.

'We've only lost five goals in the last four games, Boss. That's not so terrible?'

Bob, apparently irritated, was glad in fact to seize the first real opening that Arnold had given him. 'Arnold, I'm too old a hand at this game to be conned by you. And you've been much too good a goalkeeper to con yourself. You had a shut-out on Saturday last, and you were diabolical. You hesitated virtually every time a forward was through. You *know* that kind of save is pure instinct. If you think, you don't go at all and lose a goal — or you go too late and wind up on a stretcher instead of rolling away with the ball.'

There was a tap on the door and Enid clacked in. 'Sorry to disturb you, Mr Calderwood, but Les Frith would like — '

'Get out!' The manager's voice seared like frozen metal. 'I'll see you later.'

For once Enid's pertness and sophistication could not come to her aid. Flustered and angry, she withdrew.

'Sit where you are, Arnold,' Bob commanded. 'I'll have her guts for garters for disturbing me with a player.'

'Go easy on her, Boss,' Arnold said unresentfully. 'We've all to learn our trade.' He shifted his ground slightly. 'Supposin' I were to take a cut in terms for next season? I'd be quite happy playin' in the stiffs.'

Bob shook his head. 'It wouldn't do, Arnold. For a start, I don't know that we'll be running a reserve side next year, we drop about three hundred every time they play. And even if we did, I'd want a youngster that I could bring on in goal.'

Arnold came as near to pleading as it was possible for him to come. 'You can believe this if you like, Boss, but I'd miss the game more than the money. Since I was a boy, Saturday's been like no other day. You read the papers, see how they think you'll do, then come up here early. Y'know, I've been playing senior for twenty-two years now, and I still look at my name on the team-sheet every time I pass the board. I'm bloody angry when I'm dropped, even when I deserve to be. I can never understand how you can send somebody who's replaced you a good-luck telegram. When young Fred took over from me in August last season, I used to hope we'd win 5-4 and he'd play like a nana.'

Bob suppressed a smile; the veteran keeper had touched a chord. With gentle raillery and affection for this uncomplicated man, he said, 'But you'd be quite happy in the reserves! Well, you're not quite going there yet, although another performance like Saturday's and you'll find 5-4 will do me well enough. I'll stick with you for the time being, Arnold, till season's end if I can. I'm not sure the defence have quite found you out yet, and I don't want panic changes at this stage of the season.'

He had to look away for a moment; his distress was totally genuine. 'You've been a good servant to this club, Arnold, and from what Bob Cuthbert tells me, you were just the same at Oldham. If it was doing you any real good, I'd try to carry you for another season, but you're three years away from your third benefit. Even if by some miracle you lasted that time, this lot would be no certs to pay you. I've talked the chairman into letting you go and I'm giving you the word early, before the transfer market gets cluttered up.'

The goalkeeper stood up slowly, his mind casting back to an early remark of his manager's. 'Ireland, eh? I'd have to be pretty desperate to go there.'

'The South's very pleasant. There are clubs like Cork and Waterford looking for fellows like you, fellows with experience who could coach a bit.'

With totally unexpected wit, Arnold adopted the famous Rodin pose. 'Arnold Dearson, one of the game's great thinkers,' he intoned solemnly. 'Now you are having me on.'

'I swear I'm not. Lots of players far less intelligent, far less responsible than you, stay in the game. You've always been a value-for-money merchant, Arnold, you'd be a good example to young players. I'll put a couple of feelers out if you like, one there, one non-League. You'd maybe do OK there where the pressure's not so great. But I'd chuck it, Arnold, you *will* get hurt.'

The old player looked at him searchingly then looked away, satisfied that, though the manager might be mistaken, he was genuinely concerned for his player's well-being. Shoulders hunched, he wandered over to the window, looking out at the field which was receiving its first clipping of the year.

'You're right, Boss,' Arnold said slowly, hard up against end-of-the-road reality. 'I'm not the keeper I was. I know my eye got better after that bang with the car two years back.'

'Four,' said Calderwood softly.

'Was it?' Arnold exclaimed, in honest amazement at the rushing time. 'Well, choose how, I can't convince my muscles that my eye's OK. I'm hiding in the goal area at corners now. God, Boss, even two years ago I'd have gone through my own centre-half to get to a cross-ball.'

'You did, Arnold,' Calderwood spoke with a grimly jocular relish. 'That's why Nagger Tupliss carries a scar on his

71

forehead today.'

Arnold's grin was reminiscent and quite free of malice. 'He was a moaning bastard.' He burst into an outlandish imitation of what he conceived to be Nagger's Glasgow accent. ' "What's up with ye, Arnold? Hit him wi' yer handbag." '

Arnold smiled contentedly. 'I handbagged *him*! Too bloody right!' He sighed sadly. 'Changed days now, Boss. Martin, my lad, came in crying from school t'other day. Seems his pals were chanting, "Your old man's Count Dracula, he can't face the cross." '

He turned aside Calderwood's word of sympathy. 'No, no, I mind more for the lad. The chaps as pay their money, they're entitled to shout.'

He fell silent for a moment and when he resumed, it was almost as if he was speaking to himself. 'I will miss all this. I think I liked October best — if you got a sunny day and a touch of frost, just enough to firm the ground. At the end of the game I liked hanging back, waiting to shake hands with the other keeper, go in together, knowing I'd played well, made good saves that no one would even notice unless *they'd* been a keeper.' He smiled deprecatingly. 'Joy says I carry on like a poet about my old football.' He swung round to Calderwood, seeing his difficulty and helping the end of the working relationship with a real dignity.

'I'm grateful for what you've done.'

'Forget it, Arnold.' Brusquely he jerked a thumb in the direction of the dressing room. 'Just don't, if you can manage it, mention it along there yet.'

'You don't advertise the sack, Boss. Do something for me?'

'If I can.'

'Give me twenty-five minutes or so out on the pitch, you dribbling in on goal, me coming out at your feet?'

'You're on.' Calderwood grabbed the chance to lose the sadness and irritation of the day in physical action.

Ten minutes later they were changed and out on the field. Arnold's occasional reluctance to snatch the ball from Calderwood's toes was over-compensated for by the occasional scrum-half flying leap that in a competitive match would have cost a penalty, and in practice simply bruised Bob's thigh and shin. In another ten minutes he knew beyond any trace of doubt that Arnold had to go, and that he himself was being dangerously indulgent in allowing him even another Saturday. Yet in their crucial League position, who was to say that a youngster might not prove to be a bag of nerves where the old fox might just be able to fake his way through.

He came from the field vindicated and slightly winded, irrationally furious at the passage of time. There were days when this rage would have turned in upon himself. Today, for a variety of reasons, he would settle with Enid. With a lowering face he showered and quickly threw on his outdoor clothes. Arnold had found one of the apprentices to fire the ball into goal and was flinging himself about happily.

9

Quite unknowingly, Enid had picked a bad day to tangle with Bob Calderwood. Joan and he had been involved that morning in one of their rows which appeared to come along with increasing frequency. As so often happens within a marriage, the subject of the quarrel was trivial. Derek Naughton's staff dance was to be held the following Saturday night in the Spread Eagle and they were both invited. Bob, having failed to signify a definite refusal early in the campaign, was now making withdrawal signals, and Joan was furious.

'I might just as bloody well be a widow as married to you. I'd be better as a widow, I could look around.'

Bob, in domestic situations, was not able to command the control he showed at Jubilee Park.

' "The triumph of hope over experience." '

Joan looked bemused. 'I don't understand you.'

'Samuel Johnson on second marriages.'

'Look, Bob, I'm not in the market for your smart-Aleck

cracks. Why won't you come? You're being totally selfish.'

'You know very well how I feel about going out on Saturday nights after a match.'

'It's a home game. You could come back, change and be out again by eight o'clock, easily.'

Bob retreated to his second line of defence. 'I wouldn't know a soul there except you and Derek, and he's the host. He'll have to swan around talking to people.'

'There won't be more than fifty or so altogether. We've only taken over the Wensleydale Suite. Be a good lad and come.' Joan's voice was cajoling but failed to bring out the hoped-for response.

'I'm no good at trivial social chit-chat, Joan. Why don't you go alone, or take Phyllis with you?'

Phyllis and Joan had immediately made common cause against this outrageous suggestion. His daughter, normally Bob's 'sticker', was on this occasion quick to condemn him.

'I think you're really horrible, the way you don't take Mummy anywhere. People will think you're some kind of . . . hermit, or something.'

Even in his irritation Bob was amused by his daughter's fumbling for words. Invective had never been her strong point. She was a taller version of her mother, but her hair was fair and her eyes were those of her father. She was even prettier, Bob reflected, when her hair was not flecked with vermilion as it was currently, but such was Phyllis's zest for experimentation that she was quite liable to come in from the salon some evening with her head done in Buchanan tartan.

'I'm not even a good dancer, honey,' he said in mild self-defence. 'Your mother would be much better with you.'

'As it happens, Clifford and I have plans for Saturday evening. We're going to a twenty-first birthday party in Harrogate.'

'That'll be nice. Whereabouts in Harrogate?'

'The Cairn. And don't change the subject. It would serve you jolly well right if Mum took a fancy to somebody else.'

'He wouldn't care if I did, Phyllis.'

'That's enough, Joan. And quite enough from you, young lady. If you want a husband who dances, set your cap for Fred Astaire. He's maybe a bit geriatric, but a damned sight better than most of us.' He turned to Joan. 'Why not let me have a word with Derek and get him to pick you up?'

Joan looked at him levelly. 'I want you to come to this dance with me, Bob. I'm sick and tired of being the spare wheel on these occasions.'

Her husband bristled. 'You know, you're damned lucky, woman. Back in Lanarkshire, if a man doesn't fancy going dancing, then his wife doesn't go either. Simple as that. Now I think *that's* selfish. I wouldn't stand in your way.'

Phyllis, attempting to re-enter the conversation, was choked off by her mother, and huffily went upstairs to her room.

'I could understand it, Bob, if it was an away match. But with a home game, you might have made the effort, surely.'

'I'll have been away the previous night.'

'How's that? You haven't anything entered on the kitchen calendar.'

'I'm going to have to go to Walsall. Our goalkeeping position is critical. That tip-off I got from the chap in the Cleansing Department was useless. The youngster couldn't clutch, couldn't punch and couldn't kick. Walsall have a keeper going spare. He's not the greatest, but he could do us a turn. He's playing in their reserves tomorrow night.'

'I see.'

He knew from Joan's set face that she would not argue the point any more.

'And I'll see too. If Saturday's not too bloody, I'll maybe put in an appearance. But no way will I stay much beyond eleven. Tell Derek I'll do my best to be there, but there may be snags.'

They had left it at that. He wondered again momentarily whether Derek had a notion of Joan; and, if he had, did he contemplate doing anything about it? He rather thought not; Derek probably just liked having a pretty woman working around him. He wondered, even more fleetingly, what his own reaction would be if he ever found out that Derek and Joan were more than employer and employee. Would he be enraged? He was pretty sure that he would not. Then wasn't that very situation something which ought to worry him?

Well, such questions were not for the club's time. Enid was making departing sounds — the lavatory had flushed noisily, and there had been a brisk slamming of filing-cabinet drawers. He stuck his head into the outer office and called her into his room. She came on his summons.

'I've been a bad lass, Mr Calderwood.'

Calderwood was not deflected by the penitent, mocking approach.

'Irrespective of what your practice was in whatever other employment you followed, you will never again interrupt me when I'm in private session with a player.'

'I'm sorry, Mr Calderwood. Les said it was very important.'

'I don't care if the Pope said it was important,' Bob snarled. 'I could have been bawling a player out, telling him we were letting him go. He could have been raising a delicate domestic matter, anything. I don't discipline players in public, it's not my style.'

'You were very curt with me, Mr Calderwood.'

Bob looked at her. 'If you ever do that again you'll realise just how lucky you were today. I'll tell *you* off in front of whoever is there, visiting directors, your uncle, Les Frith, whoever.'

'Please put it down to inexperience. I won't let it happen again.'

In this kind of situation, Bob had a fatal vulnerability. He could always in his mind's eye see someone berating Phyllis at *her* work. He said, 'We'll say no more about it then. Anyone can make a mistake and anyone had better not make two. Just before you go, what did Frith want?'

Enid smiled mischievously. 'He wanted to know if you would give me tomorrow afternoon off to go to Leeds with him.'

'No.'

'Don't you want to know why?'

'No. It's none of my business, and as I'm not letting you off, the question doesn't arise. I'll need you here tomorrow afternoon. I'll be leaving just after three to go to Walsall to see a young keeper.' He looked at the girl with distaste. 'You could always go over my head, of course, to the chairman, and get him to overturn my decision.'

Enid, smoothing her dress, shook her head calmly. 'Poor Les! He was looking forward to buying me a ring.'

'Congratulations,' Calderwood muttered sourly.

'Oh, I wouldn't have allowed him. He's great fun, and *very* good-hearted. I like him very much — and that's all.'

Bob had listened with polite scepticism to this encomium of Les. 'I'm glad he's stayed in character. I'd have been quite concerned if he'd asked for an extra training session or volunteered to coach one of the younger players. Your Les is heart lazy.'

'He's not really my Les, Mr Calderwood. We had a thing going for a while, and he's certainly star material in bed, wherever else. But I know he'll be off to Swansea soon, and who'd want to go there?'

At such moments Bob, who could actually feel himself flushing, realised that he was in truth of a different generation. The coolness of his young secretary, who appeared to have the morals of an alley cat, took him aback. This brazen admission of a liaison — she'd laugh herself silly over the word — and the considered assessment of her partner in it, made him feel like some beached sea creature from an earlier world. He had a squirming feeling that Enid might just as well have been describing him as a lousy lay to a girl friend or to Les. And how did she know about Swansea anyway? — a question he put directly to her.

'Oh, Les has got wind of it somehow.'

'Well, don't broadcast it to all and sundry. The deal's far from finalised. There are a lot of snags to be ironed out. If Swansea cough up for him they'll be wanting money's worth. We'll have to sell him to them as a good trainer, a steady type.'

'Isn't it a little dishonest to do that?'

Calderwood realised angrily that he had been justifying club policy to this insignificant club employee for the last ten minutes.

'Swansea can look after themselves. There's an old saying, *Caveat emptor*. And you were beating Les's drum only a few minutes ago. Good fun, good-hearted, and a first-class bedmate. What more could Dai or Myfanwy want?' He went on with unbecoming sarcasm, 'Engrossing as this discussion of our local stud is, and late in the afternoon though it be, shall we attempt just one stroke of work for our employers before we go? Good. Then book me a room for tomorrow night at the Three Pines Motel — it's near Sutton Coldfield. I'd enough of overnight driving when the Planet and I went to Edinburgh.'

'With bath or without?'

'It's a motel, there are no withouts. Be sure to tell them I shan't be arriving until 10.30 p.m., but that I'll definitely be in then.' He looked at Enid impatiently. 'Shall I run over it? Single, with breakfast. Book me a call for seven in the morning, and I'll confirm it when I check in. Right, that's that, then.' He moved off towards the door.

'Right, Mr Calderwood, I'll see to it now. By the way, a Mr Dampenay's secretary phoned from the BBC while you were out at lunch-time. She said that the transmission of our programme would be put back a week because of the run-up to the election. It'll go out a fortnight tonight.'

'I'll count the minutes,' said Calderwood. 'Still, I suppose we should watch the Planet bid for stardom out of loyalty. That reminds me, if I don't get a move on, I'll miss *Question of Sport* on the box tonight. Good night, then.'

He went off down the corridor and across the yard to his car, which he always left at the far side of the car park to compel himself to walk the extra hundred yards or so.

Enid's hand was poised on the receiver to make the call when Les Frith materialised from nowhere.

'Is the boss in, Enid?'

His lover looked at him despairingly. 'No, he's not, and well you know it. You wouldn't be here if he were.'

'It's quite reasonable to ask for the boss, Enid love.' Les was the acme of sweet reason. 'It's his office after all.'

'Well, he's not in it at the moment. That was his Toyota that disappeared out of the gate a moment ago, just in case you didn't notice.'

Frith was not his usual equable self. He was trying to be good-humoured and failing to bring it off.

'I beg your ladyship's pardon. You are the chairman's niece after all, while I am but a humble striker.'

Enid coloured, more amused than annoyed.

'Don't be sarcastic with me, Les. I've explained about tomorrow night.'

'You enjoyed Tuesday night fine,' Les muttered edgily.

'Ye-es!' drawled Enid with a lewd emphasis. 'But Uncle Jack has these dreary business friends in tomorrow night and I've got

78

to drive them to Leeds for the 11.15 sleeper.'

'Why can't he drive them himself?' Frith demanded.

'He's got an important call coming in from the States about then. A man in San Diego may want one of our players over there for the summer, I gather.'

Frith's face lightened. 'Is it me?'

Enid looked at him narrowly, a little cruelly. 'I've really no idea.' Then, a thought apparently striking her, 'But of course it can't be you, can it, Les? You won't be a Barford player by then.'

'Well' — gloomily — 'see me afterwards.'

'I won't be back until well after midnight. It'd be far too late.'

'It's never too late.' The footballer used the suggestive tone of Enid minutes before. 'I could come along in the car to keep you company.'

'I don't think that'd be a very good idea. Aunt Lucy'll come, more appropriate altogether.'

'But I want to see you, Enid,' Les said piteously.

'I know what you want. And what you want, you can't have. I'm out of action for the next three days.'

Frith, for the first time in the conversation, achieved his normal pleasant grin. 'I love you for your mind, Enid. How about Saturday?'

Enid was glad to allow rein to her genuine fondness for Les. 'I'll see. I hope Uncle Jack doesn't ask Colin Barber in later on. That'd make it awkward.'

'Who's Colin Barber when he's at home?'

'Colin's my intended.' She looked at Frith, who was comically taken aback. 'Don't worry, Les, he's a wet. Uncle Jack intends him for me. I might well have other ideas.'

'I've other ideas,' Les said optimistically.

'You've *one* idea, Les Frith. I'll tell you on Saturday afternoon if I can slip Colin.'

'Slip him,' Les said masterfully. 'If you do, I'll show you my deadly duo.'

Enid burst into giggles. 'You're coarse, Les Frith. Now let me do some work.'

'Do you fancy him?' he asked slowly.

'Colin Barber? I told you, he's a wet.'

'Not him, dummy, the boss.'

'That's idiotic. I hardly know him, and he certainly doesn't like me. He's humourless, a real haggis-basher. He's hell to work for. He doesn't fancy me one bit.'

'What's that got to do with it? Do you fancy him? He's not bad-looking for his age,' Les allowed chivalrously, 'and I noticed he ran you home the other night.'

'While you were noticing, did you also notice that my car was missing from outside the office here?' The girl was angry again. 'I won't be checked up on, Les, we've always worked on that basis. I don't want to know what you get up to on away trips — '

He interrupted her. 'With eleven other blokes, the coach, and the manager? You've got to be joking.'

'That's not what I heard about Newport. Still, as I say, that's none of my business. And if Bobby boy gives me a lift to the garage, equally that's none of yours. Why not go out and train or something?' she snapped in exasperation. 'Give these Swansea people something to see on Saturday.'

'I wouldn't want to go to Swansea and leave you here, Enid love.'

'You do and you will.'

Frith gave a rueful, capitulating smile and departed for the dressing room, shouting over his shoulder, 'Let me know about Saturday.'

Alone in the office Enid, having lost the slip of paper with the motel number on it, spent an anxious moment before she remembered Three Pines, and another before Sutton Coldfield swam back to her recall. She dialled directory enquiries, clicking impatiently at the delay. At last she was provided with the number and got through to reception.

'Three Pines? Can you take a booking for tomorrow night, one night only? The name is Calderwood— Robert Calderwood. Mr Calderwood will want a twin-bedded room, and he'll be leaving early in the morning, about seven thirty. He'll confirm that when he arrives, which will not be until about half past ten. Yes, by all means, make it a guaranteed booking. Thank you so much. Goodbye.'

With a satisfied look, she replaced the receiver.

10

Never, till now, had Bob Calderwood been unfaithful to his wife. Throughout his playing days, he had looked on the casual couplings of some of his fellow players with an ill-concealed dislike. He found it difficult to understand the compulsive skirt-chaser, such as Ellis Hernon, from his days in the Midlands. Ellis had such a powerful sexual drive that by comparison Les Frith appeared reticent. His finest hour had been in a Leamington hotel when, actually on the way out to training, and in his track suit, he had waylaid the chambermaid coming in to make up the bed and persuaded her to postpone that operation for fifteen minutes or so.

If Ellis was at one end of the sexual barometer, Bob had occasionally wondered if he himself were at the other. He knew how to do it, in the old phrase, and he'd fathered two children so his virility was scarcely in question. His experience of women, nevertheless, was extremely limited. His generation had, as youths, been comparatively immobile, restricted in opportunity as in transport. Towards the end of his schooldays there had been a few enthusiastic fumblings after dances, but his immediate removal thereafter to England, and his fierce desire to establish himself as a top-flight player, had led him, quite voluntarily, to curb his social activities. Those trainers and managers he had worked under had almost to a man propounded the idea that sex weakened the young athlete. It took years in management to turn Bob to thinking that perhaps a club's real objection to women was that a wife or steady girlfriend very soon turned the conversation to what the club was paying her man and to what was the proportion of bonus to basic wage.

He would not have described himself as a highly sexed man. He thought he could not be since, although he enjoyed a bawdy joke, he seldom or never used sexual innuendo in his own speech, and twenty years around dressing rooms had not reconciled him to the classic Anglo-Saxon noun.

So how in God's name did he come to be lying in a bed in the

81

Three Pines, watching Enid, stark naked, stretching at the window to the lightening morning? Her clothes were scattered lavishly around the room. Blouse and tights were tossed casually on one chair. Bra and pants had not even made a chair, but her pleated skirt was hung neatly on a hanger. She turned and smiled down at him.

'Up and away, Mr Calderwood. You've merely made a good beginning to the day.'

Bob thought bleakly and inconsequentially that he should have felt more like the Grand Seducer. It struck him at once that the reason he didn't was because it was Enid who had done the seducing.

He had certainly not been drunk. He retraced the sequence of the previous evening as he muttered a reply to Enid, swung his feet to the floor, and watched her undulate nudely to the bathroom and to the running shower.

The trip had been worthwhile from the football point of view. The young keeper had performed well and the loan transfer had been arranged. The lad could not be registered with the Football League in time for the next day's game, but that was of little consequence really. It removed, in fact, any temptation to break a promise to Arnold. He swore softly as he remembered how one of the Walsall players he knew had tried to persuade him to put up overnight. He had excused himself on the grounds that his early start in the morning would disturb the family.

He had got back to the Three Pines about half past ten, sure enough, had thought of a quick omelette in the restaurant, and decided against it. He had ordered tea and sandwiches, the girl brought them, was tipped and went off. Five minutes later, while he was watching a chat show on TV in an uninvolved manner, there was another knock at the door. When he opened it, Enid was there.

He was never completely in control when she was around. He asked her in; there seemed little else he could do. She offered no reason for being there — no letter overlooked, no visit to an aunt in the area. Calderwood had taken his usual post-match single whisky, no more, no less. Enid sat, poised, smiling. Calderwood, increasingly edgy under an increasingly desultory conversation, then announced that he was going to bed.

'May I come too?'

'Look, Enid, I don't want a row, a scene, a fuss. I can hardly throw you out of my room.'

'It would be an interesting change from the usual set-up.'

He glared at her. 'I'm going into the bathroom, and when I come back out, you will be gone.'

He ignored her look of disappointment and stalked into the bathroom, where he did everything slowly and with an emphasised attention to detail. Possibly about ten minutes had passed when he thought he heard the outside door slam shut. He gave it another five minutes, then emerged.

Enid had stripped off everything but bra and pants and was lying, relaxed and inviting, on the bed. He had not quite known how to react. His dislike of a scene was a very real one, and he was pretty sure that the motel was not especially interested in how its guests spent the night.

And suddenly he had succumbed, was casting his own clothes to the four corners of the room and was, with trembling and inept fingers, removing those wisps of clothing which still adorned Enid. The unfamiliar contours and zesty athleticism of the girl excited him. It had been a fine lovemaking, if rather hurried, a deficiency which he had later put right. They had stayed in the one bed which was just of sufficiently generous provision to allow them to lie side by side.

From the shower came the noise of some indistinct singing. It seemed to be more like 'On a Clear Day' than anything else. Bob wandered over to the window, looking out at the pale, promising spring morning. A small launch was chugging along the canal which moated and muted the motorway. The view from the window was of brown, freshly-turned fields, a reminder that even thus near to Birmingham there were still traces of an older, rural Warwickshire. He moved the russet and gold curtains farther apart.

His thoughts should have been all of Joan but they were not exclusively so. A silly phrase ran through his head from his elementary school days. A Scots nobleman, Randolph, had agreed to give the English defenders of Stirling Castle a truce of a year and a day to see if help for them might be forthcoming

83

from England. King Robert the Bruce, clearly feeling that Randolph was being chivalrous to an uncalled-for degree, had rebuked him stingingly in the memorable phrase, 'Randolph, a rose has fallen from your chaplet.' He could still see the eager eyes of his young teacher, Miss Oliphant, passionately involved with the story she was telling her class.

A rose had most certainly fallen from *his* chaplet. From this morning, trite though it might be to say it or think it, things could never again be as they had been. When he thought of Joan he had a sense of guilt, although not quite the expected over-bearing, all-mastering guilt. It was when he thought of Phyllis, so near to Enid in age, that revulsion overwhelmed him. Mixed with these reactions was a feeling of anger that he had, to his own lasting disadvantage, transformed an office relationship into a lover/mistress one, while he candidly admitted a sense of relief that he had acquitted himself creditably in bed. It would have mattered had he been unable to do so. He would like to be able to do so again, soon.

Enid came out of the bathroom carrying a small toilet bag. In place of the Manchester City blue of last evening, she was wearing apricot-coloured briefs. He tried to make his glance unobtrusive but she detected it, and he felt like a schoolboy caught out.

'A toothbrush and an extra pair of pants and you can fly to the end of the world, Mr Calderwood.' She began to dress, quite briskly.

'I think that in the circumstances you could call me Bob when we're together.'

'Not a good idea,' Enid said decidedly, putting her hair up and gazing into the mirror. 'It might spill over into the office situation. Unless, of course, you feel you have to fire me . . .'

That was exactly what Bob felt he should do in logic and cold reason. But it was a filthy trick to take advantage of a girl (never mind that perhaps it was the other way round) and then get rid of her.

He merely said, 'It may not come to that. We can see how it goes.'

'I promise you I won't presume upon the change in our status,' Enid pledged, wriggling and zipping herself into her skirt. She sat down at the dressing-table mirror to apply her lipstick, but before she did so, filled and switched on the electric kettle.

Bob stooped to switch it off. 'Don't bother with that. We'll be having breakfast in a few minutes.'

Again came the stymie from Enid. 'I wouldn't advise it. Even this early on a Saturday motels are stiff with football folks on the move. *You'll* have breakfast, I'll have a quick swallow of coffee, go downstairs, saunter out casually, and off up the road. I'm going to make a point of being at the ground by about eleven o'clock.'

Bob made the coffee and they sat side by side on the unused bed drinking it. He looked at her, young, very pretty, well-groomed, challenging.

'Enid, I'm not proud of what happened last night.'

'You've precious little to be ashamed of. You're very, very good, Mr Calderwood. Even though the third time was just a little bit of an effort.'

He looked at her with a genuine sorrow. 'I can't pretend to understand people of your age group, Enid. Do you simply take any man you have a notion for?'

She gave an elder sister smile. 'Or, "What's a nice girl like you doing in a place like this?" That's the traditional line, isn't it? I'm comparatively chaste, Mr Calderwood. Les, three boys at college, and yourself, that's the total score to date. You're my first married man.'

Sharing a girl with a player whom he had just disciplined, and might have to go to town on again, was folly heaped on indiscretion. Momentary anger forced him into an undignified and stupid observation.

'I'm glad at least that I stand comparison with our striker.'

Enid shook her head. 'I didn't quite say that. I did say that you were very, very good.'

'Let's hope I manage to avoid relegation,' gritted Calderwood, clutching the flapping rags of his dignity round him while feeling scaldingly jealous of his randy predecessor. He attempted to pull Enid to him, but she eluded him and stood up to go, totally self-possessed.

'No second house. At least, not for now.' She came over to

Calderwood and laid a hand on his arm. 'You've got so much more going for you than Les. Don't have it in for him simply because he was there ahead of you. Bob for the first time and Bob for the last time, you *were* really very good. I'm a truly satisfied girl. It was a lovely night, Mr Calderwood.'

As unexpectedly as she had arrived she was gone. Bob flicked the radio on, his mind in a turmoil. Even so, he registered that Trevor Francis had failed a fitness test and would not be playing for Birmingham City, while Ray Clemence had passed one and would be in the Liverpool goal against Derby. How was it possible to assimilate such trivial facts at such a time?

Did he tell Joan? Did he move Enid on? If the former, was he doing it for any other reason than the transference of a burden? If the latter, then he owed an explanation to the chairman of directors, who would most certainly expect one.

He hunted around the room, cramming pyjamas and toilet bag into his holdall, checking the wardrobe, dressing-table drawers and bathroom for things left behind and for tell-tale indications of Enid. A final glance for lipsticked tissues in the wastepaper basket and he let the heavy door slam to. Very much to his surprise, he was extremely hungry.

The dining room was set out like an old farm kitchen, with some of the cooking done in front of the customer on what appeared to be, but doubtless wasn't, a traditional range. Bob had a great notion for bacon, sausage and eggs, but settled for the more austere grapefruit juice and scrambled eggs on toast. As he ate, he was looking at the sports page of the *Daily Mail* but not seeing it. He settled his bill, all the while wondering vaguely why he did not feel the least bit washed out from his strenuous night.

'Good morning, Bob.'

His heart thumped as, hearing his name, he turned. Enid's caution had been amply justified. Before him stood Dr John Layton, one of his directors, a pleasant man in his late sixties, who as a young man had been an amateur player of repute with Northern Nomads. Raised in the Corinthian tradition, he was at all times willing to believe the best of his fellow men, but lacked the necessary resolution — and, indeed, shareholding — to stand firm against the chairman at Board meetings.

The two men explained their presence each to the other. Dr Layton agreed that something had to be done to plug the goalkeeping gap. He wished Bob and the side all success against Southport and was sorry that the medical reunion he was going to attend at Oxford would prevent his being at the match — at his age it would probably be the last such reunion he would attend.

They went their separate ways, Bob to the car park, Dr Layton, too unworldly to fill adequately the role of director of a Football League club, to breakfast. The Scot rolled his car into the drive, crossed the hump-backed bridge over the canal, and turned down the slip road to the motorway. Involuntarily he gave a backward glance to his room, their room.

For most of the journey home he was certain that he would tell Joan immediately and fling himself upon the mercy of the court, if there was mercy to be had. He had forgotten that she would of course now be working that Saturday as any other. He rattled through the empty house, made tea, had a bath, and phoned her to say he thought that, after all, he'd look in on the dance. He hugged her pleased, relieved tones to him like a hair shirt.

11

I should have backed my hunch, Calderwood told himself morosely some twelve hours later. The Wensleydale Suite, normally the preserve of small wedding receptions and equally small funerals, resounded to the notes of the Joe Ackroyd Trio, clarinet, piano and drums. Anything was better than that bloody discothèque music, but in the modestly proportioned Wensleydale Suite even Joe Ackroyd and his supporting cast of two were loud enough.

About a dozen of the guests, the younger set mostly, were on the floor performing something called the Slosh, all arm movements and side-kicks like the routine of an under-rehearsed chorus line. Joan was up dancing, as was Derek Naughton, an assiduous host. It was no news to Bob that Joan danced well; what was more surprising was that Derek was also proving to be a 'lovely little mover', as Bob's younger players would have said. Relaxed and cool, he even managed to appear elegant as he and Joan chorused the ridiculous words, 'Hey, hey, hey, what a beautiful day'.

The band finished in a scatter of applause and the dancers made their way back to the tables. There weren't too many there who were known to Bob, only Leonard Steele, the club secretary, and his wife, and Dave Adamson and his wife, who had looked in briefly but were going on to something else later.

It had been a good day, now that he was able to divert his thoughts momentarily from last night. Barford had won in a canter against Southport, 4-0, a result which allowed them to clamber out of the re-election mire on the heads of their fellow strugglers. He thought Southport's days must be numbered. The club existed in the perpetual shadow of the great Liverpool sides, and in a town which was fast considering that Association Football was a disreputable pastime bringing neither kudos nor money to the town. The occasional Open Golf Championship in the vicinity would earn enough of both for the promenaders of Lord Street.

The musicians, breath restored, struck up a slow waltz, 'Moon River'. Bob offered his services to Joan, who accepted delightedly. He was well ahead of his dancing quota, having already been up for three quicksteps and a waltz.

'We are going it a bit, Mr Manager, sir. Better watch, it's catching.' Then with an anxiety at odds with her tone, 'You are enjoying it, Bob?'

He looked down at the appealing face, the trim figure in the rather severe dove-grey evening dress. 'You know me, Joan. I've never been much of a dancer. But the chat's good.' He hummed the tune, cracking slightly as he rose on the word 'river'.

'Try to do the rounds, will you, love? Not too much time with Dave and Leonard Steele. It would be nice if you gave Derek's sister a dance. She is the hostess after all.'

'I don't think Joe Ackroyd and his boys are into gavottes.'

Joan smiled. 'If they were, you wouldn't be able to do one. Dance with her for me, or as a duty to society.' She put the last three words into vocal inverted commas.

He was on the point of demurring further when the prismatic lighting distinctly showed a lighter strand in her copper hair. She has grown grey in my service, he thought, and even as he told himself not to be a pompous ass, he was all too well aware of the truth in the trite thought.

'All right, love, I'll pay my dues. I'm surprised Elsie's here tonight. I wouldn't have thought it would be her scene at all.'

'It probably isn't. But somebody's got to front for Derek and there's nobody else.'

> It's waiting round the bend,
> My huckleberry friend,
> Moon River and me.

Where did this leave the mysterious Evie, wife to Derek? Were they divorced, separated? Was she in an asylum like some modern Mrs Rochester? In jail perhaps? His musings took him through the last spins of the waltz.

Back at their table with Derek, Elsie and the Steeles, he was irked when Derek forestalled his attempt to buy a round of drinks.

'Won't hear of it, Bob. It's the firm's do tonight, old chap. Drink up, all.' He raised his glass theatrically. 'Here's to the Albion carrying on their winning way.' He cocked an ear to the music — 'The Nearness of You'. 'One of the all-time greats. Can I borrow Joan from you, Bob?'

Calderwood nodded graciously. He supposed he'd have to follow on with Elsie, but mercifully that lady excused herself and set off for the ladies' room, a vision in lilac and black. While making banal conversation with the Steeles — even on football Leonard was a lightweight — he watched his wife dance with Derek Naughton. The man could dance, no doubt about it, the slow foxtrot sorted out the gliders from the robots. He could see why Derek might be thought of in some quarters as a ladies' man. He crowded his partner slightly. His style of dancing was commanding, almost domineering. Still, Joan was enjoying it. He must enquire a little as to Evie, for he was beginning to revise his earlier opinion rather. Derek didn't look like a man who could do without a woman for very long.

The last dance before supper was a quickstep and Bob discharged his obligation to Elsie. She proved unexpectedly adept at following his limited lead, and was loud in her praise of Joan.

'Best head we've got in the main shop, Mr Calderwood. She'd make an excellent manager, but I hear you're not too keen on her coming to work full-time.'

'There are one or two difficulties, Miss Naughton.'

'Elsie, if you please.' She regarded him searchingly. 'You've no young children. You don't look the sort who'd lash out in a rage if a meal wasn't on the table the moment you walked through the door.'

This was exactly what Bob was prone to do. Flustered a little and on the back foot, he said, 'My job imposes very odd hours. If Joan worked a full day we'd hardly ever see each other.'

Elsie's eyes glinted behind rhinestone spectacles. 'Why don't *you* get a nine-to-five job?' She half checked herself. 'No, don't take heed of me, I'm a bit of a feminist at times.'

I'll take heed, Calderwood muttered to himself. I can be every bit as direct as you are. Aloud he said, 'I thought we might have seen Mrs Naughton here tonight.' He was unprepared for the vehemence of her reply.

'Are you being deliberately offensive, Mr Calderwood? I think you are one of the rudest men it's ever been my misfortune to meet. Thank you for the dance' — which had mercifully finished.

There was now an interval for a buffet supper and Bob, seeing that Dave Adamson and his wife were on the point of leaving, semaphored to them desperately. He accompanied them downstairs to reception and as Eileen Adamson collected her coat, he briefly recounted to Dave the incident with Elsie.

Adamson smiled thinly. 'No wonder she bit your nose off. Do you mean to say you don't know the background? The story is that Evie left when Derek was on his fourth lady, and I speak literally. Worth keeping an eye on, our Derek, especially with

Joan around. Well, I really have to go. Come on, woman!' He prised Eileen away from a rack of travel brochures. 'We'll go to Scarborough this year if you insist' — and they were gone in an amicable bicker.

Bob turned to go upstairs again and was passed by an enormously tall young black fellow. Bob recognised him from his newspaper pictures as Marshall Gordon, the new professional of Barford Cricket Club, a fast bowler from Nevis. At six feet five and with those shoulders, he would be a distinctly nasty customer on a damp wicket. Calderwood took a moment to wish him well, then hurried back to the Wensleydale Suite. The sight of the young cricketer was a harbinger of his own season's end.

'We thought you'd gone home, Bob,' Derek twitted him. 'Food's nearly all gone. We've saved some for you though. Get a plate from the table.'

Murmuring conventional thanks, Calderwood transferred two thin slices of roast beef and a little salad to his plate and picked up a glass of white wine.

'Sorry to be so long. I'd a couple of things to check with Dave Adamson.'

Derek turned to Joan in mock dismay. 'Does this chap never stop working, Joan? Do you ever see him?'

'Only at the firm's dance, Derek', Joan said with a winsome smile. (Damn you, woman, watch how you smile at a man like him.)

'I hate to mix business with pleasure, old chap, but would you consider letting Joan come to us full-time?'

No, I would not, you middle-aged lecher. That's what he wanted to say, but impossible to say it to one's host. In any event he was not supposed to know of the lechery, and he was reluctant to play the heavy Victorian husband in company. What he did say was, 'I'd have to think about that, Derek. There'd be one or two things to consider.'

'Of course, old chap. I hope your decision's yes. We'd pay well to have Joan — she's very capable. But if you decide otherwise, there'll be no hard feelings.'

'If you decide otherwise.' Calderwood thought it was said quite deliberately to create the impression that Joan had no control over her own destiny.

They left not long after eleven, as he'd planned, resisting all invitations to stay on for another hour. On the way out they met Enid, who had Les Frith in tow and, less predictably, Phil Gifford, the student forward. The two players had the certain awkwardness felt by those who meet their manager in a place of entertainment even on a Saturday evening.

Enid, flamboyant in a primrose trouser-suit, was poised and welcoming. 'Mr and Mrs Calderwood, good evening. Did you enjoy the party?'

'Very pleasant, Enid,' Joan said. 'I didn't know you knew about it.'

'I was in the market shop the other day and Miss Naughton mentioned it. We've just had dinner in the restaurant. I wouldn't recommend it, the steak was as tough as old boots.'

'We were luckier then,' said Joan. 'We were the cold meat and salad brigade.'

They parted company. Calderwood's face was expressionless as they went to the car but his mind was seething. He wanted Enid. Seeing her slim figure going off with the two boys had made him realise that with hammering certainty. Which of those two would she end up with tonight, that lout Frith or the quieter Gifford? He thought back to last night, to her athletic improvising, to his own physical delight in penetrating her.

They were in the car when Joan made a chance remark that she hoped Phyllis was enjoying herself at Harrogate. He thanked God for the dark; he could swear that he was flushing in revulsion. If Phyllis or Fraser were to find out! He had a fugitive notion that his daughter might just be the more understanding of the two. Fraser would certainly see the episode as a deadly insult to his mother. He managed to drive out the Tarkington Road, doing the right things with the car, making adequate conversational returns.

'It wasn't too awful, was it, Bob?'

'No, quite enjoyable. I'd a good natter with one or two people. At least the band wasn't out to deprive us of our hearing.'

'Derek shouldn't have raised the subject of the job again. That wasn't fair.'

'Well, a good gal is hard to find. Maybe I've been a bit stuffy over it.'

'You haven't changed your mind, have you?'

He slammed the car door shut as they drew up at the house. 'There'll be no frost tonight. I'll just leave her in the drive. The job? Perhaps we should talk about it.'

I am allowing my wife to do what she wants. I am putting her at risk with a predatory employer. I am salving my conscience for Enid. State the alternative preferred, give reasons for your choice. There were three choices; strictly speaking they could not be alternatives.

They made coffee and over it Joan looked at him, her face pretty, honest, sensible. 'Your win today, Bob, will that keep you in the Fourth Division?'

He paused, the cup halfway to his mouth. 'If I were at the ground, or talking to the press, I'd give them the bit about being in danger until four other sides are mathematically worse off on the last day of the season. But seeing it's you, I think I could say yes, we'll make it.'

'So your contract's all right? Will they think you've done a good job?'

'Yes. To keep this bunch in the Football League in my first full season and with no money to call on, it's not a bad performance. If you add our FA Cup run, it's a rather good one.'

'How's Enid shaping up in the office?'

He glanced obliquely at her, but the question was patently guileless.

'She's all right. She's certainly not a Vi Black but she's coming on. With luck she'll eventually be adequate.'

Joan broke into peals of laughter. 'You Scots lay it on with a trowel, don't you? "She'll eventually be adequate." Sooner her than me. Well, I'm off to bed. Coming?'

'In a while. I'll have a look at the late-night golf first. Has Phyllis got a key?'

'She ought to have. Just close the storm doors to.'

She went out, pottered around the kitchen for a few minutes, then went upstairs. He switched on the set and saw Enid everywhere in the galleries and in each of the short-skirted markers. He used to laugh pityingly at heroes in books — or

93

even villains — who wanted a woman with their loins. He was not laughing now. He wanted Enid with that intensity, and he would have her again. In the meantime Joan would be expecting him above. He switched off the television set, turned out the lights, and thoughtfully, slowly, climbed the stairs to their bedroom.

12

It was with a definite feeling of unease that Calderwood settled down in his sitting room the following Friday evening to watch the promised transmission of *Sidelight*. He would have preferred to watch it alone. Joan knew this and had considerately gone over for the evening to see her friend Jean Ogden. Fraser had arrived home for the weekend, however, and Bob saw all too little of his son to want to drive him out of the house when he showed no signs of going. He let it be understood, notwithstanding, that Fraser's silence would be appreciated during the programme.

It began with the compulsory mock-urgent theme music that had become a current affairs cliché. A pitch-black studio flared to light, bringing to view a casually dressed, spectacled young man who appeared confident of being able to solve at least some of the world's problems within the compass of half an hour. He was introduced by a credit as Simon Falconbridge.

'Good evening, and welcome to another edition of *Sidelight*, our own particular way of looking at the world in which no corner is too remote, no issue too unimportant for us. Last week, we discussed the change of government in Upper Volta and the likely repercussions in Central Africa. Tonight we turn the spotlight much nearer home, to a northern industrial town where the local football team, Barford Albion, has for nearly a century conducted a battle for survival. Barford Albion personifies the challenge facing many of our Football League sides.'

So saying, Simon Falconbridge ended and the programme moved outdoors. It was taken in charge by Cosmo Eele, the reporter who had come with Oliver and the crew to Jubilee Park on their return visit. The lady who looked after the tearoom, Mrs Armitage, had told Bob with a fascinated horror that after the film had been shot, Mr Eele had downed three gins and five egg sandwiches in the boardroom in the space of less than twenty minutes.

The programme was slick, professional, failing only in its total lack of insight. Shots of scattered handfuls of Albion supporters on the terracing at the Darlington match were skilfully inter-cut with frenetic crowd scenes from a Manchester United-Leeds United Cup-tie. Somewhat censoriously, Eele made the point that more people had passed through the Old Trafford turnstiles on that day than would watch Barford Albion over an entire season of home matches.

Oliver's shots of patched fencing, rusty turnstiles and the ancient stand were certainly there. Calderwood sat, his jaw tightening as the exposé took its course. Albion's record since joining the Football League was put under scrutiny. Accepted as Second Division members by the League, they had exchanged that membership for Third and then Fourth Division status almost as soon as each became available. The club's one success, a Yorkshire Cup win in 1936, seemed like the ultimate bad joke, the spotlight trained on a single object in an otherwise empty, massive trophy cupboard.

Jack Schofield appeared briefly and spoke well. He gave the impression that yes, it was a struggle, but he enjoyed it, and in any case it was an inherited responsibility. Changes in taxation and therefore in disposable income made it more difficult with every year that passed, but there was an onus on him to keep League Football in the town, that was important. His grandfather and father had been prime movers in the club, and he did not want to be the generation which broke that family connection, hanged if he did. The Arsenal results showed what could be done with enthusiasm and hard work. The players were in good heart, and they had one of the best managers outside the

First Division, indeed including the First Division.

Quite successfully, Schofield had projected the image of the concerned, philanthropic legislator, serving his town at some considerable personal cost. The rest of the programme consisted of an interview with the Planet. Oliver, ever on the *qui vive* for local colour, had persuaded the reluctant Joe to spend a few minutes in conversation with Cosmo Eele. The interview had been filmed in the home team's dressing room at Jubilee Park, and Calderwood, watching, noted that the intrusive Cosmo seemed much more at home on the Planet's patch than did the sweatered veteran. This, too, in spite of drawing a blank with a first question which a more sensitive director would have ensured that the programme editor managed to lose.

The two men sat side by side on the bench seating. In front of them was the campaign-weary massage table, behind were rows of pegs on which at various times on a Saturday hung strips and civvies. Cosmo, in dark blue button-down shirt and light blue Slazenger pullover, opened proceedings.

'I have here Joe Staples, one of the club's unsung backroom heroes. Ask anyone at Jubilee Park for Joe Staples and they may hesitate. But ask for the Planet and that's another matter.'

He half-turned on the bench towards Joe, who was sitting in the bolt-upright stance of an Aston Villa team photograph from the eighteen eighties. 'I understand they call you Planet around here, Joe. That's a bizarre piece of nomenclature surely?'

'Eh?'

Cosmo quickly rephrased. 'It's an odd name.'

'Aye.'

It was going to be a working interview.

'How did you happen to come by it?'

The Planet glared at the camera reflectively. 'I got it during the war. I was out in Cyprus. I'd really chucked playing by that time, but I were helping unit side out at left back. Played with a lad Jock Gilchrist at right back. He was a Scot,' the Planet added superfluously. 'We got to the final of the island cup and there was a write-up in the local paper. The reporter said that Gilchrist were a star in defence, but that I were a planet.'

Calderwood had rarely heard the Planet go on at such length. A *bon mot* had occurred to Cosmo and he leapt in nimbly.

'It should have been the other way about, Joe. You know, Jock Gilchrist, Superstar.'

'You could say that,' the interviewee said impassively, either ignoring the witticism or more probably not comprehending it. Cosmo got back to cases.

'Tell me, ah, Joe, how long have you been here at Jubilee Park?'

'Since 1930, near enough. I'd a few years off for killing Germans.' With a much greater pride he went on, 'I played in the side that won the Yorkshire Cup when we beat Halifax.'

'Would you say that was Albion's best side?'

Joe nodded definitely. 'Oh, aye. We'd some good players.' He stressed the adjective lovingly. 'Bill Nimmo, another Scot — from Glasgow he was— what a left-half. He was that cool you could have put a snowball in his armpit and it wouldn't have melted.'

'Did he play for Scotland?'

Joe looked at him pityingly. 'With Albion? No chance. If he'd been Irish or Welsh now, they cap from the smaller clubs. But not the Scots. Besides, Bill was like some others of us, didn't train too hard.' The Planet's gums hove into view as he cackled, 'Some of us trained on Guinness.'

'Did Bill?'

'Well, let's say he were no Rechabite.' He caught himself in sudden anxiety. 'Here, maybe I shouldn't have said that?'

Oliver had not believed in sparing the unsophisticated. The cameras had kept running and Cosmo unctuously smoothed over any awkwardness.

'I wouldn't worry, Joe, it was all some time ago. If you're watching out there, Bill Nimmo, no offence!' He turned back to the Planet, exchanging his good fellow's voice for that of the enquiring sociologist.

'What changes have you, in your own lifetime, seen in the game?'

At home, Calderwood stretched his legs in exasperation with the sub-literacy of the question. 'How the hell could he see changes in the game other than in his own lifetime?' he enquired peevishly of Fraser. His son enjoyed telling Bob to let them listen in silence.

The Planet pondered the question momentarily. 'Well, mostly the gear. We played in boots like canal barges, you'd to sit and work the dubbin into them or they were as stiff as boards. These lads today could hardly lift a pair of our boots, let alone play in them. And there were the jerseys with lace-up collars. And the shorts past the knees.' He chuckled reminiscently. 'Knickers, we called them in our day.'

Cosmo at this stage had either decided, or been told, that the Planet was good value for money. He kept his questions short.

'What were you paid?'

'About four quid a week. Mind you, that were good money in them days, in the thirties. I'd a mate who was a fitter and turner. When he was in work, and he drew dole for nearly two years, he were only getting two pounds five a week.'

Even in his annoyance Calderwood was mildly amused that Joe said 'he was' when he remembered, and 'he were' when he didn't.

'And other differences?'

'It were a more manly game. You liked to charge your opponents, 'dunt them' Bill Nimmo used to say. But we'd none of the sly fouls you get now. We'd a full back here, Ben Davis, a proper terror, "King Kong" they used to call him. I never saw Ben foul a man from behind in my life, not in all the time I played with him. He was a manly player.' Clearly the word 'manly' ranked high in the Planet's terms of praise.

'What about crowds then?'

'Oh, we'd get about five or six thousand then. We seemed to get the better sort of working man in those days. The toffs watched rugby and the dross stuck to the pubs and the bookies' runners.'

Cosmo raised an eyebrow. Like many radicals he had not been much exposed to such robust social attitudes. Criticism of the working class by same was not what *Sidelight* was really about.

'Where have the crowds gone then? You're only drawing about two thousand per home game these days.'

'They don't work Saturdays now,' Joe explained patiently. 'They can go to Leeds or Sheffield. When I played they didn't finish till one o'clock, even some of us players didn't

98

finish till one o'clock.'

Cosmo shifted. It was time for the matador to move in for the kill.

'Tell me, Planet,' he enquired solicitously, 'is there any future for clubs like Barford Albion in modern League Soccer?'

The Planet retreated to prepared defensive positions. 'If there's not, I'm out of a job.'

'But let's face it, is there?'

'As much as there's ever been.'

Cosmo's eyes flickered slightly before the cameras. He was obviously taking a wind-up.

'Well, thank you, Joe Staples, and may you help the Albion to further triumphs.' His hand almost imperceptibly restrained an already rising Joe as he intoned. 'And that wraps up this week's programme which came from Jubilee Park, Barford, the home of Barford Albion, a struggling club not, perhaps, emerging as fast from depression as its locality is doing. Now back to Simon Falconbridge in the *Sidelight* studios.'

In the studio Simon moved into his peroration with the air of one who had done his best to set Barford on the straight road. 'Next week, *Sidelight* features film from Rangoon and we pose the question, "Can the Burmese Prime Minister survive the threat to his government created by the Shan hill tribes?" Till then, goodbye.'

The lights darkened, the strident music shrilled as the credit titles came up, Oliver Dampenay's and Pam Correll's amongst them. Then the fade-out and a few seconds of gazing at the station identification before it was time for *Come Dancing*. Calderwood snapped the switch off and looked at Fraser.

'Well?'

'Very interesting, Dad.'

'Come on, Fraser, you can do better than that.'

'Can I speak frankly?'

'When has that ever stopped you before?'

The boy hesitated, a caring look on his personable face. 'Let me get a lager from the fridge first. Shall I fetch one for you?'

Calderwood shook his head. Fraser went to the kitchen, opened the ring-pull, filled a tumbler, and was back in what seemed thirty seconds. His lanky frame writhed in the deep armchair.

'I think I'm on to something, Dad, in my own mind. About why I've come to prefer rugby, I mean. It's not the game itself — soccer's a splendid game. But with a rugby club there's far more chance to get . . .' he fished for the word, 'involved. I can run the bar, act as match secretary, coach the mini-rugby, spearhead fund-raising activities. But basically all Albion want of me is to pay my admission money and then shout for ninety minutes in the stand or on the terracings. I think football's got to think seriously about this.'

'So you think,' Calderwood said bitingly, 'that the Crewe Alexandras and Barford Albions of this world are not worth seeing or saving. You think that people like me, not to put too fine a point on it, are mugs?'

Fraser flushed protestingly. 'I didn't say that, Dad. I haven't even thought it. People nowadays, though, want to be something more than just turnstile fodder. They want involvement, they want any skills they may have to be used.'

'Real Madrid and Ajax don't seem to have any shortage of turnstile fodder,' Calderwood said in a nettled fashion.

'Maybe there's a reason for that.' Fraser was hesitating between the chance of helping his father and the probability of seriously annoying him. He decided to take the chance. 'And I don't just mean that they're good sides. You see, you can be a member of those clubs just like I'm a member at the rugby club here.'

Calderwood regarded him sourly. 'You've been doing some deep thinking, Fraser.'

'Not me, this is Eric Bond's theory. He's a pal of mine, a sociology student.'

'Oh! A sociology student!' scoffed Bob, as if that explained everything.

'Come on, Dad, they're not always wrong. Eric's theory is that only in Britain did the game develop with clubs as limited liability companies. That's a form of organisation that's inevitably exclusive of the general public. Apart from the Board, players and ground staff, how many people can actually do anything for Albion?'

Calderwood was spared answering by the telephone. It was

100

Dave Adamson, ringing to get the manager's view of the programme. He himself had thought that it had been pretty slanted.

'I don't know, Dave. There was nothing that was not factually accurate. Our fat friend Oliver had done his homework, I'll say that. And our chairman did mention publicly, very publicly, how important League Football is to a town.'

Fraser whispered to his father that he was going round to the rugby club for an hour or so. Bob jerked his head in acquiescence as he listened to the voice on the other end of the line.

'What you say is true enough, Bob. Certainly Jack Schofield has made it much harder for himself not to keep the club going.'

The two men agreed that the Planet had come over much as he was, and that it would be interesting to see what Schofield and the players thought of the programme. Dave was still inclined to think that Bob should have taken the proffered opportunity to appear, and although the manager demurred, in his heart of hearts he felt the reporter might have the right of it.

It was about fifteen minutes later when he replaced the receiver, and the same amount of time elapsed before the chirk of the key in the front door signified the return of Joan. She had not seen the programme, having been too occupied in discussing with Jean Ogden the recent marriage and honeymoon of the latter's daughter. Calderwood was partly piqued at this lack of interest, partly pleased that there was no present necessity for further discussion. What the hell right had Fraser to unsettle him like that? Savagely he crushed the small voice which said, the right you gave him in asking him. He thanked God that the next day was Saturday, a day of doing, a day for leading Albion, in the immortal phrase of Cosmo Eele, to further triumphs.

101

13

The April days lengthened, the season drew to a close, and Albion inched visibly to safety. They had gone five games without defeat, so Crewe and Southport now had to finish below them no matter what. In all probability Darlington would, too, and even Newport and perhaps Hartlepool could be caught. The team had found its scoring touch, despite the fact that Swansea had at last come for Les Frith. The timing, after the transfer deadline so that Frith could not play in any match affecting promotion or relegation, was surprising, but Calderwood thought he followed the Swansea reasoning. They were going nowhere this season, neither up nor down, and a new signing at this time would keep the fans interested over what might have been a dreary last month. So sudden indeed had the transfer been that Frith had had to return to Barford the following week to tidy up a few loose ends. He had sought, and gained permission, to train at the Jubilee ground, and now, after training, stood on his familiar spot in Calderwood's office.

His hair, still damp from the showers, was plastered over his good-natured softish face. His bearing had that mixture of subservience and gauche independence of a problem pupil returning to his school for the first time after leaving. Bob was prepared to allow Les to brighten his day for ten minutes or so. It had been a good morning. There had been a few very early enquiries for season tickets for the following year and a rather interesting, a very interesting, letter from the United States. He looked at Les almost with affection and his tone was heavily amiable.

'Well, Les, and how is Welsh Wales?'

Frith shrugged and rolled his eyes. 'Bloody terrible, Boss. I can't hardly make out a word they say, they talk that queer! And the pubs, Boss, in some parts they still shut them on Sundays.'

Trust Leslie to get his priorities right, Calderwood thought grimly, congratulating himself that the club was minus one boozer and plus forty-five thousand pounds. Aloud he condoled, 'War's hell, Les! And how about the football? I saw you took a bit of a hammering on Saturday.'

Frith, who had frequently in his time at Jubilee Park expressed the conviction he would shine in better company, was torn between defending his new clubmates and saying what he thought. To his credit as a footballer, it was objectivity which triumphed.

'Tell you the truth, Boss, we've not got much. We're playing four-two-four with a couple of fairies in mid-field. They seem to think tackling's been outlawed. They won't win a fifty-fifty ball all season, either of them.'

Must be bad if you've noticed it, my son, Bob reflected. Les had never exactly been renowned for his teethy tackling, as 'Jubilee Jottings' would have put it.

Les carried on with his analysis. 'Centre-half makes up for it though, he's a rough bugger, kicks everything above grass height. He's on his fourth booking.' He sighed disparagingly. 'Chinky Hamilton's the only footballer in the team.'

Professional football is a fairly small world and Calderwood's eyes lit up with recognition tinged with disapproval. The distinctly occidental Chinky was a wild man.

'For God's sake, don't tell me you and Chinky are in the same side. There won't be a woman safe in West Wales.'

Les beamed, as if Calderwood had delivered a lengthy eulogy on his own and Chinky's virtues. In the world of professional football a reputation as a serious drinker or as a womaniser is not always something to be shunned.

'Aye, he's a lad is Chinky. There I was the first morning, miserable as sin, you know what it's like, Boss, with a new side, four of them glaring at you, as they wonder who's going to be left out for you? Well, we'd started doing lapping, when suddenly I hears this great shout, "Frith, you bastard, you can play none." He laughed appreciatively — to be accepted in football involves the jocular insult.

'Chinky?' Bob enquired rhetorically.

'Chinky, Boss. He was a bit late for training.'

'That figures.'

'We're in the same digs. It's nice to have a human being to

103

talk to.'

'That's the greatest compliment Chinky will ever receive in his natural,' said Calderwood with an overlay of irony.

'Come again, Boss?'

'Never mind.' He got up from his chair. 'Look, Les, I don't want to rush you, but I've got things to do.'

'Sure, Boss.' He held out his hand awkwardly, unsure of his reception. 'Well, thanks, see you some time, eh? I'd hoped to see Enid.'

'She's just running her uncle out to the airport.' Calderwood's tone was distinctly less cordial.

'I'll maybe see her later then. I don't have to go back till tomorrow morning.'

'Fine. If not, I'll tell her you called.' He choked down his rivalry. 'Take care, Les. You'll be okay after a couple of weeks. Settling in's always tough. Don't write them off too quickly, they've a couple of fair players besides Chinky. Give it a go.'

Frith nodded solemnly, sighed, brightened. 'Yeah. The digs are quite good and there's a really beautiful little bird next door. Her name's Angharad, I think. It's Welsh anyway.'

In exasperation that was only partly assumed Calderwood shooed him out of the office. 'For God's sake get off back to Wales. I'll follow your career in the *News of the World*.'

Frith grinned cheerily. 'No, Boss, the *South Wales Echo*.' He broke into the sing-song tones which he always reserved for his press cuttings. "Once Les Frith settles in, he should prove a valuable acquisition to the Vetch Field side in their quest for promotion." Ta-ta, Boss, give my love to the *Examiner*.'

'And to Enid?'

'I'll likely do that myself.' He was gone.

Calderwood sat for a minute in the suddenly quiet and somehow diminished office. He had heard other managers talk about 'their boys' and wanted to throw up, but there was a sense in which it was true. Still, he wished his colleague at Swansea joy of Les and Chinky. 'Somebody else, not me,' as the old song said.

He turned back to the desk and the light blue airmail

envelope on it, postmarked Milwaukee. Quite unexpectedly an old team-mate, Pete Rossington, from his Northampton days had offered him a two-month engagement, mid-May to mid-July, coaching with the club that he was managing in the North American Soccer League. There would be a little work in schools, but he would make in eight weeks what it would take him half a year to earn in Britain. There seemed at first sight no irreconcilable clash with his duties at Jubilee Park. The American club would provide accommodation for himself and Joan. Not that he'd consider taking Joan, nor did he think it probable she'd want to come.

He looked up to see the other woman in his life, Enid, who had come in very quietly and was now putting her scarf and raincoat on a hanger which she then hooked over the coat-stand.

'Chairman get off all right then?' he enquired.

The girl shook her head. 'There's a delay of forty-five minutes. He said just to leave him and come back here, in case you needed me.' She looked calmly, quite unflirtatiously, at him.

'I would have thought London had convinced you of that.'

They had managed two nights in London, more accurately Finchley, when Bob went down to attend a meeting of Third and Fourth Division managers. Enid had taken a couple of days to see an old school friend at Beckenham which she did with great assiduity during the day.

She smiled reminiscently. 'London was . . . very nice.'

He moved towards her, touched her hair. She stood off a little.

'This is an office, Mr Calderwood.'

'Have you thought about next time?'

'Yes.' No hesitation, no dressing-up. 'Uncle Jack's gone off, Aunt Lucy's already in Brussels. They'll be away for three days. Why not come over tomorrow evening?'

'Why not tonight?'

She shook her head. 'I've someone to see.'

Frith, Bob thought savagely, but pride inhibited further probing. In fact it was a girlfriend, but Bob would spend the evening twisting on a spit.

They dealt with routine correspondence, largely requests for information on the club from earnest teachers in the town schools, who seemed simultaneously and desperately to have decided that the history of Barford Albion might provide a project to stimulate the listless and charm the rebellious. He wrote a holding letter to Peter Rossington, thanking him for the offer and promising to phone him within seven days. Then he told Enid to scrap it, that he would phone Rossington that night.

'You're quite interested, aren't you?'

'Quite.'

'Milwaukee is where it's at?'

The glib, alien phrase displeased him. He was short with her.

'No, not yet, but the States might well be where it will be in a few years. Anyway, I'd have to get your uncle's permission. I'd appreciate it if you don't mention this to anybody, I mean *anybody*, until I've had a chance to talk to the chairman.'

She looked at him appraisingly, approvingly. 'You really are a man for observing the due forms, aren't you?'

'I've never found short-cuts honourable or profitable in this business. Barford wanted me long before Milwaukee. I've a duty to them.'

They finished work for the day. Bob helped Enid on with her coat and would have kissed her had she been co-operative. She was not, her voice was chilly.

'When I'm taken in adultery, *Mr* Calderwood, I don't want it to be by the Planet. I'd hate to confirm his fondly-held prejudices. We agreed that this was a small town.'

She was totally right, Bob raged. All that she was saying he had said to Les Frith a mere three months ago in this very office. He gave the brusque nod which meant that he had been in error, and she smiled forgivingly.

'Come round about half eight tomorrow night. I'll have a meal ready.'

Calderwood's hesitation was noted.

'All right, if it's awkward, no meal. Better come in by the side gate, you could leave the car up in Wharfedale Lane. You are remembering it's my day off tomorrow?'

'I'm remembering.'

He was threading his way through the town on the way out to Tarkington when he saw Jean Ogden, package-laden, waiting at a bus stop with the weary resignation of one who'd been doing it for some time. He pulled alongside the kerb and after she identified him, she clambered in gratefully.

'C'mon, Jean, you had me figured as a kerbside crawler.'

'Chance would be a fine thing.'

They both laughed. She was one of his favourite people, still young of face despite pepper and salt hair, and with large hazel eyes that were outstandingly lovely.

'You're a godsend, Bob. The damned Mini's packed in — Tim's going to have to come up with the wherewithal for another.' She indicated the parcels. 'I've got arms like a gorilla with this lot. Sally and Norrie' — referring to the newlyweds — 'are coming over for dinner tonight with Norrie's folks. You've no idea how set Tim is on flying the flag on such occasions.'

'Do you miss her?' Bob asked, eyes on the road ahead.

'Oh, yes, Bob. Tim's worse. I find him sitting in her room sometimes. You'd think she was in China rather than Knaresborough.' She looked affectionately at him. 'You'll miss Phyllis too when she goes.'

'A treat in store,' Bob began, then shook his head ruefully. 'I can't do the flippant father bit, Jean. There'll be another of us sitting in an empty bedroom. It seems a little in the distance as yet.'

'What about the young Frenchman, Yves, was it?'

'Yvon. Like a lot of other young Frenchmen, more attractive in St Malo than in Barford.' He smiled at the memory. 'She wrote him off as a wet three days after he came to visit us. I'd to take him in tow for the rest of the week. I thought he was a fine lad. No, it's young Clifford who's the front runner just now.'

Jean had the relaxed coquetry of the attractive, fortyish woman who knows exactly where the boundaries are.

'They go far too soon, just the same, Bob. Mind you, you don't look old enough to have a marriageable daughter.'

'Surely I'm supposed to say that?'

107

'If you wait on the Scotch for a compliment you'll wait for ever.'

They took the turn-off for the Ogdens' house which was about two miles from The Owlies. Jean looked at Bob with a fond concern.

'I thought the programme was a bit rough on the club the other night, Bob.'

'Did Tim see it?'

'We both saw it. Fat chance of our missing it. I'm surprised you ask.'

'It's just that Joan said that you and she hadn't managed to see it for nattering about the wedding.'

Jean had always reminded Bob of high school and Girl Guides, a wholesome girl who was doubtless, within the marriage bond, a sensual wanton. A glance in his angled mirror showed him that Girl Guides from high schools could lie with wondrous efficiency and speed for their old friends.

'Oh, that. No, no, what actually happened was that Joan got caught up with Tim's mother over the wedding photographs, and wouldn't disappoint her by breaking off. You know how good she's always been with Mother, who can be rather tiresome. She insists on identifying every last uncle and cousin.'

Bob nodded pleasantly. 'I've an aunt back home who's the same. Heart of gold really, must send out about sixty birthday cards in the year. She could give you the address of every Calderwood between here and Melbourne.'

There was a soft swish of tyres on gravel as the car swung into the drive of The Wickets. Bob drew up at the front door, skirting the traitorous Mini. He helped Jean in with the parcels and shopping bag.

'Thank you so much, Bob. You are a life-saver.'

'Oh, we go around doing good by stealth.'

He declined a cup of coffee, saying that Joan would be expecting him and in any event she would have a thousand things to do with the in-laws coming to dinner.

'That's true. Never mind, we'll try not to let the side down. Love to Joan, and be sure to thank her from me again for being so patient with Mother.'

Bob promised he would do that and got back into the car. It

was logical that women would cover for each other, men did it in pubs, on golf courses, on weekends, but he had not experienced it up till now. He would bet a month's salary that Joan had never been anywhere near the Ogdens on the night of the broadcast. So, where had she been? With Derek Naughton? Nowhere she felt she could tell him, that was certain.

If it were Derek then he was not flattered. He passed the 'Welcome to Tarkington' sign, turned left at The Two Plovers (known locally as The Two Soft Lovers) and swung into his own driveway.

In the kitchen Joan was making the last adjustments to the table.

'Have a good day, love?'

'Yes, ye-es. One of those days where everything went well. Les Frith looked in.'

'I thought he'd gone to Cardiff.'

'Swansea. He's back north just for a couple of days.'

'I rather liked Les,' Joan said musingly.

'Randy little tyke,' her husband growled in displeasure.

Joan served the soup. 'We'll soon be beyond the season for this,' she observed.

Bob nodded. When he spoke, he had not quite finished his spoonful and a faint slurp brought a censorious 'Daddy!' from Phyllis. Calderwood despatched an Arctic look in his daughter's direction, but his remark was addressed to his wife.

'I picked up Jean Ogden at a bus stop in town and gave her a lift home. She was in a bit of a flap — Sally and her husband and his people were coming over tonight and the Mini had conked out.'

Jean nodded as if the news were expected. 'She's a bandit with that car of hers. She never has it serviced, never tops up the battery.'

'She speaks highly of you too,' Bob said, his tone intentionally light and bantering. 'She asked me to be sure to thank you again for talking so much with Tim's mother on the night of the programme.'

Joan, as on countless other nights, collected the soup plates and stacked them on the sink.

'Well, Mrs Metcalfe's a lovely person. I'd rather have

109

watched your programme, but a couple of hands at crib's not much to give, is it?'

'Not too many would take the trouble,' said Bob. 'I'll trouble you for the celery, Phyllis.'

Later, over coffee, Bob told Joan of the offer he had received that day from Milwaukee. Joan assumed that if he accepted, he would be going out on his own and he took no steps to disabuse her. She could hardly, he told himself, start in a job full-time, if that was what she wanted, and then immediately turn round and ask for two months off.

14

In the end, avoiding re-election had been like pushing at an open door. On the last Saturday of the season but one, Barford Albion were still in some slight peril. They faced a tough home fixture with Lincoln City while Hartlepool and Newport had, on paper, much easier tasks. But, as every dullard of a coach and manager that Calderwood had ever known used to say, with the air of one coining an eternal verity, 'You don't play this game on paper'.

And so it had proved. Bob had known very few games in his time on the bench as a manager in which the minutes did not fly when Albion were behind, or crawl if they happened to get in front. The crucial Lincoln match was, however, as stress-free as League Football was ever likely to get. Albion's new centre, Sam Ellis from Hardington Colliery (an additional source of satisfaction that, since the pits had seemed to be losing their historic tradition of producing footballers) had at once struck up an on-field understanding with Vic Slocombe. The new-comer's bustling, tearaway style complemented the thoughtful suavity of Slocombe's play to perfection. Within ten minutes of the start each had found the net. A brief Lincoln flurry was quelled by the calm professionalism of Arnold Dearson, and just before the teams went in at half-time Ellis was tripped in the box and Phil Gifford put away the penalty kick.

The second half was merely a wait for the passage of time. It was highly unlikely that Lincoln could manage four away from home and, when Ellis scored his second on the hour, totally impossible that they could rattle in five.

The final whistle went and Calderwood got up from the bench to hurry to the dressing room. Stand and terraces cheered him lustily and although he tried hard always to appear expressionless in victory or defeat, he relaxed to the extent of a little victory wave and jig. At once he was put out with himself for this departure from dignity.

There was the usual post-match babel. A transistor radio brought the news that both Newport and Hartlepool had obligingly dropped points at home. It was certain then, whoever had to go cap in hand to the Football League for re-election, it would not be Albion. It had been done by hard work, some managerial skill in motivation, and the good fortune without which the most gifted manager is helpless.

He thanked the players, with a special word for Sam Ellis, the youngster, and Arnold Dearson, whose last game it would be at Jubilee Park. As he made his way back from dressing room to office he was stopped in the corridor by a tall man who looked vaguely familiar. He identified himself as a scout with one of the Sheffield clubs and expressed an interest in Ellis. Bob promised to let his Board know, the scout said he'd try to get his manager to have a look at the youngster in Albion's last League game. The two men parted amicably.

He went into the office and sat down. Enid was upstairs, helping her uncle entertain. The whiskies might just be that little bit more generous today, not that Barford Albion had ever been Fourth Division in their standards of hospitality. He'd let the socialising finish before he reopened the subject of America with the chairman. Schofield had seemed reasonably receptive, certainly he hadn't knocked the idea back.

He took a couple of congratulatory calls. Dave Adamson looked in briefly; he gave it as his opinion that Albion in the closing six weeks or so had played as well as at any time over the last five seasons. He seemed quite euphoric.

'I think you've got things on the right lines, Bob, nice blend of runners and know-how. Young Ellis is rough-edged but he's got possibilities.'

'Somebody else thinks so.' Bob told Adamson, off the record, of the scout's approach.

'There you are then. Your Uncle Dave can spot a good 'un.'

Bob looked at him, friendship contending with the professional's dislike of outside judgments and disregard for them.

'I'll mention it to the Board, of course. But I wonder about Ellis. The kid's only played two games, both at home. He's done well, I grant you, but what's he like on a cold February day at Millwall with the crowd baying for blood — his? To me Slocombe's the far better bet, I'll find six chasers for every one thinker.'

Adamson was, in his turn, slightly pinked. 'You're not the run of the mill manager though, Bob. Most managers are afraid of clever players. Even more afraid when they're clever off the park.'

'You might be right. I'll let you know if there are any developments.'

Adamson grinned. 'Eat your heart out, Les Frith, eh?'

Bob shook his head. 'I heard that he'd got a couple in the first half at Barnsley.'

Adamson made a mental note. 'Happy endings all round then. I'll do a par on Les next week. And send him the cutting. I bet his cuttings book's bigger than Gielgud's.'

Bob looked at him, his tanned face tired and lined in reaction. 'In this business, Dave, you have to reassure yourself from time to time.'

His friend nodded. 'In mine too. Though I don't find reading my old articles is a particularly good way to do it. By the way I'll want a "Look forward to next season" piece in about three weeks or so. When I come back off holiday.'

'Always assuming I'm not in the U S of A.'

'Of course. Mind you, even there they have stamps and a postal service. Might be worth an extra ten quid from the editor with an American dateline.'

'I'll tell my agent. Of course the chairman might put the

kibosh on it since I've kept them in the Football League.'

Adamson wouldn't hear of it. 'He's changed his mind, I shouldn't wonder. There's no need for him now to crawl to other chairmen for support at the League AGM. I ran into him on the stairs — he was very gracious. Complimented me on a piece I wrote last week . . . and called me David, Robert' — Adamson's way of showing that another idiosyncrasy had been observed.

'I sometimes wonder why he does it,' Calderwood admitted.

'I know,' said Adamson. 'He always wants to give the impression of standing in special relationship to somebody. Well, I can't give you any more of my valuable psychologist's time. I'm due at home for an in-depth session with Eileen.'

'Have a good holiday, Dave.'

He managed to see Schofield for a few minutes on the twin subjects of Ellis and Milwaukee, and tried to make his points quickly as Schofield seemed in a hurry. The chairman registered his appreciation of the Sheffield interest, and like Bob expressed a little surprise.

'Well, Robert, every man has his price. Ellis is a man, therefore Ellis has his price. My reaction's to sit on it for a bit, let the *Examiner* run a couple of ' "Eighty thousand pounds won't shift Ellis', say Jubilee Park Board." Then maybe later we can tell Sheffield on the phone, "But try fifty-five thousand." '

He looked at his watch. 'Damn it, I've got to run, and this is important business. It's lunatic to attempt to rush it. What are you doing Monday morning?'

'The usual. Checking on injuries, run of the mill admin.'

'You can leave that to Enid. I'm awarding you a morning off with pay. Come on out to Barford Castle. The course is lovely now after last week's rain and that bit of heat.'

'I haven't played in months,' Bob demurred feebly.

'Then I'll beat you all the more easily, Robert. Let's make it eleven o'clock on the first tee. That suit?'

* * *

It was one of the greatest advantages of a Scots upbringing that

113

golf for a boy had been available and cheap. As he looked at the long, low, well-appointed clubhouse at Barford Castle, Bob realised that he would never, from his economic background, have been a junior member here. In Scotland, though, he had played Carluke and Carnwath at home and the glorious Fife course at Elie during the summer holidays.

Golf had gradually been squeezed out of his life, but good early teaching and innate skill meant that even after the longest of lie-offs he could be reasonably sure of shooting around eighty-five. Schofield was very obviously a manufactured golfer with a handicap of twelve which he had rather to struggle to hold.

It was a lovely, still day and the moorland turf was springy underfoot. Gorse bushes abounded for the unwary and the course was long, but the manicured greens were true and holding. Calderwood could feel all his love for the game surge back.

Schofield was a good host. He had organised coffee but made sure they were on the tee at eleven as planned. He had chosen that time because the course, quiet on a Monday anyway, would be at its most spacious. Few members came out immediately following the weekend, but there was an outing of bankers from Hull who had started to go off from 8.30 a.m. Schofield had allowed a couple of hours for the hackers and sclaffers to get well out on the course.

He took his game seriously. He made it plain that there would be no business discussion until the nineteenth and confined the conversation to pleasant generalities. Once he asked if Enid were giving satisfaction in the office but Bob was confident that the question need not be taken at other than face value. Apart from that, Schofield restricted himself to exclamations of 'Bad luck!', more frequently 'Shot!', and sound advice on distances and clubbing.

After four holes Bob was three down. Then he began to put his game together and around the turn won four in a row. Schofield hung on desperately until Bob began to tire not from lack of fitness but from unwonted concentration. They came to the seventeenth with the chairman one up. It was a short hole, up to a plateau green. Schofield had the honour and played a

114

seven iron, well struck, slightly pushed out on the very edge of the green. Bob, bunkered, came out to twelve feet and just missed on the left. Schofield had putted up indifferently to about seven feet.

Larks were singing overhead as he lined up the putt. 'This for the match, Robert?'

Bob nodded; his training was not to speak after his opponent stood over the ball. The putt never looked like going anywhere else but in the hole. Calderwood extended his hand. It had been a most enjoyable round.

'Well played, Robert. If I'd your ability I'd be out on the golf course a damned sight oftener.'

They stood on the eighteenth, and elevated tee, almost five hundred yards downhill to the clubhouse. In the background the town sought to gain a toehold on the lower slopes.

With the pressure off Schofield hit a moderate drive but Bob relaxed and, swinging slowly, hit such a tee shot as he had seldom if ever bettered. Schofield could afford to be impressed.

'That's the kind that brings you back again, Robert. With the run that's three hundred yards near as not. You're looking for a birdie here.'

The birdie was six inches short of being an eagle. As they entered the clubhouse the last of the visitors from Hull were setting out on their second round. The two men had a quick shower, Bob noting that there were real hand-towels in the gents' washroom. Then into blazer, collar and tie for the bar.

'We find you have to spell it out for dress, Robert. Otherwise before you know it, the bar'll be full of people in scruff order.'

He was right, thought Bob, although he himself would never warm to much of the pompous formality associated with a certain type of English golf club. Many of the most famous and prestigious Scottish clubs got by very well without a tenth of all this palaver. He had been at the Barford Castle Golf Dinner in October at the chairman's invitation and been dourly amused at the compulsion to appear in hunting pink coats which seemed unanimously to afflict the club captains of the area. Scarcely less risible was the club ceremonial toast, the vice-captain solemnly intoning, 'Mr Captain, sir, will you take wine with

115

me?' and on receiving his assent, the two men linked the little fingers of their left hands while they drained their glasses to sustained applause.

Still, there was a sense of style, no denying that, and the lunch could not have been bettered anywhere in the county; the loin of pork had been quite outstanding. Getting good service would never be a problem for Schofield anywhere. At a golf club where he had already served as Greens Convener, was currently Match Convener, and a very possible future captain, the staff were obviously prepared to put themselves out for him.

The chairman called for a couple of brandies and suggested that they go through to the small committee room in the interests of quiet. He took the opportunity of showing Bob the revisions he had made to the system of keeping handicaps. The clarity and efficiency of the scheme were at once apparent to Bob.

Schofield let the golf of the morning go with some reluctance. 'As good a morning as I've spent in a long time, Robert. We're mad, dashing around working our backsides off. We should be out here on the moors, drinking it all in.'

'You played well, Chairman,' Bob said ungrudgingly.

'Thank you. I know you mean that. And, I had to, because that's one of the nice things about you, Robert, you don't play a customer's game. However, duty calls, to business. Ellis first of all.'

The two men were in agreement. Bob said that while building a team was his priority, Ellis was raw, might go off the boil any time. He hadn't been long enough at Jubilee Park to entrench himself in the fans' affections and if they could get that kind of money for him, they'd be better picking up two seasoned players.

Schofield nodded. 'Right. Now, about your safari.'

'Well, I've told Peter I'll phone tonight. I'm second choice, as it happens, a Hungarian, Bela Nagy, pulled out. I thought I had to be anyway from the timing of the invitation. However it depends on whether you think there would be any clash with my duties here.'

'Do you?'

'Not really. I could fly back July 14th or so, that's plenty of

116

time for pre-season training. Leonard Steele could handle routine correspondence — for that matter anything the Board felt needed initiating. We could hold off any Ellis move till I got back. I don't see that my going would interfere with our preparations for the new season.'

Schofield nodded. 'You're right, Robert, it wouldn't at all. You see, the question doesn't arise. There isn't going to be a next season for Albion. We're relinquishing our membership of the Football League. That's what I asked you out here to tell you.'

15

The rows of red-bound *Golfer's Handbooks* glowed from the shelves. Through the small side window Bob was conscious of the club professional on the practice-ground with a portly member, endeavouring vainly to replace lunge with swing. He could notice all this although the man sitting opposite him in the round-backed chair had just deprived him of his living. He was aware that Schofield was looking intently at him, seeking some response. When it came it was inadequate.

'What do you mean, no next season?'

'What I just said, Robert.' Schofield's voice was not unkindly. 'We will not be renewing our application for membership for next season. The club has an offer for the ground. Around the three-quarters of a million mark. I've decided to accept it, or rather' — he caught himself — 'I've recommended that we do.'

'Does it matter if the others disagree?' Calderwood asked, his tone ragged with bitterness.

'Not at all,' the other said firmly. 'As it happens, the Board's unanimously in favour. We'd an unofficial get-together out of town at the Packhorse on Saturday night. We'll have to put it to the shareholders at an Extraordinary General Meeting, of course, but I see that as being a formality.'

'What about the League?' Bob asked thickly.

'We simply give notice that we are resigning from membership. I'll spread the word that the club is not confident of being able to honour its financial commitments for another entire season. That'll alarm the League, who're haunted by the clubs which went bust in mid-season in the nineteen twenties. It'll scare the PFA lot stiff, in case there's any danger of their lads not being paid. It has one further advantage,' he went on, in the act of lighting a cigarette, 'it happens to be true.'

'Are you saying that you couldn't continue to run the club?' Calderwood was floundering helplessly, unable to make any impact.

'I'm not saying that. What I am saying is that the club is not viable through the turnstiles and I'm not prepared any longer to give it the kiss of life. There's no law that says you *have* to subsidise a football club indefinitely. Or, thank God, that a man can't do what he likes with his own.'

Calderwood swallowed, dazed. The man had to be stopped. How could he appeal to him?

'Have you thought, Chairman, of the gap it would leave in the life of the town?'

Schofield laughed out loud. 'Don't give me that crap, Robert. You make it sound as if we should be on the Chamber of Commerce brochure. "Visit historic Jubilee Park, home of struggling Albion." Where's the town any Saturday afternoon? Three thousand through the gates and we get claustrophobia.'

There was a diffident tap on the door, repeated, after which it opened slowly to disclose the rotund, spectacled form of the club secretary.

'I'm awfully sorry, Jack,' he said uneasily, 'but we are down for a Secretaries' meeting this afternoon to fix dates for the Armathwaite Putter. I could try to find a corner elsewhere.'

Schofield's brow cleared. 'Not at all, Steve. Your chaps'll be here?'

The secretary nodded dolefully.

'We'll find another corner, never mind about us.' He smiled winningly at his manager. 'Shift-ho I'm afraid, Robert.'

Once outside Bob suggested that if matters were settled, he was wasting time that could be better spent at the office. His employer would have none of it.

'We'll get a corner in the members' lounge here. I'll put my card on the table, that's a sign we're talking shop and we'll be left alone. It'll be a good hour before the first of the Hell, Hull and Halifax brigade come down the last fairway.'

He steered Bob to an alcove table, placed a rather large business card ostentatiously on it and called across to the club steward, 'Ben! Bring us a pot of coffee, there's a good chap. Thank you so much.'

He turned back to Bob. 'There are a lot of people to be considered in this. You don't close a club lightly. You yourself, you've put a lot of hard, honest work into this season, you're entitled to know why.'

'All I know is that we're not the worst team in the League,' Calderwood said sullenly.

'Indeed we're not, Robert. I read this morning's *Examiner* too. There are five sides below us in the Football League. Or, put it another way, eighty-six above us.'

He swung his arms around in an expansive gesture. 'Look around you, and then think of Jubilee Park. This is an amateur club, golf's an amateur game, but the quality of administration here is frighteningly professional. Soccer's a professional game and yet the standard of administration . . . and I'm speaking of three clubs in every four . . . is pitiful.'

It was unusual for Schofield to develop an argument at length, but he warmed now to his theme.

'Our club has lived with failure, total, perpetual failure, for fifty years. It's almost physical at the ground, you could reach out and slice it with a knife, cut yourself a plug of thick black failure. One county cup in eighty-two years — because Leeds went on tour that season and Huddersfield wouldn't compete. The year we won it they wrapped the bloody competition up. Thanks, Ben, just put it down there. No, that's all right, hang on to that.'

He came back to the attack even as he poured out the coffee. 'One? Without! And what about those pennants in your office? A tour of the Channel Islands and one of Ireland.' His voice rose

119

in unfeigned scorn. 'How pathetic can we get?'

'Malky and Eddie and the other old men that come every week don't think we're pathetic,' said Calderwood stubbornly.

'Exactly. *Old* men. Even that pansy Oliver noticed that in his programme.'

With an angry flash of insight Calderwood snarled, 'You set it up! You meant him to!'

His companion shrugged negligently. 'I don't deny it. As majority shareholder I've always had power to accept what seems an advantageous offer. The programme simply made a few points for me to a helluva lot of people.'

'I'll bet it did. Like what a responsibility the running of Albion was.'

'Not on. If private enterprise is going to be screwed into the ground by both political parties, we can't be expected to keep the Albions of this world going for ever. Why not invite one of the unions to exercise the power of patronage? Little fear of that, my friend, the brothers aren't that daft.'

Calderwood pushed his coffee miserably away and there were a few seconds of silence. Then the Scot spoke in a persuasive, advocate's manner.

'Mr Schofield, I can understand you being a bit disappointed with the way things have gone this season.'

Schofield's smile was eminently reasonable. 'They go like this *every* season, Robert.'

'If you're dissatisfied with things, won't you give the club another year? Perhaps a change in personnel, here' — he indicated his own seat.

'Don't talk soft, Robert.' He poured some more coffee and in putting in the sugar, slopped a few drops on to his cavalry twill slacks. He swore quietly.

'Look, I've no complaints with the way you've handled things, quite the contrary, you've done well. You're no Clough or Shankly, but you are hardworking, honest, socially presentable and potentially a first-class golfer. The blame in no way lies with you.'

The testimonial flowed past Bob unheeded as he sought ways and means. He cast around with the vigour of desperation.

'Is there any chance of somebody buying you out? Would

120

you sell your shareholding?'

The chairman seemed genuinely baffled. 'To whom?'

'Well, the Supporters' Association.'

He would never have said a stupid thing like that in a less agitated frame of mind. He knew at once from the businessman's half-scornful, half-pitying tone that Schofield had him marked indelibly as a financial lightweight, a commercial nonentity.

'Stick to things you understand, Robert. That's sheer stupidity. Our Supporters' Association gives us about a hundred pounds in cash and a thousand pounds in bother every season. They couldn't raise enough money to put a down payment on a goalpost. Afternoon, Frank,' he nodded at a passing member who, seeing the card on the table, returned the nod affably and passed on. 'That's Frank Selby. His father was a wool merchant on Bradford Exchange when that meant something.' He looked earnestly at Bob.

'See here, business is for the professionals. It needs flair and understanding. Have you ever looked at the shares register for Barford Albion Limited?'

A shake of the head was his answer. It was many a day since Bob Calderwood had felt himself to be so thoroughly inadequate.

'You surprise me. I think I might, in your shoes, have made it my business to find out. No matter. The situation is this. I hold about seventy-five per cent of the issued share capital and the rest is split amongst dozens of little men who have five, ten or twenty shares because they were left to them by their fathers. The sentimental stock.' He looked out of the window as one of a pair coming down the home fairway left a wedge shot stiff at the flag. 'Shot! He'll not need to putt that. But to answer your question, anyone who likes can have Albion, lock, stock and bloody barrel, for three-quarters of a million pounds. That's the asking price.'

'Is it just the money?' Calderwood wondered.

'Yes. Very largely. *Just* the three-quarters of a million. Seems a good enough reason in itself, I must admit. Stand by for "Jack Schofield . . . This Is Your Life". Shan't take more than five minutes, I promise you. Can't anyway there are the first of the financiers going up the sixteenth.' He looked narrowly at Bob.

'You've been a player and a manager. You genuinely believe you know the other side of football, the boardroom. You don't. Most directors would almost bankrupt themselves to stay in the Fourth Division. You see, essentially they're little men — oh, competent enough in their own lines of business, but basically of little account. My own father's a good example, and in anything I say I'm not knocking the old boy. He did very well by me.'

He looked up and motioned to the steward.

'Will you have a sherry? Soft drink? Just as you like.' He commanded a sherry from the toiling Ben. 'He was very much the local lad, my father, and proud to subsidise the local club from the profits of the engineering works. It paid off well for him too, in a way. He got on the FA Council quite young, became a selector eventually, and got drunk in seven European countries. Did you know he was introduced to Hitler? He was with the national side in Germany in 1936. Mother hid the photograph when war came.'

He laughed reminiscently. 'That's what I mean about the game being amateurish, Robert. Here you had a businessman who, as results show only too clearly, couldn't pick a team to beat Crewe Alexandra, yet he helped pick the national side. It let him talk in the Conservative Club about Wilf Copping and Eddie Hapgood and what he'd said to them before the match. But I'm different, Robert, I haven't that gut commitment, being the second generation, third actually,' he corrected himself. 'For one thing I went to a rugby-playing school even if I can't stand the game.' His voice rose in shrill, inaccurate mimicry: "Let's have a clean long service, Nigel" — that's in the afternoon, then it's "The Harlot of Jerusalem" in the clubhouse at night. If I learned one thing at that school though it was that there's a world outside Jubilee Park, a more attractive world.'

He lit a second cigarette. 'There's not much more, I promise you. Do you know that I sit on nine different boards, and the shambles we call Barford Albion causes me more bother than the rest of them put together? I can't make it work, nobody can, and I don't like failure.'

'What about the casualties then? There'll be a few.' The raw Scottish tones left Schofield in total mastery of himself.

'Understand, Robert, I'm explaining, not apologising. I'm doing nothing crooked. I'm simply realising an asset and, as a by-product, leaving room for another town where perhaps they care more for League Football.'

'Stalybridge?' The word was a whip-crack.

'Stalybridge,' the chairman agreed softly. 'Or Yeovil. Or King's Lynn. Times change, Robert. You don't see many Rileys or Armstrong Siddeleys on the roads these days. As for Malky and Eddie and our other ancients, Leeds is just down the road. They can go and watch them.'

Calderwood had begun to get really angry, quite irrationally, when his chairman used the alien word soccer. He now exploded in puzzled wonderment, his voice well above conversational pitch.

'You *really* don't understand a bloody thing about this game, do you? Malky and Eddie hate Leeds, hate Huddersfield, they've been hating them ever since they could see over the top of a boundary wall. Their loyalty's not to football clubs in general, it's to Albion, it's total.'

Schofield held up his hand firmly. 'Please! I can understand your distress, but we must conduct this conversation within decent limits. I understand this much about football, too. I understand that what you've just said about the old boys is a damned poor reason for my turning down a seven hundred and fifty thousand pound offer.'

'I'm sorry. I have a duty as your guest,' Calderwood muttered grimly, 'which is, as you say, why you invited me here.' He looked angrily across the table. 'There'll be a lot of opposition, you know.'

'I shouldn't bank on it, and it'll certainly be nothing we can't handle. I'll tell you how it will be, Robert. The *Examiner*'ll have a field day. We'll be strolling down memory lane for a fortnight with your pal David Adamson recalling past triumphs that never were. Some clown at the Town Hall will have a go at me at the next council meeting. I'd even put a little money into "Save the Albion" stickers, they'll definitely be bullish in the short term. But that'll be all and it'll do no good. We're going to join

New Brighton and Accrington Stanley in the great League in the sky.'

Calderwood simply wanted to get away, but he had to ask. 'The players, have you considered them?'

Again the answer was immediate, uncompromising. 'Yes. They're covered to the end of the season anyway. I'll consider paying those who are on their options, although I'm sure we don't need to. There'd be a damn sight more hardship if I closed any of my other eight concerns.'

'What'll become of them?' Calderwood persisted.

'Their registrations vest in the League. If any of them attract a transfer fee we can be allotted a proportion of that fee to cover our costs and winding-up expenses.' He paused. 'Always providing that we leave as a member in good standing.'

He looked out of the window again. Three distant figures stood up on the eighteenth tee. Schofield rose and prepared to go.

'We can get two-thirds of the proceeds from any later transfer of one of our players, provided we haven't been expelled from the League. That's what it comes down to.'

There was a wrenching admiration in Bob's next remark. 'You have this all worked out, haven't you?'

Schofield looked down at him. 'It's a good job that one of us has. People have told me for years that football's a business. I've decided to pioneer the application of business principles. If it really catches on there'll be about eight clubs left in the Football League ten years from now.'

The two men walked out to the car park, Bob astonishing himself by managing to dredge up a parting civility for the club steward while Schofield indicated that he'd want a table for four for lunch that Sunday.

The chairman watched as Bob loaded his caddy car and golf bag into the boot. His words were tinged with genuine respect.

'You haven't asked, Robert, which is greatly to your credit, but it goes without saying that your contract'll be honoured for the fourteen months it has to run. There'll be six month's severance pay too.'

Sharp as a tack, thought the manager without a club to manage. He's no choice but to honour the contract, he makes the gesture over severance pay, but can't bring himself to make it a year's salary.

'One thing more. The club'll place no obstacle in the way of your going to America.'

Calderwood gazed at him incredulously. 'I can't walk out blithely on this mess in a fortnight's time.'

There was a suggestion of flint in Schofield's disclaimer. 'It isn't a mess. And your going or staying won't help or hinder. But you must make up your own mind.'

'Do the press know?'

'If they don't, it'll be the first thing that's happened around here that they've missed. If you mean can you tell them, it'll do no harm now.'

'Shouldn't we hold the news until after the last match?'

'No real reason why. If the news is out some of our lads can use the game as a shop window. That reminds me, I'll phone over to Rochdale and get them to triple their programme run. They'll sell them easily to collectors if it's our last appearance.'

He opened the door of his Audi. 'I'll look in at the ground on Wednesday, Robert. Thanks for the game. I really enjoyed it.'

Calderwood stood transfixed. The bastard meant it. He *had* enjoyed the round. And he *was* closing down the club. And Bob, who had always imagined that he knew his way round, was much brighter than some of his managerial colleagues, more aware of the real world, had been brought to battle on ground of his adversary's choosing and destroyed utterly.

To whom could he turn? Where, if at all, could he mobilise support? He must phone Dave, and with the thought remembered that Adamson was on holiday.

Joan had been working full-time for a fortnight now. The urge to confide in her was strong but he would either have to tell Derek or make polite conversation to him and he wished to do neither. He was by no means confident in any case that Joan would treat the news as a disaster.

He stood in thought as the bankers made their noisy way to the clubhouse. He got into the car, backed out carefully and headed for the ground. He was still manager of Barford Albion for a few days yet. Besides, Jubilee Park would be quiet, and he wanted to see Enid.

16

It was not often that Jubilee Park managed to look attractive. In its daily existence it appeared dour, hand-to-mouth, shabby, but on this beneficent late afternoon of spring it appeared almost picturesque to Calderwood as he returned to his office from the golf course. In the background a mower whirred pastorally out on the pitch, even the Toytown stand had a certain charm.

As he parked the car, he thought of the difference which a few hours could make. He had left the ground as manager of a League club, not the greatest but one which had survived. He was returning now to preside over the final rites. He should start by announcing the death, but to whom? The Planet had a clear claim to be told first, but he felt himself shrinking from that task and he headed for his office. It was getting on for five o'clock, and he half-expected that Enid would have gone home, but she was still there, working methodically through an old ledger, scoring a few names out and making annotations against others.

'I'm back, Enid,' Calderwood announced superfluously. 'What are you doing?'

She glanced up at him happily. 'I'm going through this list of complimentary tickets we issue. It badly needs updating. Ex-Chief Superintendent Graham, for instance, he's been dead for years. I had a spare half hour so I thought I'd put it in order for next season.'

Calderwood shook his head in a dogged hurt. 'A good idea, Enid, but I shouldn't bother now. There isn't going to be a next season. For you, for me, for Albion, for anyone.'

'What on earth do you mean?'

Briefly he related the earlier events of the afternoon at the golf club, the decision her uncle had made and the reasons which had prompted him to it. He had a strange compulsion to present Schofield's case as fairly as possible. Schofield's niece was furious, and unimpressed by the apologia.

'But that's outrageous! Uncle Jack doesn't need the money.

He's got more than he knows what to do with.'

Despite himself Calderwood smiled wryly at this chivalrous assessment, then sobered as the girl went on with transparent sincerity.

'And what will you do? You've worked so hard to keep the club going. Not that he'd give any consideration to that.'

'He did, Enid. There's nothing he hasn't considered. The club will honour my contract.'

'So you're all right for a year or so. What then? Can you get another job at . . .?'

'At my age, Enid?' Bob asked gently.

'Don't be foolish, when has that mattered?'

Looking at her, Bob was more conscious of the distance in years than he had ever been before. Normally Enid dressed and made up to look rather older than her years, but today in her anger on his behalf she seemed very young and almost vulnerable.

'I needn't be put out to graze just yet. Pete Rossington told me if I changed my mind about going to Milwaukee he could certainly use me on the coaching staff. I'd be over there for about four months. I'm certain now that the chairman won't stand in my way.'

Not 'Schofield', Enid noted, or 'your uncle' but 'the chairman' even in disintegration. He turned from the window, the soft afternoon sunlight shining on his short, wavy hair. He was suddenly urgent, beseeching.

'Will you come with me, Enid?'

'To Milwaukee?'

He nodded.

'I couldn't possibly.' She was musing rather than denying. 'Where would I stay?'

It seemed to be the logistics of the exercise rather than the morality of it which gave her pause.

'That's easily taken care of. There's an offer of accommodation with the job. It's standard procedure for this type of short-term contract.'

'There's an offer of accommodation for you and *Mrs* Calderwood, surely?'

Bob shook his head impatiently. 'Joan wouldn't want to go,

and anyway, even if she did, she could hardly walk out on Derek Naughton having just gone full-time.'

'Does she know she's invited?'

'No. Will you come with me?'

The answer was a few seconds in coming.

'No.'

'Why not, Enid?'

She looked at him with real fondness. 'For your sake, chiefly. There's no way you could keep it quiet.'

'Who's to know over there?'

'Your friend Rossington.'

'I can't remember that he's ever met Joan. Even if he had it's of no consequence to him. He's running a pro football team, not a boy scout camp.'

'It'd still get back here and you know it. Football's a goldfish bowl even over there. I've read enough to know that the Los Angeles Aztecs and the Houston Hurricanes are simply Leicester and Birmingham transplanted. It's only a job you've lost here, you could lose your marriage and your family there. I don't think you're strong enough for that.'

'You don't?'

'You're a decent man. I don't want to see you held up to ridicule. Some First Division managers can survive that. They're the flash boys with the big city clubs. For them it's part of the glamour, it's expected. Here' — she looked around the dingy office — 'it'd be . . .'

'Pathetic?' Calderwood's voice was harsh.

The girl did not flinch. She nodded, consideringly. 'Pathetic.'

Calderwood, conscious that antagonism was futile, was nevertheless stung to ask, 'How come you're so perceptive? Have you been playing God for long?'

There was no anger or resentment in her reply. 'When you're left an orphan early on, you tend to think a lot. I don't say that out of self-pity, not for a moment. I've been very lucky. Aunt Lucy has been wonderful, almost better than a mother to me. But you know me well enough to know that something of Uncle Jack's rubbed off on me too. I'm very much the chairman's niece. My father was the gentle brother. You're a gentle man too.'

'Never mind that. I'm asking you again. Will you come to the States with me if I take the job?'

'No. Positively not. Apart from anything else I'll have to think about getting a permanent job. This was always just to fill in.'

'And you and I? Was that also just to fill in?'

'That's all it is at the moment. I don't see you rushing to leave The Owlies. It needn't be the end for us, I can still see you if you want. We can enjoy each other as we have done.' With an impish grin she added, 'You've a good mature body, Mr Calderwood, and a quirky mind. We'll be safer in Wales or London, you'll see. Poor lamb, the Schofield family haven't exactly made it a great day for you.'

He could not budge her and there was a point soon reached at which it was undignified to try. Leave it for a couple of days then perhaps reopen the subject. In the meantime there was his duty to the players and the Planet. He sat at his desk as Enid prepared to go home.

'Enid.'

'Yes?'

'Don't say anything about the closure on the way out. The players are entitled to hear about it from me.'

'I'd have thought they were entitled to hear about it from the chairman.'

'They will. Your uncle doesn't shirk the tackle, say what you like about him. I like you much better though.'

'I should hope so indeed. Look, we need a night soon to talk.' With a smile she was gone.

He sat down at his desk and almost unwittingly riffled through the contents of a couple of the drawers. An exercise book with the names of a few players who might be gettable jotted in it. Given Barford Albion's financial position, the players fell exclusively into one of two categories. They were either the occasional schoolboy of promise that the big clubs had missed on the first trawl, or durable veterans who might 'do a job' over a couple of seasons or so. All academic now, Albion would have no need of either crabbèd age or youth.

Academic too was the paper he'd prepared for the Board on

129

the pros and cons of continuing to run the reserve team next season. No reserve team, no first team. It was a first team training night but he decided that Steve Birkenshaw could take the session. Curiously, Enid had got it exactly right, the news of the closure should come from the chairman. Bob fired in penny numbers when it was a case of a player being transferred or freed, but this mass sacking should be announced by Schofield. The decision not to continue was his. Besides, Calderwood did not wish to tell his tale again today.

The Planet, though, had abundantly earned the right to prior notification and Bob went in search of him. He found him in the mower shed behind the enclosure and there, amidst goal nets, sawdust, corner flags and broken seats, he told Joe Staples that he would shortly be jobless. The Planet took it calmly enough.

'Better at my age, Boss, than for the young lads. Or Archie with that wife of his, that money was very useful to him.' A thought struck him. 'What about yourself, Boss?'

'You and I both, Planet. Though I suppose nobody'll miss the place as much as you'll do.'

'I don't suppose so. But it's been coming, Boss.'

'The TV programme, you mean?'

'No, I don't rate that. Little things. Chairman's father, old Geoff Schofield, he were in this hut every week, checking out equipment. Young Jack's never been in here since he was fifteen. I'm not surprised at all.'

'I've suggested to the chairman that you're made a special case for length of service, Joe.'

'That's good of you, Boss, but there's no occasion. I've liked my work and they've paid me regular. Three or four years at most they'd have got shot of me anyway.'

He finished painting the last of the corner flag poles and carefully stood it sloping from the wall. Then he came outside with Calderwood. They crossed the field to the main stand past the terracings where for four generations Barford men had stood on Saturday afternoons. Their Saturday evening entertainment had gone in that time from temperance concerts to music hall to talking pictures to Palais de Danse to discothèques, but Saturday afternoons had been immutable. Till now.

The two men halted on the touch-line under the overhanging

stand roof. Already the tentative spring growth was beginning to repair the ravages of six months of sliding tackles in goalmouth and centre circle. Idly Calderwood wondered whether the chairman had included plans for the disposal of the turf in his detailed arrangements. The answer was almost certainly yes. He switched back to the present and repeated to the Planet the warning against premature disclosure which he had given Enid. If Schofield decided to release the news to radio or TV then that was his affair.

He watched from the car park as the Planet trudged off home phlegmatically. Funny, he'd have thought the old lad would have created more, shown anger, perhaps even shed a tear or two, rather than this surprisingly passive acceptance that his working days were over.

Yours too, my son — Calderwood reminded himself. Before that there would almost certainly be fights with Joan about future direction. He hoped these could be postponed — for the moment he lacked stomach and energy for them.

Luck was on his side for the first time that day when he got home to Tarkington. He was met by a still house and a note from Joan to say she'd gone to Leeds to her cousin Vivian, who was undergoing some sort of domestic crisis. She might not be back till tomorrow, in which case she'd go straight to the shop.

The golf had honed Calderwood's appetite. He disregarded the lasagne which Joan had left out for him to heat and instead hard-boiled a couple of eggs while he opened a tin of corned beef. He looked at the jar of mayonnaise which normally he would have ignored, hesitated, then smeared the eggs liberally with the contents. On a whim, he telephoned the *Examiner* and Bob's phone call and invitation to come round later that evening forestalled by seconds Adamson's own hand on the receiver.

While he ate and waited, Calderwood forced himself to take rigorous account of his situation. What could he do? What options were open to him? He could manage again, he was pretty sure of that. Papers were fond of talking about managers being tossed on scrapheaps but the reality was otherwise. He'd often thought whimsically that football managership was like a gigantic *Magic Roundabout*. The difficult thing was persuading somebody to let you straddle a hobby-horse in the first place.

131

Once on, you might tumble off on several occasions, but if you waited by the side of the roundabout, there would soon be a riderless horse along and you could remount.

He'd done not badly at Barford, he knew that, and he also believed that Schofield would put the word out about him. A Third or Fourth Division club might well be interested in him, especially now that there was a shift away from the long-haired, one-of-the-boys school.

Conceivably a Second Division or even a First Division club might be interested in him as an assistant manager. He thought himself that was a bit ambitious, but it was a growing trend, and there had been some spectacularly successful essays in joint managership, such as Matt Busby and Jimmy Murphy, Brian Clough and Peter Taylor, Joe Mercer and Malcolm Allison. He wasn't sure whether he'd find this attractive even if asked. His managerial philosophy was basically that it was better to be fired for your own mistakes.

Had he been a Revie, an Allison, a Docherty, he could have filled the time between jobs very lucratively by fronting a column or appearing on the Saturday lunch-time TV sports shows. He was objective enough to know that as Barford Albion's last manager, he probably rated one five-minute slot on *Grandstand*, the same on *On the Ball*, and perhaps double that on *Nationwide* before instant oblivion set in.

Joan would want him to run a shop. He had no notion of this, and Schofield's pitiless exposure of his lack of commercial acumen had now made him very nervous of any such venture. The cobbler should stick to his last.

What was that fellow called who'd spoken to him at the end of the Rotary lunch? John Newton. "If you ever get the push, get in touch." A social politeness, no more, he couldn't see himself, well into his forties, totally untried, having much to offer Newton's company, or any other. Yet Newton could mean possibly staying in Barford, and leaving Barford was leaving Enid. It took only a couple of hours' absence from her for him to rediscover how much he wanted her. He had been genuinely surprised to find that he could be a good and vigorous lover. He had no wish to break off with Enid, no confidence that if he left her amongst younger men that their relationship could possibly endure. Football was driven from his mind in a violent onset of physical longing.

The banging of a car door and the scraping of feet on the metal door-mat announced the arrival of Dave Adamson. The reporter was genuinely concerned and angry, but his professional interest in a good story kept pushing through.

'We got it wrong, Bob. I had figured he was all set to carry on. And I had the first stirrings as far back as January. But he can't be allowed to get away with this.'

'I thought you were on holiday,' Bob murmured inconsequentially.

'I got a call from the man himself, would you believe? I've had to leave Eileen, she's furious. But you don't get the town's football club closed down every day, or at any rate an attempted closure.'

'Do you think Schofield can be stopped?'

'I'm sure of it.'

It took only half a dozen sentences from Adamson for Calderwood to believe that closure was inevitable. It was uncanny the way in which Schofield had anticipated the opposition's probable strategy. Mobilisation of public opinion, appeals to the council, sticker campaigns, an *Examiner* series, all were trotted out by Adamson, and his listener knew with stark certainty that they would fail for the reasons which Schofield had adduced. Eventually he got Adamson around to discussing the unthinkable, partly to clarify his own thinking. What would happen in the event of Albion becoming defunct?

The reporter showed an understandable, if macabre, interest in the details of decomposition.

'You tell me the registrations of all the players would vest in the League, Bob?'

'As I understand it.'

'Who would bring money of our lot? Phil Gifford, I suppose?'

'I suppose so. Don't forget that in this particular situation it's very much a buyer's market. I think at the end of the day we might get more for Vic Slocombe.'

'He's always been a favourite of yours, hasn't he?'

'I've got no favourites,' Calderwood said coldly, hitting the

133

word. 'Inevitably a manager will find some players more to his style than others. I think Vic's got the little touch of class that'd sustain him at top level.'

'We're a long way from closure, Bob. There'll be great resistance in the town.'

The manager looked at his watch. 'I make it we're about twelve hours from closure. And I'm not banking on popular resistance. I don't recall the barricades being manned in Barrow or Gateshead. It's not that people are all that anti. They're just not pro any more. Honestly now, would you recommend a new start on your paper to concentrate exclusively on sports journalism?'

Adamson blew an imperfect smoke-ring and sent a look of dissatisfaction after it.

'That's the kind of question I try not to ask myself and do occasionally, in the fastnesses of the night. We can still kid editors that we should devote two pages every week to football. More folk in Barford go to the bingo, yet we don't devote any space to that.'

He looked quizzically at Bob. 'We scribes do think about the game in our unguarded moments, old friend. There's next to no money coming in through the gates and I wonder how long the sponsors will want to be identified with punch-ups, barrack-room chants and empty terracings. To answer your question, I'd advise my budding reporter to acquire a working knowledge of local and national politics.'

He stood up with great decision. 'Bugger me backwards, Bob, I'm going home to me empty nest. I'm beginning to depress myself and you're not exactly Pollyanna tonight either. We'll see tomorrow what's to be done.'

'If anything,' Calderwood said dispiritedly.

'Even if it's only to get the garrison to capitulate on better terms, that'd be something. I'll phone my oppo at Rochdale, he should be useful — there's a club that's been revived on the mortician's slab for years. And I'll tell 'em there's a good bloke who might be going spare soon.'

'Thanks, Dave.'

He stood in the driveway as Adamson reversed out and on the instant thought of Joan. Still early enough to phone Leeds, he

thought, if she's there. Perhaps there's another game of cribbage scheduled for tonight. He was surprised when Joan
answered the phone, more surprised by her first words.

'How are you, love?'

'Fine. Why?'

'We've just heard about Albion. On the ten o'clock news on
the radio. It's just this moment been announced. What are you
going to do?'

'Take the phone off the hook for starters. Thanks for the
tip-off, Joan. Everything all right your end? Good. I'll see you
tomorrow, then.'

He did not replace the receiver.

17

Long afterwards Bob was to marvel at the comparative ease
with which he got through the day when the closing of Barford
Albion was announced by its chairman to the world. He said
little, felt nothing, as one does at the funeral of a very close
relative. The parallel was reasonably exact. They had come to
bury Albion and to praise it.

Television journalists who had needed to check the location
of Barford on the road-map the previous evening were queueing
up to deliver their tuppenceworth on the irreparable damage
which the social fabric of the town was about to sustain.
Schofield was in tremendous form. Bob, who had been present
at the dress rehearsal so to speak, was much impressed by the
calm way in which he deflected the barbs of BBC and ITV.

'We could possibly have staggered on into the beginning of
next season,' he told an ITN reporter, 'but if we pull out now,
we can discharge all our obligations, to the players, to all our
employees, and to the Football League.'

The phrase 'a member in good standing' flickered through

135

Calderwood's mind. The small boardroom was a chaos of lights, microphones, self-important sound-engineers and earnest enquirers probing amidst the cigarette smoke.

'What will happen to the ground?' asked the *Daily Mirror*.

'We have an offer for it for industrial development,' Schofield said with an air of sad defeat. 'Clearly I'd like to see the club continue in being under other direction if, say, there were to be a takeover bid for Albion. Of course any such bid would have to approximate to what we've already been offered for the ground. It wouldn't necessarily have to match it exactly, but it would obviously have to approach it pretty closely.'

'Can you give us an indication of what that sum might be?' The question came from the *Sun*.

With a deprecating smile Schofield said, 'You'll understand, I'm sure, the need for confidentiality between the prospective purchaser and ourselves. Naturally if another serious buyer were to emerge, we would disclose to them the original offer.'

As he had earlier done on the *Sidelight* programme, Schofield came through as thoughtful, courteous, humane, a Cincinnatus who had lost a protracted, unequal battle, and was now going back to the plough. He paid particular and graceful tribute to the manager for his efforts on the playing side, and he avoided the tactical error of publicly castigating the citizens of Barford for their non-attendance. The whole performance was mellow and elegiac.

Two other interviews were tacked on to the piece on *News at Ten* that evening. The Secretary of the Professional Footballers' Association said that perhaps the events of the day would give pause to those who thought the footballers' description of themselves as wage-slaves was exaggerated. He himself would do his best to see that all the players found clubs.

The Football League spokesman said that the orderly withdrawal of Barford Albion— he picked up the reporter on his use of 'collapse' — should not be seen as symptomatic of a general crisis in professional football. Perhaps what was most noteworthy about the event was its comparative rarity. In the thirty years or so since World War Two, only Accrington Stanley had provided a remotely similar case.

With one exception — Jesse Rydings, a reserve mid-fielder

and schoolteacher, who the Education Committee with its habitual, punctilious parsimony had decided could not be released — all the playing staff were on the ground, drawn by a mixture of curiosity and fear. Bob decided to turn this to advantage by calling a players' meeting and the professionals crowded into the home dressing room.

The manager was as brief as he felt he could be towards his shell-shocked players.

'Right, lads, you've heard the chairman's announcement. I've one of my own for you. I'm calling an extra training session for this evening and I want everyone here. It's short notice, I realise, so if anyone has a cast-iron previous arrangement, I'm prepared to talk about it privately, although I'll be a hard man to convince.'

'What the hell have we got to train for?' The disgruntled voice was that of Phil Gifford.

'Pride,' rasped Calderwood. 'Self-respect, that's what being a professional footballer means to me. Your best efforts whether there are five thousand out there or five hundred. We have two games to play yet, that's two lots of pools money to be won for starters. I'll remind you that our match result against Rochdale will probably determine who has to apply for re-election. That doesn't affect us now, but we've a duty to all the clubs involved to give of our best.

His eyes, determined and commanding, raked the group as they stood in a semi-circle. 'There's another reason. These two games are shop windows for you lads, perhaps the last you'll have. You're all available, everyone knows that. Nobody here is a world beater maybe, but there are some good honest journeymen amongst you.'

He paused for a moment, as if convincing himself of the fairness of what he was about to say.

'As you know, normally I pick what I think is the best twelve we have. I might play them for seven/eight weeks at a time, and if we're winning or even not losing, hard luck on the rest of you. Clearly though, the times are not normal. I intend to give as many as possible a run over the two games, certainly fifteen or sixteen of you. You'll improve your chances of selection by being at training tonight. One thing more. I'll be in my office

137

for the next couple of hours. If you think I can help any of you, come and knock on my door.'

Two players availed themselves of his offer. The first was Arnold Dearson who again thanked Calderwood sincerely and profusely for their recent talk. Clearly the goalkeeper was under the impression that Bob had then known of the coming dissolution of Albion and had been anxious to smuggle Arnold out of Jubilee Park ahead of the impending holocaust. The manager decided to let the veteran goalkeeper take this charitable notion into retirement with him. His other visitor, Vic Slocombe, had really come on his, Bob's, specific invitation as he left the dressing room.

'Sit down, Vic, I particularly wanted a word with you. I suppose, with your background, you're finding this interesting?'

'I may do in a little while,' said the young banker thoughtfully. 'At the moment it's all rather close to home. I've wound up companies in theory and I'm beginning to be allowed in on it in practice, but this is different.'

'Cards on the table, Vic, and if you quote me, I'll deny it. I think I'm a pretty good judge of a player. More important, other people in football think so too.'

Slocombe nodded politely but remained silent.

'What I'm saying is that in my opinion you are the one player on our staff who is capable of performing at top level. Yes, at *top* level. I don't think the First Division is beyond you.'

There was a look of almost schoolboy pride on Slocombe's intelligent face.

'That means a lot, Boss, coming from — '

'Would you like me,' Calderwood said over the top of him, 'to speak to one or two of my friends in the game for you? I've got good contacts at Ipswich and Villa. I know any recommendation I might make would be taken seriously.'

The player thought it over for a little space then half-shook his head.

'I don't think so, Mr Calderwood, thank you nevertheless.'

The manager's ears took in the subtle shift from 'Boss' to 'Mr Calderwood'. The answer was coming with obvious reluctance and equally obviously had been pre-considered.

138

'I'm afraid that what I'm about to say may sound patronising and snobbish. If it does, it's not meant to and I assure you it's not said off the top of my head. I've thought about this a lot.'

'Let's have it then,' said Calderwood, a little put out by this unforeseen opening.

'I'm more pleased than I can say that you think me First Division material. But I decided some time ago that if the chance for full-time football came my way, I wouldn't take it.'

'May I ask why not?'

The young man flushed. 'I don't think full-time football's a worthwhile occupation for an intelligent person.' He cut into Bob's glower with a hasty, 'At least, not on the playing side.'

'Go on.'

'I know one or two of the Leeds and Wednesday boys quite well. Their life frightens me. It's not the playing, I think this is the most skilful and enjoyable game in the world. It's the travelling. I don't want to go to Southampton cooped up in a bus playing Solo with someone like Les Frith. No harm to Les, but it's a waste of time.'

'You don't have to play cards. There's no law against reading a book. I've been known to do it myself in unguarded moments.'

His player disagreed with him. 'You have to be one of the boys unless you're a super-star, Mr Calderwood, a Beckenbauer or a Stanley Matthews. It's a team game.'

Calderwood let him talk on.

'You see, you can't eat, sleep, talk football all week. There's a limit to how much you can train. There's a limit to how much tactical discussion you can absorb.'

'Would your answer be any different if you were a miner or a factory worker?'

'Possibly. There's no doubt the bank tolerates my playing rather than likes it. If I were a three-quarter for Sale or Headingley, that's another thing. A couple of Rugby Union caps are a great recommendation for a young banker — more so if you work for a building society. Even if I never got that far, I'm much more likely to meet and cultivate important clients in a clubhouse rather than here. And then there's Europe. If you sign for one of the really big football clubs you've almost an

139

annual European commitment, to say nothing of close-season tours.'

'They do pay reasonably well,' Calderwood interjected mildly.

'I'm in risks, Mr Calderwood.'

Two lessons in economics in two days, Bob thought, am I so much of an innocent abroad? The boy had echoed Fraser in an eerie way. Two intelligent young men who for differing reasons seemed to be turning their backs on the game.

'So you'll give up then, Vic?'

'I didn't say that. If you'd be good enough to recommend me to a Division Three or Division Four club within fifty miles of here, I'd be very grateful.' The young man stood up. 'I'm greatly honoured by your good opinion, Mr Calderwood. I've much enjoyed playing for you. I'll do my very best in our last two games, should I be selected for them.'

The rest of the afternoon was a jangling of telephones, brief interviews with press men— 'Nothing to add to the chairman's statement'— and the usual preparations for a Saturday match. Enid was in a particularly friendly mood which drew some of the stress from the day. The Owlies loomed and Joan. But not decision, no decisions today, this month, maybe even next.

Joan was home ahead of him and had his meal ready. He had got perhaps halfway through it when the phone rang. His meal grew cold, Joan tried to rescue it by restoring it to the oven, and then as time went on, grew sulky and resentful. It was fully fifteen minutes before he reappeared in the kitchen.

'Your chops are ruined. They'll be as dry as a board.'

'Sorry.'

'What was it all about anyway?'

'A call from Scotland, from Lanarkshire. Brandon United. The manager's job's going there, they'd like to interview me.'

'You told them no.'

'No.'

'What does that mean?'

'I told them I'd consider the offer. They want me to go up tomorrow.'

'I won't go.'

'It's me they want to see.'

140

'I won't go if they offer you the job.'

'They're offering good money. Better than here by about three thousand. It's a club with a good reputation and it's ten miles from where I was brought up.'

'You can go on your own if you take it.'

He still shied away from the collision course. 'What about "Thy people will be my people" and all that kind of stuff?'

'You can go on your own.'

'I may very well do that. I don't see that in our present position I can afford to reject any promising offer out of hand.' He looked at her narrowly. 'Perhaps I should say in *my* present position. Lanarkshire is rather a long way from Derek Naughton.'

'What do you mean by that?' Her voice had become quiet and wary.

'Just that the next time you look after Jean Ogden's mother-in-law, you'd be better to liaise with Jean as to whether you're showing the old lady photographs or playing cribbage with her.' He held up his hand and continued coldly, 'Don't blame Jean, she lied like a trooper, but lie she did. Derek.'

The last word was a statement rather than a question. Joan nodded wordlessly as he followed up.

'At his home? Or in the storeroom in the shop after closing time? That wouldn't be very comfortable, but as we both know, it needn't take long and excitement's a great thing.'

The little figure stood dumbly, head bowed.

'I'll refrain from asking you if he was good, although I believe that's the conventional question.'

'We made love and beyond that I refuse to discuss it.' Oddly, she proceeded to do just that. 'I've no excuses, I'll not tell lies. Like most first times it wasn't particularly marvellous, that was much more my fault than his.'

'He's past it.'

'By no means. That's from experience and report. Let go of my wrist. I don't think he'll try again, and if he does I don't know that I'd let him.'

'Obviously you'll leave the shop.'

'It's not obvious to me. We parted very amicably. Unless I found I was being unduly harassed — and he's not that type of

141

man — I'd be perfectly prepared to carry on.'

In the face of her quiet determination, he found himself blustering.

'And do you think I could possibly allow that?'

'You're in a position of great strength, Bob. All courses are open to you. I'm neither proud nor delighted at what Derek and I have done. I do see marriage as important, I doubt if I could bear Phyllis and Fraser taking against me as a result of this. We've had over twenty years together. It's not been as marvellous as either of us once thought, but it's not been bad.' There was a flash of the old stubbornness. 'But I won't come to Scotland with you. I'm sorry.'

For perhaps half a minute Bob was tempted to set the record straight by confessing to the nights spent with Enid. For half a minute this was a possibility but the moment passed. The initial flash of anger dampened. He simply did not know what he was going to do. The remnants of the meal were now a write-off and he sought refuge in the activity of throwing a few things in an overnight bag.

'I'll go off straight after training tonight and put up about Carlisle. My appointment's for half ten tomorrow — I'll be home about the usual time.'

Joan gave no sign that she had heard. He came over, put his hands on her shoulders and tightened them so that she could not turn away.

'Look, it's probable they may not want me anyway. I really don't know the Scottish scene at all. If they take me, they're virtually committing themselves to the squad of players they've already got. But I'm entitled to consider the job absolutely on its merits and I will. We've done our work with the children, we have ourselves to consider primarily. If Phyllis decided to marry young Clifford and move to Venezuela, she'd be unlikely to put our comfort very high in her priorities.'

He was in the doorway, feeling that he'd reacted very well. A thought came to him which he did not resist, although he should have tried.

'I wonder where Elsie-the-she-dragon was while you and Derek were having it off? I must ask her next time I see her.'

'You could run an advert in the *Examiner* requesting

142

information. If you're strong enough for that kind of ridicule,' Joan replied. 'She stood outside the bedroom door and kept watch for us.'

He drew back his hand as though he would strike her, but brushed past, slamming the front door sufficiently violently to shatter one of the coloured panes of leaded glass. Joan knelt automatically to retrieve the pieces from the tiled floor and gashed her thumb on a long, sharp sliver.

The marriage might be saved. If she wanted to save it. Or she could be her own woman. Fine at forty-five. Dodgy at fifty-five. Derek would attempt her again, she was fairly sure of that. He would need to for his own self-esteem and she felt little stirrings of interest at the thought.

She went back into the kitchen to clear away the meal and switched on the radio, where the *Petticoat Line* was giving advice on keeping hubby happy. It seemed to boil down to feeding the brute. She switched off, crying bitterly.

18

The gently-rounded folds of the Dumfriesshire hills rose greenly on the morning sunshine, and for the first time in almost a month Calderwood felt something near contentment. He had been very taken with the little pub in which he had put up near Wigton, the Toyota was running well, and it was nice to know that someone wanted him.

The accepted professional wisdom in football was that any move to Scotland was to be regarded with shock, horror, outrage. The equivalent in politics would have been the sending of an out-of-favour Soviet politician to run an electricity station in Ulan Bator. Bob did not totally subscribe to this professional wisdom. For one thing, as a reasonably patriotic Scot he could hardly be expected to, for another, he thought that Brandon

United, the club making the offer, had real possibilities, although it was in something of a trough at the moment. There had been a time in the late fifties and early sixties when the Scottish side had taken on and defeated the best of European and South American opposition in floodlit friendlies.

The Brandon United tradition was based on elegance of style, the classical Scottish game, but the abolition of the maximum wage in England had seen the cross-border transfer of six of that particular side and dealt a mortal blow in playing terms. They had been Calderwood's local team as a boy, and he still had some emotional regard for them. He thought, however, that he had been sufficiently distanced by time and space to be able to consider the job offer objectively.

It was a bonny part of the world, Upper Lanarkshire. The trig stone houses, huddled in the lee of small canting copses, had an astonishing fireburst of colour in their gardens. He drove down the long right-hander into Abington with the Clyde winking in the sunshine.

He had no reason to doubt that Joan meant what she said. When they were first married he had brought her up to Scotland a couple of times, but although she had quite enjoyed the West Highlands she found the country stark and its inhabitants abrasive. Well, considering the Brandon managership objectively entailed considering life without Joan, in the short term at least. His marriage seemed to be foundering amidst the waves of indifferent amity.

From the motorway he could see the small town where he had been born and, away to his right on a hill-top, the floodlights of Whitehill Park, the ground of Brandon United. He shot a glance at the clock on the dashboard. His appointment was in fifteen minutes, his timing had been spot on. Three minutes before half past ten he drew up in the players' and officials' car park in the shadow of the commodious cantilever stand. The doorman at once showed him upstairs to the boardroom.

Four of the club's five directors were there, and he was cordially received by the chairman, Will McQuaker, an actuary, younger than he was himself, Calderwood noted with a jab of surprise. McQuaker introduced the others, David Lumsden, a baker, David Ogg, a retired headmaster, and

144

Donald Robertson, a steel stockholder. Bob nodded to all three men, shook hands with them in turn, and waited for the blur of faces to assume individual identity.

After a few conventional pleasantries — the chairman asked him if he were correct in thinking that Bob was from their part of the world and was a Lanark Grammar School former pupil — they left the boardroom for a tour of the ground. Bob had been in too many grounds not to be impressed. Whitehill Park was beautifully maintained. The seating in the stand was freshly painted, the tea stalls were clean and obviously well looked after, most of the crush barriers were of concrete, but where they were of metal, they were rust-free.

The good impression was confirmed on the return to the boardroom. He was surprised at the amount of money available for players. If needed, the board could spend two hundred thousand pounds, an astonishing sum for a Scottish club. He asked McQuaker how it was done.

'Well, Bob — I can call you Bob? — we have a very flourishing social club, you'll see it in an hour or so when we go there for lunch. We have nearly three thousand members, and we operate a two-tier system. I suppose you could call it lounge bar and saloon bar. We have a thousand people in here every Friday, Saturday and Sunday night, and the social committee pay out some big money for the best club acts. We've had Shirley Bassey and Cleo Laine here, y'know.'

Calderwood came to the point. 'How many do you get through the gates?'

McQuaker nodded, taking the point, not in the least resenting his bluntness. 'On a run of the mill Saturday, five and a half to six thousand, against Celtic or Rangers about four times that. The ground holds twenty-five thousand, quite big enough for all practical purposes, in fact too big for most of the time.'

'What would you need as a weekly gate to break even purely from backsides on seats?'

This was obviously the aspect of the club which interested Will McQuaker most strongly. He launched on his exposition with marked zest.

'We work on what our home attendances have been over the last full season discounting the Celtic and Rangers matches.

145

They take care of themselves. We have to try to get the extra thousand in against such as Aberdeen, Hearts and Dundee. We'd break even at eight thousand.'

'What makes you think I'm your man? My track record's not all that marvellous.'

'We think you may be. You kept Barford Albion in the League on playing ability. With the resources you had to work with, that's almost a better performance than winning the League with Liverpool. You come very highly recommended, you know.'

'By whom?'

'Jack Schofield. I've known him for some time. We met at Wembley years ago when Scotland were down there and our two companies have actually done business since. I've a high regard for your chairman's judgment and he has a high regard for you. Hence, here you are.'

He stood up from his chair at the boardroom table. 'The Scottish Tourist Board wouldn't be very pleased with our hospitality — it's after twelve and you've had a long drive. Time for a bite of lunch. Let's go over to the club.'

The social club was a long, low building, functional where the main stand was elegant. It was as spick and span as the rest of the surroundings, with the exception of a black splash of graffiti across the red bricks to the left of the main door. A furtive hand had sprayed the message, 'Fuck the Pope', and Calderwood's memory was jogged by the similar outpourings he had seen driving to the ground. His first thought had been that the simple letters F.T.P. must be some kind of political slogan. He now realised his error and realised too the meaning of the scrawled ripostes which disfigured other doors and walls, F.T.Q.

The pleasant, homely waitresses reminded Calderwood of his mother's friends. The directors' table was beautifully laid — the plates were patterned china, the glasses crystal, the napkins linen. A genuine Scotch broth was followed by roast lamb or steak and kidney pie. Puddings rather than pallid ices were the order of the day. Calderwood had resisted the offer of a pre-lunch whisky, that could be a barbed invitation at an interview, but he allowed himself two glasses of red wine and the opportunity to decline a third.

The Scottish club had done its research well. The directors knew that Calderwood's children had long passed school age, so that it would be less difficult for him to move north should he take the job. David Ogg, the director who was a retired headmaster, commented on the absurdity of having two educational systems cheek by jowl which differed so much as those of Scotland and England. Bob, with memories of his own school days in this part of the world and his more recent bafflements with the academic struggles of Fraser and Phyllis, was able to agree feelingly.

The meal drew to an end and still the conversation stayed general. It became clear that the really hard talking would be done in the boardroom after lunch with Will McQuaker. Coffee was brought and liqueurs. Again, Calderwood turned down the offer, a genuine enough refusal, although it occurred to him that Schofield would almost certainly have spoken highly of his temperate consumption when he was enlarging on his other qualities. As they were leaving the social club, he was introduced to one or two people who were obviously members of more than ordinary importance. The second of these was a burly, florid man in a particularly well-cut and beautifully muted tweed suit. He had clearly been a good-looking young man and although middle age had coarsened his features and dilated his veins, he was still vulgarly handsome.

'Murdo, this is Mr Calderwood of Barford Albion. He's just paying us a brief visit. Bob, this is Murdo Ellis. If you decide to trade in your car while you're up, Murdo's your man.'

The two shook hands.

'How are you, Mr Calderwood?'

Without waiting for a report or reply, he put another question to the chairman. 'I take it he's one of us?'

'Born and educated within ten miles of here,' said McQuaker, a little too quickly, a trifle too conciliatingly.

'That's not what I meant, Will,' the other said with no trace of a smile lightening his lips or eyes.

The chairman, seemingly embarrassed, made no reply and they parted on Ellis's, 'Nice to meet you, Mr Calderwood, enjoy your trip.'

147

The other directors also took their leave on various pretexts. The chairman would negotiate and speak for all.

The panelled boardroom was quiet after the bustle of the social club. Pennants of the most distinguished clubs in Europe added colour to the expensive, understated décor. Real Madrid were there, A.C. Milan too, and there was a South American presence. Estudiantes from Uruguay and Flamengo from Brazil had played here, at Whitehill Park.

The photographs of previous teams on the walls represented solid achievement. Brandon United had, in their time, won the League Cup, the Scottish Cup, and reached a quarter-final in Europe. Only the Scottish League Championship had so far eluded them. It was a far cry from the seedy desperation of Jubilee Park.

McQuaker, a small brisk man with a mop of very blond curly hair, sat relaxedly in an armchair. The real talking could now start.

'Well, Bob, you've seen over the policies. What do you think?'

'I'm genuinely impressed. You've transformed this place out of recognition since I used to come here in the days of the old Dutch barn stand.'

They got down to discussing terms.

'I indicated to you on the phone the kind of salary we'd be thinking of paying. I believe it's about two and a half thousand more than you're getting?'

This was conventional, polite sparring. Schofield would have told McQuaker what his current salary was, but it was courteous for McQuaker to assume that he was getting slightly more from Barford than he was.

'Three thousand, actually.'

'I see. The contract would initially be for three years. You'd have no objection to that?'

'None.'

Three years was perfectly fair. If a manager couldn't make an impact in that time he was most unlikely to over a longer period. No club could reasonably give a longer-term mortgage on its future. McQuaker was speaking again.

'You'd have a car, of course. Murdo Ellis usually sees us right there. We'll see to the removal. We have options on a couple of houses, but you know the district, you'd probably have your own ideas on where you'd want to live. Or Mrs Calderwood might.'

'She has very definite ideas. Barford.'

McQuaker shot him a warily interested look, but said nothing, inviting further comment.

'She'd be hard to persuade, no doubt of that. But if everything else were all right, it wouldn't stop me. It's my job and I'm professional about my job.'

McQuaker spoke slowly. 'I won't deny your wife's hesitation about coming to Scotland creates a new dimension. The fact that, knowing this, you've still travelled up, makes me think you're serious about the job. In fact "serious" was a word Jack Schofield used a lot when talking about you. Let's carry on then on the assumption that Mrs Calderwood could be persuaded — or left behind for the time being. We'd want to know that whoever we appointed would stay. The Premier League is probably our last chance in Scotland to get it right.'

He looked at Calderwood with a reassuring smile. 'I usually find it useful at this stage to ask whether you've any questions you want to put.'

'Staff,' Calderwood said laconically. 'How many?'

'Nineteen full-time professionals, seven part-timers, eight or nine schoolboys on S forms.'

Calderwood went on to ask about coaching and transfer policy, then came to his last question. 'It's maybe got very little to do with football. Or, allowing that I've been away a long time, maybe it's got a lot to do with Scottish football.'

'Well?'

'Your man Ellis's question, "Is he one of us?" '

'Oh, that was Murdo's way of asking would you fit in?'

'I don't think so, Chairman.'

McQuaker reddened slightly, his face appearing even more youthful. 'You know the West of Scotland, Bob, tribal loyalties die hard. Murdo's from Stonehouse, a bitter area on the whole. We have to try to keep a balance in the club. The last manager was a Catholic, the next can't be. That's the reality.'

'Supposing he was Matt Busby and available?'

'Supposing he was Matt Busby and available.'

149

'Christ!' gritted Calderwood. 'No wonder our World Cup record's so abysmal.'

'Christ has quite a lot to do with football up here,' the chairman said quietly. 'But it *is* getting better. Twenty years ago we'd never have had a Catholic manager at all, and even a Catholic player would have been a rarity. That's changing. Nevertheless we've still many supporters who'd rather lose every match with a team of paid-up Covenanters than win with diluted stock.'

'I find that appalling. I went to England because I wanted to play professional football.'

There was a note of displeasure in McQuaker's voice now, although he sought still to persuade. 'All of us would wish that things were otherwise. Some of us are working for change. Haven't you a duty to do what you can to help us try to change things?'

Calderwood looked earnestly at the little actuary. 'Management's a hell of a job anyway, Chairman. The chop rate is one in three, any year. At least in England I could pick the eleven players I thought best even if they all happened to be Jehovah's Witnesses.'

'I really don't believe you could,' McQuaker said. 'Supposing you managed Bradford or Leeds, or Birmingham City. I could easily see a situation arising where you could justify playing half a dozen Pakistanis or West Indians in the side. Are you telling me that would meet with universal acceptance from your Board or from the support? That's not what I hear.'

Calderwood was not totally confident that he could make a disclaimer.

'Look,' McQuaker went on, 'I know they fight the Reformation all over again here every Saturday. Buses pass this ground for Ibrox and Parkhead. But I know we can get them in if we have an attractive side. We can't get gut loyalty like the big two. That's why this is a real job. At Ibrox or Parkhead you'd only be a totem pole.'

'It's not without its attractions,' Calderwood said thoughtfully. 'There's Europe too. With Rangers or Celtic liable to win the three major trophies every season there's a lot of scope for getting in as defeated finalists.'

'I'd say our supporters have missed Europe more than anything else.' McQuaker got up from his armchair, went to his desk and brought out an envelope. 'You've a long drive back ahead of you. That's a copy of the contract we'd be prepared to offer you. Take it away with you and let your own club lawyer look it over. Better still, your own solicitor. And see what you can do with Mrs Calderwood,' he added with a smile. 'She'd find we're quite human. And you yourself might not find it such a back of beyond in the football sense if you ever wanted to work your way back south.'

'It's a much more professional organisation than the one I'm with.'

'Well, Scottish First Division ought just to shade English Fourth out, wouldn't you say?' — in tones of velvet rebuke.

The two men agreed that there was no point at all in Bob seeing any of the players until he had decided to come. Anything else would merely have been unsettling.

'By the way,' McQuaker said, looking up at Bob as they moved out to the car park, 'when you write to us, let us have an account of your expenses. It would help if you can give us receipts. We'll expect to hear from you by Tuesday — that'll give you five days. Goodbye now, thanks for coming up and safe journey back.'

You're losing your grip, Calderwood told himself, as he moved out past a couple of articulated lorries on the A74. You know you don't need five days to make up your mind about the job. It's an attractive post, the terms are very fair, the club has possibilities . . . and you won't touch it.

Not on Joan's account. He had realised that she wouldn't be moved in the same moment when he knew that he wouldn't have let that deter him had he wanted the job badly enough. The miles and the gentle beauty of the Lowlands slipped away. How could such a peaceful environment produce such a raw society?

It appeared that Brandon United would be better served by the Secretary-General of the United Nations. 'A wunnerful oppertoonity for somebody, somebody else, not me.' Staunch Protestants and devout Catholics, the curse of his native heath. Sorry, lads, he'd been away too long for that nonsense. 'Is he one of us?' He bloody well wasn't and he wasn't one of them either. He wondered vaguely if there would be any merit in fielding a complete team of atheists, then dismissed the thought and his birthplace from his mind for good. He cast a look in his driving mirror, moved out and drove past Ecclefechan at the five miles above the speed limit which was his normal rate. Ecclefechan, a music-hall name, birthplace of Thomas Carlyle. All he knew about Carlyle was that he too had gone south — to Chelsea.

He wondered as he drove how long it would take for a US visa to come through.

19

It took just over a fortnight for the visa to come through and in that time he had written to Brandon United declining their offer.

Bob had been surprised when John Newton had asked if he could drop in at The Owlies some evening. It was difficult to find a reason for saying no, and he felt slightly obligated to the Rotarian for his interest. Newton was convinced that Bob had something to offer on the personnel management side. After all, this was surely an important aspect of football management?

'It is, Mr Newton. You have to know who to lead, who to drive, who marches to a different drum. But I imagine that's a comparatively small part of personnel management.'

'More important than you might suppose.'

'I'm forty-six years old.'

'Am I supposed to throw up my hands and faint away? You'd be dealing with people, common sense'd be your greatest stock in trade. Your age is a recommendation rather than otherwise. I've had my bellyful of abrasive whizzkids who know it all and empty a shop floor before you can say knife.'

It was another genuine offer, and again Bob refused. It had been a piece of bad luck that Joan had come in just as John Newton was leaving.

Joan knew that she had to resist attacking her husband but

found herself doing so.

'Another offer bites the dust. It's running at one a week, Bob — or shall I call you Rockefeller?'

'Call me whatever you like. I rather got the impression from a few hints you threw out that you didn't want me to take the Brandon job anyway.'

'Don't change the subject.' Bob had done no such thing. 'What was Mr Newton offering you?'

'A job as trainee personnel manager. Less than what Albion are paying me but with prospects.'

'Here in Barford?'

'Yes.'

'And you turned it down?'

'Yes.'

'Just like that?' Her voice grew more strident with each question.

'Yes.'

'Is your wife allowed to know why?'

'If you like.' Had he said 'yes' again, she would have struck him. 'I don't think I'd be very good at the job or very interested in it. I couldn't start when he'd want me to because of my stint in the States. Neither of those is the real reason.'

She did not feed him the question, and the blue and white ceramic clock ticked noisily in the silence.

'I hoped that some day, Joan, you'd realise that I'm a manager from choice. I'm not a failed schoolteacher, or a banker who couldn't make it, or a thwarted doctor. I'm a professional football manager.' He gave each of the last three words a hard, slow emphasis. 'It's a job with its own lunatic rules and demands maybe, but it's the job I do best and it's what I'll continue to do if I can.'

'And you're walking out of here on Saturday night?'

'For four months. I feel I need a couple of days in London before flying out.'

'I read in the *Sun* this morning that George Lambert's going out to coach in Seattle and is taking his wife along. Is his job more important than yours?'

'I saw that too,' Calderwood said slowly. 'It's the same job.'

'Why weren't you asked if you wanted to bring your wife?'

153

'I was.'

The brief answer, which she must have foreseen, jolted Joan like a heavy body punch. Her husband this time did not stand back to await another question.

'I felt you wouldn't want to leave the shop, even before recent developments there. And even if you had, I'd much rather go alone. There'll be a vast amount of work to do, promotional as well as coaching. If I do well, I could easily be asked to do another couple of summers. Their season and ours dovetail very well.'

She looked earnestly at him and in the set of her face and her copper hair there was a look of the girl he had courted so long ago in Northampton.

'Bob, do you care about Derek and me?'

'That's a helluva stupid question.'

'It's just that I get the feeling now and then that you're . . . almost relieved.'

'Sure I am. I'm running three mistresses and it helps to balance the books.'

'It's not even worth serious discussion to you?' She was crying quietly.

'Indeed it is. It's a serious matter. Whether it's serious enough to bust up a marriage that's been going for twenty-two years is yet to be seen. Are you frightened that Derek will wreak his randy will if I go off to the United States? Why should you be? I couldn't save you when I was here.'

He got up, went into the kitchen and, seated at the scrubbed wooden table, began to prepare a detailed checklist of all the things he would need to take to America. The evening passed in a numbing, vicious silence, the silence known only to those who have loved each other, the silence one feeble, kindly word could shatter, the silence in which that word becomes, literally, unutterable.

*   *   *

The last day of the season dawned hot and sunny and bade fair to remain so. The weather, like the world, was looking ahead. Had it been a home game, 'Jubilee Jottings' would certainly have proclaimed 'Farewell King Soccer, Welcome King Willow'.

For the last Saturday afternoon, ever, the Golden Triangle coach purred along the roads of England with the large cardboard sign on the windscreen which said, 'Barford Albion Football Club'. A blow to P. Atkinson and Sons, proprietors of Golden Triangle coaches, thought Bob, for many a season the Albion account had been a useful one. He wondered, not for the first time, why Schofield used an outside coach firm.

The coach had tables and fewer seats than was usual, to give the players leg room. Some played cards. Vic Slocombe, with the new-found courage of his convictions, was reading the *Guardian*. Arnold, whom Bob had restored for the day, was listening, rather unexpectedly, to a Country and Western cassette. Bob could just pick up the nasal, keening sounds.

Yuh ask, why do the tear-drops fall?
It's that saddle, a-hangin' on the wall.

It was no occasion for hilarity, but Bob found himself smiling as he watched the grizzled goalkeeper. Arnold seemed deeply affected by the banal words and was mouthing them solemnly in time with the singer. Rest easy, Arnold! It was very fitting that he should ride this last train from San Fernando into the depot.

Barford's loss was Rochdale's gain. Curiosity doubled the gate that interest would have attracted — by twenty minutes before kick-off there was not a programme to be had. In the boardroom the Rochdale directors were genuinely sympathetic towards Schofield, Dr Layton, and the other members of the Barford Board, but already there was a curious atmosphere, a distancing, as if Albion did not even have the two hours of life left which the game would require.

Everyone died in character. Slocombe scored a fine goal early on, Gifford watched his legs for ninety minutes, Arnold was injured when going down at the centre's feet ten minutes before half-time. Ian Gregor went into goal and his defence, panicking quite unnecessarily, for Gregor was far from negligible as a keeper, conceded three goals in those ten minutes.

Since the injury had occurred close to half-time, Bob had delayed committing his substitute until he could ascertain the extent of the damage to Arnold. By the time the teams were ready to re-emerge for the second half, the Rochdale doctor had put four stitches in Arnold's forehead and the latter flatly refused to be taken off. He joined his colleagues swathed in bandages like a swami to the genuine roar of appreciation that was becoming so rare for visiting players on Football League grounds. More than that, within thirty seconds of his return he had plunged once more into a ruck of players, this time emerging unharmed with the ball.

The stupid bastard, Calderwood thought, in partial fear and total admiration. We'd have given him a free and there he is, risking his neck when it wouldn't matter if we lost twenty goals.

But it would matter, and those in the Barford dug-out in the next few minutes heard how little different manager and goal-keeper were in their approach.

'Close up on him, Archie! Harry him, Phil, for God's sake you're not out there for the air! That's it, Ian son, move him out, move him out!'

As on every Saturday much of this exhortation was not implemented, indeed much of it went unheard. The Barford rally which followed was possibly quite unconnected with the manager's touch-line coaching, and in the best traditions of the club it was unsuccessful.

Gifford emerged from self-preservation long enough to volley a spectacular second goal, but the final whistle blew with Albion at 2-3 cast in their accustomed role as losers.

End of the match, end of the line. Nobody lingered in the dressing rooms — within half an hour of time-up the coach was on the road again. An attempted sing-song died away in a tailing of discordant sound. All the goodbyes had been said, nobody hung around Jubilee Park. With an offhand 'See you, Boss,' the players took their separate ways. No directors had returned with the coach. Bob gave the Planet a hand into the pavilion with the skip.

He had no intention, any more than the players, of hanging around. He had to get home, to pack, to say his goodbyes to Joan and the two children. Yet even on this Saturday night there was his report on the referee to do, and a wish to leave things decently in order. And there was the phone, and a fellow manager anxious to sympathise, while in a totally non-malevolent way anxious also to profit by Albion's disappearance. Unseen, Calderwood smiled wryly into the receiver.

'Jubilee Park, manager speaking — hello, Frank, I should have said ex-manager — well, I might have been phoning you, it's the name of the game, isn't it? We can't win — I don't see why not, *we're* not going to be needing anyone next season. You'd suit him very well, being nearby, his wife's an invalid. No, Archie's not that old, he's thirty-two. He is, I saw it on his form the other day. He'd do you a turn for a couple of years, he's brave and he'll graft. I should try twelve thousand, certainly no more. Well, I've a few feelers out, you're not rid of me yet. That's right, Milwaukee, I'm off in a few hours. I'm quite looking forward to it, it'll give me time for thinking. No, she'll mind the shop while I'm over there. Thanks. Right, Frank. See you.'

He put down the phone to see the Planet standing aimlessly in the doorway. He didn't want to be kept back, Tarkington beckoned him, but he was suddenly aware that his working relationship with Joe Staples was finally over. They would meet again, most likely, on his return from Milwaukee, but never again on that level of intensity which involvement in a common task brings. Their next meeting would be in street or pub, and after the initial exclamations of genuine delight would come the striving for topics of conversation.

Already the Planet looked rudderless and Calderwood felt the old anger against Schofield flare up anew.

'Well, that's that, Joe.'

'Ay, that's that.'

'Everything stowed away and locked up?'

'Aye. I've left the strips in the hamper for Mrs Lovell to wash. What's happening to them?'

'No idea. I'd like to think we'd give them away to some youth clubs. The chairman might have other ideas.'

'Such as?'

'Flogging them to some other League club as a change strip. Might make sense now that things look a bit tighter all round.'

He stood up. The last manager of Barford Albion took a last look round his office. Joe held his ground, clearly with something to say.

'I don't want to go without telling you you've been a good 'un to work for. I've seen eleven managers here, and you've been the best of the lot.'

'Thanks, Planet. I'm also the one who has closed down the club. I'm grateful for your good opinion.'

'What's going to happen to the ground?'

'Nothing immediately. They'll have to be sure planning permission is all clued up. Then, of course, they'll demolish the stand and flatten the banking on the terracing. Why?'

The Planet looked at him doggedly. 'There's a thing I'd like to have if no one else wants it.'

Calderwood was already moving to the wall behind his desk. Dexterously he unhooked the faded photograph of the County Cup-winning side.

'It wouldn't be this, by any chance, Joe?'

The Planet nodded.

'Take it, go on.' He beat down the older man's hesitation. 'Go on, if anyone notices it's missing, I'll tell them when I get back that a souvenir-hunter took it. Take it now, Planet, once the demolishers move in all these things will walk.'

The Planet stood clutching the photograph with a look of veneration that might at another time have been ludicrous. Calderwood, a thousand miles from laughter, had to save himself by asking, with appropriate gestures, 'Anything else you'd like? Can I interest you in a piece of antique silverware, the County Cup? Or perhaps a pair of pennants, once used?'

Joe shook his head, dusting the picture lovingly on the front of his sweater. He was gazing intently at the faded figures as he identified each to his manager.

'By God, there were some friends of the brewers here. Poor Tim Dyer, he was killed in Crete. Him and me travelled two hundred miles on a forty-eight-hour pass to play in a War Cup-tie in the first year of the war. We stayed over for the replay and we got twenty-eight days' jankers when we got back.'

'Did you win?' asked Calderwood, the manager's question.

Joe shook his head. 'Everton, 5 – 2.' He resumed his inspection. 'Bill Anderson, a damned good left-half. Little Tich McCall, the lads used to say he looked his wife straight in the belly-button. She was a big woman. Frank Thomson, there was a real hatchet-man. I remember one snowy afternoon at Gateshead, Boss. We were drawing 1 – 1 and this big animal of a centre had been giving me a right going-over in goal. It was snowing real hard . . .'

Calderwood, half-listening, became aware that the Planet had not completed the sentence and was looking fixedly out of the window, his face working as he struggled for mastery. It was time to go. His tone was brisk and kind.

'Come on, Planet.'

They went out into the lovely late sunlight of the April evening, shook hands and parted. As Calderwood drove away, the last sounds he heard were those of the great iron main gates being slammed shut.

*　　*　　*

Almost before he knew it, he was on the overnight train to London. It had been a draining evening, the leave-taking had been harder than he had imagined.

It had begun on a light-hearted note. Phyllis had become nineteen the day before and she was there with her boyfriend Clifford. From the meaningful looks, nudges and giggles going on between the two of them, Bob had the feeling that an engagement might be imminent, if indeed they bothered to get engaged nowadays. Fraser racketed around like a gigantic puppy. He would be sorry to lose his father, but the fact that he was to fall heir to the Toyota while Bob was away did much to temper his grief.

The meal finished, it was time to run through the checklist for the last time. Passport, plane tickets, travellers' cheques, American Express card, international driving licence, all were in order. He wrote his American address and telephone number in the address book, and they arranged that he and Joan would telephone each other once a fortnight.

Joan, Fraser and he would drive to the station — Phyllis and Clifford were staying behind. Suddenly it was time to go and The Owlies seemed unbearably familiar and secure. Nonsensical to feel this way about a house which was only one of seven they'd had in the last twenty years, a house they would very probably have to leave anyway.

159

He shook hands with Clifford, a nice, anonymous young man — not much drive there, he thought — and turned to kiss his daughter. Was it fancy or was she really stooping slightly to kiss him?

'Goodbye, love, take care.' He felt his eyes stinging even as he realised his daughter had managed to grow up without any massive help from him.

'Goodbye, Dad. Watch yourself. Send us a card and tell us all about it. And good luck with the team.'

'I'll be in touch.'

He saw Phyllis and Clifford standing in the lighted door as the car sped down the driveway. The tyres squealed as Fraser cornered into the main road, bringing an instinctive 'Easy there!' from his father. Fraser nodded amiably enough, there would be plenty of time over the next four months to see what the car could do.

They arrived at Leeds in plenty of time, time enough in fact for a coffee in the Queen's Hotel which no one wanted. The three of them crowded into the first-class sleeper and sat on the bunk. Fraser hoisted the cases.

'Watch yourself with the majorettes, Dad,' Fraser cautioned. 'They're all called Barbie and have legs nine feet long.'

'Your father's not at all like that,' Joan snapped defensively as Calderwood managed a man-of-the-world grin for his son.

'Su-rre. I'd better leave you two alone for a couple of minutes,' her son said with ponderous gallantry, 'I'm in the way here.'

'You're not taking up more than three-quarters of the sleeper. Is he, Joan?' He looked at his enormous child with great affection and held out his hand. 'Goodbye, son. Here, steady on, I'll need it again. Keep an eye on the girls for me, eh? I'll tell you all about it.'

Fraser stepped out on to the platform and the sleeper seemed to double in size. Calderwood looked at his watch.

'Five minutes.'

She nodded. 'Have you got everything?'

'I think so.' He patted his inside pocket. 'At least if I've forgotten something, it won't be anything dire.'

'I still think you should have taken another suit.'

160

'I'm going to work, love, not to socialise. I'll be in a track suit most of the time.'

'So you say.' It was a brave attempt at a joke.

'I'll be back around September 10th. We'll take it from there and see what offers.'

'There won't be any chance of a manager's job then.'

'So much for your hopes. There's little chance now, but some club will lose their first four matches come August and decide to ditch their manager.'

From outside a warning whistle blew. He kissed her cheek, holding her hands.

'Look after yourself.'

She nodded, went to go, then turned to stand on tiptoe and wordlessly throw her arms round his neck.

Through the open window they all grinned at each other inanely for a few seconds. On a second whistle, the train slipped imperceptibly from the platform. As long as they were within eyeshot they waved unflaggingly, Fraser's massive bulk dwarfing his mother. Then, on a bend, they were gone.

The train clattered slowly through the backyards of south Leeds past canals and occasional illuminated factory signs. Calderwood returned to his compartment. At that moment he most desperately wished not to be going.

With an effort of will he shook off his yearning for his family. He could jump off the train now, go back to Tarkington, and they'd be rowing again by the next day. Hardly the frame of mind to attempt the conquest of the United States. He unpacked his pyjamas, a book and an already made up whisky and lemonade. He turned his mind to London, where Enid would be awaiting him.

20

The horses cantered along Rotten Row throwing up little spurts of sand while their riders gazed imperiously into the middle distance, almost as if they totally disassociated themselves from the physical act of control. It was a lovely morning, of a freshness that London would scarcely know again all summer.

Calderwood drew Enid aside as the horses passed a little too closely, admiring the detachment of the riders, art concealing art.

'Can you ride?' he asked.

She nodded. 'I went through the usual mad-keen phase at sixteen. It's bad for the backside though, just look at that departing vision there.'

'Nothing wrong with your backside anyway, it's delightfully slim and boyish.'

'I thought you men preferred something you could get a real hold of?'

'Not this one,' said Calderwood contentedly.

They were walking in Hyde Park just before noon on the Sunday. Calderwood admired for the hundredth time the clean lines of Enid's body, the curling brown hair, the opaque whiteness of her neck. Over the last month he had lost all feeling of hesitance, of self-reproach, of timidity. With Enid, at least, he was fast becoming an accomplished lover.

'Where are we going?'

'Ever been to the top of the Hilton?'

'No.'

'That's where we're going.'

The express elevator pushed their stomachs back and shot them to the restaurant floor. Somewhat reluctantly they were served with a drink — too near lunchtime for the waiter's liking — and sat down at the window table. Georgian, Victorian, Edwardian, Manhattan, New Brutal, the capital stretched away beneath them. The Surrey hills, it appeared, were really hills, not just an invention of a bright estate agent.

'Can you see the Queen, Mr Calderwood?'

''Fraid not. Perhaps she's preparing Sunday lunch.'

'Talking of lunch . . .'

'Not here, glutton. The name's Calderwood, not Carnegie. I know where we'll go.'

She looked at him, intrigued. 'You seem to know your way around our great city very well.'

'I did once. Well, I suppose I still do, though they've pulled so much of the damned place down. I was stationed at Uxbridge when I was in the RAF, I used to come in on Sunday mornings and walk all through the City and the West End. Later, when we were at Maidstone, I'd come up sometimes with Joan.'

It was an indication of how their relationship had progressed that he could now use Joan's name in conversation without constraint. Enid sipped her Tom Collins thoughtfully.

'I'm beginning to wish you weren't going away,' she said. 'I could have done with a knowledgeable man like you to show me the ropes.'

'That's a little later, Enid. Are you still set on this air hostess business?'

'It's not air hostess business. It's the possibility of a job with Delta or perhaps Braniff in their London offices. Definitely on the ground. I've no wish to carry tons of salad or have babies throwing up all over me. To say nothing of being the star attraction of Gropers Anonymous.' She grinned cheerfully at him. 'It bothers you slightly, doesn't it, when I'm "coarse"?'

'I'm getting used to it.

> You only do it to annoy,
> Because you know it teases.

Like another drink? Come on, then.'

They made their way along Curzon Street past the burgeoning Arab banks, grateful for the shaded portions of the road. In a few minutes they stopped before a small restaurant in Shepherd's Market.

'They do very good salads here, or they used to. They also have terrific Viennese pastries. I'm holding temptation and restraint before you. Date and walnut salad and the svelte you, or the Black Forest gâteau and the horsy bum.'

'Both,' said Enid decidedly.

They ate at a little table outside, with a glass of dry white wine to assist the salad, and sat on for a while after the meal. Calderwood settled the bill and they left, their footfalls sounding companionably on the summer pavement as they turned down Half Moon Street towards Piccadilly.

'Where to now, sir?'

'You're psychic,' said Bob – and on the phrase commandeered a taxi. 'Hotel Jerome, Hans Street,' he said to the driver, and as he helped Enid into the cab, 'I have this strange need to take a nap in the early afternoon.'

'Me too. Must be a sign of age.'

They sat intensely, not speaking, hands locked, as the taxi headed west along Piccadilly past Apsley House, the beached hulk that Wellington once called home. The Royal Mews flashed by, then Knightsbridge, and finally the quiet side street near Cadogan Square with the hotel standing high, Dutch, fantastical, in its pleasing warm red brick.

They had not made love for more than two weeks so there was no very long prologue. Enid came on top of him in a reversal of roles. As he drew her down upon him he relished anew the firm lift of her breasts and the pronounced thrust of her chin. He cupped his hands round her buttocks and thrust upwards with strong thighs. There was a strenuous flurry of limbs and then a sigh of release.

They lay together in the double bed which was curiously raised by a step from the floor and heard the moderated roar of the Sunday afternoon traffic as it raced down towards the Embankment.

'What would you be doing if I weren't here?' the girl asked languorously.

'You are here.'

'I know, but suppose I hadn't come.'

'Gone to Lord's or the Oval, I suppose. I love cricket. It's almost my favourite game.'

'You're very much a man's man, aren't you?'

'I don't know. Maybe a man's man would go to Soho to a strip club or a blue movie house.'

Enid shook her head decidedly. 'Real men *do*. Others talk about it. I remember a big rugby player I quite fancied when I

164

was at school— I'd have been sixteen. He took me home from a club dance — I was besotted with him, he could have done anything he liked with me. He was pathetic. You know that poem, "The Drunkard's Address to His Penis"?'

'No,' said Bob with perfect truth.

'There's a bit in it where he's reproaching his John Thomas for failure the night before and he says, "A stricken inch was all that you could do." I doubt if that big blowhard of a rugby player even managed that.'

Bob looked in honest puzzlement at her, nestling contentedly in the crook of his arm. 'Where in God's name do you learn the poems? Not at home surely? Your Aunt Lucy would have a fit.'

'My Aunt Lucy's only thirty-eight,' said Enid, reaching for a Cinzano which she had left on the bedside table.

'Don't tell me,' snapped Calderwood, suddenly irritable, 'she's younger than I am.'

'You're obsessional, lover. I learned that poem from a girl at school.'

'I can't imagine Phyllis knowing anything like that,' Bob said optimistically.

There was a faint stirring of unease between them. Enid smiled dubiously at him.

'Probably not. It's just lusty old me.' Her tone altered. 'I shall miss you, more than I thought. At first it was just a matter of fancying you, thinking you'd be good with your muscled legs in bed, and you are. Not that I'm swearing undying love or anything like that, that's not for us, I think. Though I'm not just as sure of that as I was.'

She leant over and kissed him quite unaffectedly and he once more felt the desolation of impending parting.

'How do you see us then?'

'There's a while yet for us perhaps? I'll be moving into Aunt Marion's house at Barnes — she's Lucy's sister — at the end of the month. I know and you know that I'll meet young men in the airline job if I get it.'

'You'll get it,' said Calderwood with an oddly proprietorial pride. 'You're good-looking, sexy, and know your own mind.' He managed a real smile. 'You were even becoming quite a passable secretary by the end of the season.'

'Oh, sir, you do me too much honour. How can I ever repay you?'

He did his best to show her.

* * *

In the day and a half that remained to them, Bob and Enid attained an amity, a companionship, which had till now been lacking. There were one or two hiccups. On the Sunday night he suggested that they go to a concert at the Albert Hall. Enid agreed without enormous enthusiasm and showed herself reasonably interested in the young audience, but by the interval had plainly had enough. She sulked her way through the 'Peer Gynt Suite' which followed and Calderwood, reading the signs, whipped her off as the percussion were limbering up for the '1812 Overture'.

Her mood did not survive a quick visit to the Brasserie in Old Brompton Road and a stroll through the warm, lilac-scented back streets. They made love again tempestuously, experimentally, successfully.

Monday progressed from breakfast to early evening without visible staging posts, like a speeded-up film. Shortly after seven they were walking across Holborn Viaduct in a sunlit aureole when Bob seized Enid's hands and led her down a steep flight of stairs to the street below. Past the decrepit offices of fur companies they went, past the little sandwich bars, which for another twelve hours would be shuttered and empty. As they neared Ludgate Circus he turned up a lane to the left and after a few baffling swerves, stopped before Mother Bunch's, a wine bar set in a series of arches.

'I've ordered dinner here,' Calderwood said. 'It's almost my favourite place in London. I hope you'll like it too.'

Enid, initially slightly mistrustful of the unadorned exterior and, once inside, of the floor dusted with sawdust and the barrels which did duty as tables, soon came to share his enthusiasm. She drew his attention to the cobwebby bottles of port, to the chalked notices recommending not only dishes but those wines which could be bought and carried off.

Like most women, the passing show was the great attraction

166

for her, and she found herself comparing her lover very favour-
ably with the tall braying City youths who obviously had some
sort of office party going. There appeared to be an upmarket
trade union rule which prohibited them from appearing in
public wearing a shirt and collar of the same colour.

She looked at Bob, as he studied the wall menu, frowning
slightly, brown eyes earnest, hair curling. A man among boys,
for all that some of the boys looked reasonably attractive. If only
they would stop yapping about coffee futures and rumoured
takeovers.

The waitress suddenly appeared at their table, carrying two
large goblets, filled.

'What's this?' Enid asked.

'Try it,' It was Calderwood at his most abrupt. 'Do you like
it?'

'Yes indeed. What is it?'

They drank Buck's Fizz. 'Champagne and pure orange juice.
I like it. They tell me it's good for hangovers.'

'Don't you know?'

'No, I've never had a hangover. Can't afford one when your
body's your fortune.'

'As the actress said to the bishop. I'll have the smoked
mackerel and the ham.'

'Me too.'

They ordered accordingly and Enid was unsparing in her
praise of the food. Calderwood was gratified in the quiet,
relieved way of a man who has praised a restaurant to his girl
and seen his faith justified.

'I'm surprised at the kind of London you know,' Enid said,
dissecting her mackerel dexterously.

He looked at her in mock exasperation. 'Here we go again,
folks, it's stereotype time. You'd expect me to know Euston, a
few caffs, Piccadilly Circus, three boozers and the Tube
stations to Wembley.'

'I can't deny it.'

'Look, Enid, there's no factory out the Great West Road
where they make football managers. Denis Valentine in the
Southern League was the most knowledgeable man on classical
music I've ever met. Ivan the Terrible, up over the Pennines,

on the other hand, has compressed English to a working vocabulary of two words, the second of which is 'off'.'

Behind them, a spindly young man whose rugged individualism took the form of a blue collar on a white shirt was trumpeting that if one had never seen *The Ring* at the Festspielhaus, one was in no position at all to discuss Wagner. He then proceeded to intrigue his tablemates, who included two outstandingly pretty girls, with an answer, '9W', to which they had to find the question.

Bob could not resist a little showing-off to Enid who, in common with everyone else at Mother Bunch's, had heard the answer.

'It's "Do you spell your name with a V, Herr Wagner?" '

And so it proved. It took just a little explaining to Enid.

'How did you know that?'

'I was a great John F. Kennedy fan. It's a game the brothers played. Joan used to say it must all have got a bit much. I'm coming round to thinking she was right.'

They made a long, leisurely meal, and decided against theatre, concert or night club, a little surprised at the increasing ease with which they could talk one to the other. With a brief stop at the Running Footman in Mayfair, they walked all the way back to the hotel.

Towards midnight, Enid raised herself on her elbow and looked at Calderwood.

'We have spent a very high proportion of this weekend in bed,' she said in a reproving tone.

'You are . . . quite excellent in bed, Enid. I want to thank you now, from my heart out. Not in any "You made an old man very happy" way either. I just want to tell you that I have found your body strange and new and wonderful.'

His voice was grave and convinced. The girl felt a little embarrassed by the passion and sincerity of that voice. Very simply she said. 'Thank you' — and after a pause — 'Will you write to me once from the States?'

'If you'd like me to.'

'I would. If I land that job with Delta or Braniff I'll go out there sometime and I'd like to have your impressions.'

Calderwood had the image as she spoke of some bronzed

Californian in a motel throwing the Nile-green folds of Enid's nightdress up above her waist. It was an unnerving glimpse, and he put it aside with some effort.

'Then stand by for mail call. I'll need an address.'

'Write to me care of Aunt Marion at Barnes.' She got out of bed quickly and rummaged in her handbag for a pen. 'Jot it down now, otherwise we'll forget.'

He inscribed it in his diary dutifully. Looking at her standing there, strong, lissome, pliant, it occurred to him that he had the advantage of any notional bronzed Californian, and he laid hands on the Nile-green nightdress. The doubled and re-doubled folds resisted his lifting motion as did Enid, half-laughing but a little wearied.

'You've a long journey tomorrow.' Even at this last, his name was used sparingly by her.

'If I don't sleep tonight, I'll sleep on the plane for the first time ever, maybe. I've put my phone number on that concert programme, you can stick it in your diary if you like.'

He would leave her at the hotel after breakfast and travel to Gatwick on his own. That way it would be a more private and intimate goodbye. He could not for a moment visualise being married to Enid — although he could quite easily envisage not being married to Joan — but if he lost Enid, that was *when* he lost Enid, it would be a sorrow much more profound than he had contemplated.

Their lovemaking that night had a tender, almost elegiac, quality that had not been present before. They were weighed down with thoughts of parting, and physically weary. For a few frightening moments Calderwood feared that he would be unable to deliver. 'A stricken inch was all that you could do.' In the end he managed well; there was a glorious second when capacity vanquished self-doubt, and Enid responded to his caressing probing. Afterwards she turned her face to be kissed and fell asleep almost instantly.

For a while sleep eluded him. Through a chink in the curtains he could see the street light and the leaves of a plane tree stirring slightly and producing a curious scraping sound. From the direction of the river came the siren of a police car or ambulance dying away as it raced southwards. Enid lay sound asleep, her lips occasionally pursing and making little plosive noises, her breasts rising gently on each breath. He smiled in loving recollection as he himself fell asleep.

21

Outside, the early July heat was brutal, but the air-conditioner in the red and green Howard Johnson motel lodge at Milwaukee was chilling Bob Calderwood's room with totally admirable American efficiency. All over the United States, in scores of red and green motor lodges, men and women were thus enabled to snap their fingers at the furnace which masqueraded as the American summer.

Bob had been sitting, propped up uneasily on a double bed, casting a desultory eye on a baseball match which was showing on television. The game had reached the midway point of the seventh innings; the Brewers were out and the Orioles would bat. It was the famous seventh innings stretch, when traditionally the crowd stood up to dissipate the stiffness of two hours' sitting, and the tinny electric organ played 'Take Me Out to the Ballgame'.

He got up, opened the huge leather folder which lay on top of the dressing-table, and from it extracted some red and green motifed writing paper and two matching envelopes. Swivelling the television set round towards his new position, he turned the sound down to eliminate distraction and, after a brief pause, he began to write to Enid.

Dearest Pick of the (Mother) Bunch,
  And *very* lithe too! We're almost at the halfway mark here, Fourth of July tomorrow, so I thought I'd give you something a little better than the brief scribbles and postcards to date. It was grand to hear you on the phone last Sunday, even

if it does mean that you or I have to lose some beauty sleep. Not the first time we've done that, not, I hope, the last.

Do I like it here? Yes. I like their eagerness, their willingness to make a go of things, their hospitality. The last is frightening — I had to fake a headache to get even the early part of this evening to myself.

I'm quite used to the motel now, and though it's lonely at times, it's far from a bad way to live, at least for a while. I've got two double beds (what a waste!) and a bathroom that's like the Taj Mahal with taps. (That's Bob Hope, not me.)

To get back to the beds for a moment. One of them has a vibrator and for twenty-five cents in the slot it will massage you for ten minutes. If you'd come as I suggested, I'd have saved an awful lot of quarters.

The football, to be truthful, is not much better than what we turned on at Barford. I'm in schools a lot in the afternoons. The kids are polite, but fairly neutral. Oddly, the drive in the schools for soccer comes from the parents who think that American football is too dangerous for little Hiram or Luther or Elmer. (They really are called Hiram, Luther and Elmer!)

The razzmatazz at games is unbelievable, all flashing-thighed majorettes, club mascots and organists playing 'Charge!' à la US Cavalry when the home team wins a corner. It's exactly the same at the baseball. When the Brewers score a home run, a chap dressed in Alpine hat and leather shorts slides down a long chute into a gigantic beer barrel.

Writing of baseball made him look towards the television set and he stayed with the match for a few minutes as he watched the second man up for Baltimore hit into a double play to the clear disgust of the Orioles' manager. Two down, one to go. Bob resumed:

The long air trips I could do without and the time-zone changes. Every other game goes into extra time since they'll do anything to avoid drawn matches. They say a drawn match is like kissing your sister. I'm glad you're not my sister.

Glad too that things seem to be working out well so far with Delta. Question. Who is Alan? That's twice you've mentioned him without further description. Unless he's in holy orders I hate him, even if he is, I hate him.

Ask me what I miss. I miss the pubs, I miss the cricket, I miss the warm summer days as opposed to the feeling of walking into a flame-thrower every time I go outside. Milwaukee's a well-doing place, spends a lot of money on things cultural for a beer town, there's a fine symphony hall and a marvellous gallery of modern art.

In case I sound too like a guide-book, let me tell you what I miss most. Your breasts, your thighs, your . . . but I'll already have given Aunt Marion heart failure if by some mischance she should open this letter. I know now that lovers who have to snatch time do live more intensely but those two days in London will never leave me. I'll be home in seven weeks and, although we take it as it comes, I'd like to think that we might be as we have been. I'll be overjoyed should you find time to write before then. I'm going to the Independence Day parade tomorrow and will try to look pleased that they kicked us out two hundred years ago. We leave on the 5th for Houston.

Your legs are majestic.
The Boss

He put the red and green pen down and flexed his stiff and slightly inky fingers. The Orioles had just won by 4 – 2 and their manager was displaying a bonhomie that was even more chilling than his dug-out invective.

He should write to Joan, it had been over a week, and he could have fitted it in on the last road trip. He temporised, wrestled with himself. Going into the bathroom, he picked up the ice-bucket and then a couple of coins which lay on the dressing-table top and made his way out of the room and along the corridor to the soft drinks vending machine. With intent gaze he considered the relative merits of Coca Cola, Fanta, Root Beer and Dr Pepper, and settled on the second of these. Then round another corner to where the ice-maker was purring away happily to scoop three small shovelfuls of the cork-shaped ice into his bucket. Pouring the drink, Bob gulped thirstily and, with what was almost a sigh, began his letter to Joan. The pauses were more frequent, the red and green logo seemed to hypnotise him.

Dear Joan,

I've been trying to get a letter off to you for a few days now, but with the away match (road trip they call it here) with San José, I don't seem to have had a moment.

I was delighted to hear from you and I hope that everything is well at your end. I agree that the offer made by Fraser's pal for double-glazing is attractive, in fact it's suspiciously so. I'd want to check him out a bit, and besides, who is to say how long we'll be able to stay on at Tarkington? Keep him interested till I get back, but don't commit yourself to anything.

I'll be back right at the beginning of September unless we qualify for the national play-offs, which seems unlikely. We're playing well and scoring goals but our defence leaks like a colander. The crowds aren't all that marvellous either. We get about twelve thousand, you might say that's not too bad, but the Brewers get over thirty thousand for their baseball matches. I'm sure the club will be here next season, and I've already been sounded on that, but if Milwaukee don't make the play-offs next year, there won't be a Milwaukee season after that. They'll move the whole shooting-match to Buffalo or Tulsa. Jack Schofield would be in his element out here.

You'd be murdered in the heat. Cotton's the only thing that's bearable or wearable. I went into J. C. Penny's the other day and bought four cotton shirts. My accent slays them. 'Say something, sir,' they ask me. You feel a hell of a fool. They constantly take me for Irish too, which doesn't enchant me greatly.

They're very kind, though you, like me, would find them overpoweringly gushing at first. The girls are beautifully-toothed, scrubbed, gleaming, but for every raver there's a fatty. I don't think I'ver ever seen so many porkers of young women. But then, if you eat mashed potato sandwiches when

173

the temperature's over a hundred, you may well become a porker. Food is very cheap and very good. You can exist very sanely on salads and fruit, which is what I try to do, or go to town on the bacon, sausage, hashed browns and pancakes, short or long stack.

It's a housewife's dream here. The shops really exist to give service. Tomorrow's the great day of the year, Independence Day, and would you believe, there's a Fourth of July Sale in the big stores. The contrast with us at home is frightening — imagine Harrods open on Christmas Day. If you can't or won't sell an article, the guy next door will. Not a country to be sick in though.

I'm not too sure whether football will 'take' here, it's a fifty-fifty thing, I'd say. Artificial turf doesn't help, the heat inevitably makes the game slow, and we don't seem to interest too many blacks. Curtis Eberling, one of my co-coaches, says it's because the blacks have basketball sewn up and in the city ghettoes it's the ideal game, very little space needed, practically no equipment.

I hope Fraser hasn't wrapped the Toyota round anything. Remind him that it's due for its twelve-thousand-mile service this month. You can pass on to him my favourite ad from American television, 'If you're too old for nappy-rash, it's jock itch.' That should go down well at the rugby club.

Clifford's writing for my consent to his engagement to Phyllis seems a completely pointless exercise. Even if so minded, there's little I could do to stop it at four thousand miles' distance. I suppose it'll turn out all right. I've a notion she could do with someone a touch more domineering.

He broke off to take another mouthful of Fanta before turning back to the page.

You can let me know if there is anything you particularly would like me to bring back. It doesn't necessarily have to be cheap but it does have to be light.

Thanks for letting me know about Hereford United. It's a good choice by the League, there's nothing in that Worcester-Hereford area at all. Stalybridge's turn will come,

174

I suppose, but the League certainly have long memories where the North-West is concerned.

He fished for another sheet of paper.

That's about all my news for now, I'll post these . . .

Damn it. He crumpled the sheet and began again.

That's about all my news for now, I'll post this and then go for a swim. After supper I'll visit the motel launderette. I'm becoming a dab hand with the washing machines and can talk with authority on the various soap powders. The American matrons think I'm cute.

Take care of yourself. Make sure that Fraser and Phyllis stay with you as often as possible. Lean on them heavily to do this, especially Fraser. Don't forget to tell him about the service.

I'll be home soon.
Love and best wishes,
Bob

He addressed the two red and green envelopes, inserted the letters and stamped them. Then quickly he cast off his clothes and stepped into his bathing trunks, rather busily patterned in yellow, white and black. As he was leaving the room he had the daunting suspicion that he had put the letters in the wrong envelopes.

Clumsily he tore them open, ripping envelope and stamp alike. Enid's letter was safely destined for Barnes, Joan's for Tarkington. With commingled relief and exasperation he re-addressed the last of the Howard Johnson envelopes and put in the letters with hypersensitive care. He drew a towelling shirt over his head and went out to the motel lobby to buy two new stamps for his far-distant women.

22

Joan had not deliberately lied to her husband when she told him that she did not think Derek would try to repeat his seduction. She had, however, managed to sound much more convinced than she actually was. The first nine weeks of Bob's visit to the States passed without any attempt on Derek's part to take her to bed. By degrees she became half-accustomed to Bob's absence. They phoned each other as arranged, and either Phyllis or Fraser had always been on hand to keep her company at Tarkington.

There came a Friday night in mid-July when, for good and sufficient reason, neither would be at home. Fraser had degree examinations pending, and needed to work at Salford Technical College, and Phyllis was going off to stay with Clifford's family at Harrogate, her first visit in the role of fiancée. The prospect of being alone neither appealed to Joan nor particularly alarmed her. She contemplated asking Jean Ogden to move in with her for the weekend, then with a fierce surge of impatience decided she would manage on her own. Nevertheless, she was more receptive to a request from Derek to work late than she might otherwise have been. Summer was barely under way, but large retail newsagents were already engaged in ordering Christmas stock.

Derek was a joy to work with. Not only were his instructions clear, but he took pains to explain reasons for decisions. The town-centre shop must stock up well with the very large boxes of chocolates, the two-pounders. There would be a ready sale to the young bloods wishing to make an impression on their girls at an early stage of acquaintance — even on the girls' mothers — and to the preoccupied businessmen who had no doubt written a substantial Christmas cheque but wished something tangible to place in their wives' hands.

The Ollerton Road shop was in a poor district, so the emphasis was on small boxes of confectionery, something that grannies could run to for their grandchildren. The Crabble Park shop lay on the fringe of the wealthiest district in Barford.

There was a heavy order here for expensive desk and pocket diaries. It was a shop where the Jewish New Year was also a considerable commercial factor.

The type of shop dictated the range of greetings cards, children's games and paperbacks. Derek was quite willing to give Joan responsibility and to seek her opinion frequently as to the sale potential of various products. They worked hard, uninterrupted, in the back office of the main shop. By nine o'clock they had the Christmas orders licked.

Derek removed his glasses, snapped them shut and returned them to their black leather case. He took off a grey dust-coat and from a hanger took down a blue-black pinstripe jacket. He examined the flower at his buttonhole, decided it had served its purpose, and discarded it. He looked handsome, self-assured, the kind of man who would go from *boulevardier* to old man without any intermediate stage. He helped Joan on with her jacket, a gesture he performed quickly, punctiliously.

'Speaking for myself,' he said, 'I could use a drink to lay the dust. How about you, Joan?'

'I don't think so, Derek, thanks. I'd better get home.'

'Just a quick one. Phyllis can get her own supper for once?'

'She's away. So is Fraser. But I've a lot of things to catch up with in the house.'

'What's the rush? I'm in the same boat, Elsie's away till Sunday. Let's have a bite at the Anchor. I'll have you home by eleven. If you like I'll run you out to make sure everything's OK. Come on, eleven o'clock, I promise you.'

With the inevitability of water flowing downhill she found herself, without quite knowing how, in bed with Derek in his house. She knew that she had in the end made but a token resistance, knew also that this time she had found the loving positively enjoyable. Even in her contented aftermath, little prickles of occasional annoyance invaded her. Derek was almost too pat, his hands had assuredly unhooked many a brassière before, and his enthusiastic preference for suspender belts was manifestly a conclusion arrived at after detailed comparison.

With all that, he was very good. He asked her what she would like, and talked to her caressingly and encouragingly while they did it. She felt sensuous in a way that she did not in her silent couplings with Bob.

'Did you enjoy that, honey?'

The casual endearment did not appeal. Many honeys had been asked that question by Derek in the same tone.

'I did. I prefer to be Joan.'

'Of course.'

She was immediately mollified, conscious of having been perhaps too quick to bridle.

'You pleased me greatly, Derek.'

'You too. You're a splendid lover.'

'And there speaks the voice of experience?'

He laid his index finger on her cheek but his reproof was real enough.

'I like making love to women. Fortunately for society, and me, I like persuading them into bed. I like them while I'm pleasuring them, I like them afterwards.'

'And your wife?' Joan asked.

'A splendid, conventional girl. Once a fortnight would do Evie, right from our tempestuous days of honeymoon at Sidmouth. It's another question boy should ask girl. Not only "Where will we live?" but "How often do you want to do it?" There are enough people who're happy with once a fortnight to make the system work. Did you and Bob have any problems in that direction?'

She shook her head. 'No, and I'm not just being the loyal wife.'

She looked down at their twined, naked bodies, and said again with wry emphasis, 'I'm not just being the loyal wife. We were very adequate, but the earth didn't move for me and I don't suppose the stars fell for him.'

'How would he take it if he knew about us?'

Her hesitation was fractional. 'He does know.'

There was the merest tensing of his body though his face remained unaltered.

'He does know?'

'Since the very first time.'

'I have to point out that this is only the second time.'

She flushed unhappily. 'It was very bad luck really. I'd told

178

him I was going to visit a friend. He met her by chance a day or two later. She realised something was up and tried to cover but our stories didn't tally.'

'I see. What does he propose to do? Why didn't you deny it? He can't have had any positive proof.'

'I was taken aback when he taxed me straight out.' With a tinge of bitterness, 'I'd never done it before so I don't have your experience. I think one or two people had warned him about you beforehand.'

He smiled uncertainly at her. 'I'm not blaming you, Joan.' He caressed her breasts and thighs. She wished herself out of the situation at the same time as she hoped he would continue.

'What do you think he'll do?'

'I don't know. He was angry at the time, naturally. Since then he's taken it very calmly. He made a few digs at me about how my cribbage was coming along — I'd told him I was playing crib with my friend's mother.'

'No wonder he had the antennae out,' Naughton said ruefully. 'We've got to think here, Joan. Has he talked about divorce? Does he mention it in his letters?'

'He hasn't said or written a word about it since he went to Milwaukee. What's the usual pattern in these affairs? Surely you know?'

'I don't know. Almost all my ladies have been maidens, technically anyway, or widows. To be candid, I had a run-in with a husband once, but we were able to come to an arrangement.'

He lit a cigarette, lit another for her from it. They sat up in the last shafts of the evening light. He spoke as if trying to work out a problem in his own mind.

'What I don't see is why he should be taking this so calmly. Would you describe him as a proud man, Joan?'

'Very much so. Principled to the point of stubborn.'

'Hmm. So would I. I've been around the Jubilee Park boardroom several times in the past two years. He's been unfailingly polite to the Board but he's very much his own man. I'd have thought he'd have thrown the book at us.'

'He may not think I'm worth bothering about. He may be thinking of the children.'

'Hmm,' said Naughton again. 'But he's the totally innocent party — your children aren't toddlers. In normal times he would have got a few dressing-room sniggers but if he stays in football he's going to have to shift anyway.' He looked at her almost apologetically. 'Has he a girl somewhere?'

'No, at least, I don't know of any. He's never been a ladies' man in that sense.'

'That's what disturbs me. A ladies' man would be much more likely to take a tolerant view. I feel someone like Bob ought to react strongly to a situation where another man has had his wife's skirt off and her pants down. I think he'd see it as basically as that. And if he doesn't see it that way, I just wonder why. But you think there's no girl.'

'No.'

'None of your girlfriends he's ever taken a special interest in?'

'He'll make the occasional flirtatious joke with them, and under great social pressure, give them a duty dance. He'll give *me* a duty dance under great social pressure. You saw yourself at the staff dance what he's like.'

Naughton was not disposed to let it go. 'He's a virile, attractive, youthful-looking man.'

'I know. It used to bother me when we were first married. There are camp followers even at Third Division level, and I could have seen it being a real problem if he'd gone to Arsenal as he hoped.'

Derek was like a dog worrying a bone. 'Somebody younger then. A friend of Phyllis?'

'That's insulting.'

'I don't mean it to be.' A thought struck him. 'How about his secretary, young Enid Schofield? She's a highly attractive lass.'

'He describes girls like Enid as jail bait.'

'A way of getting back at her uncle perhaps, if she were willing? No, don't get angry, Joan, if we get this one wrong we're all over the papers.'

She was angry and at the same time she saw the logic of his position. Thoughtfully she said, 'He could come to divorce another way.'

'How do you mean?'

180

'He wants to stay in football. If he'd taken the Brandon job in Scotland I'd told him I wouldn't go with him. If he got a job in Plymouth I wouldn't go there either, not if it was in football.'

'Constructive desertion, eh?'

Joan shrugged.

'Do you hate the game that much?'

'Yes. I've given it a fair try — twenty years of it entitles me to speak my piece. I've seen an able man devote his mind and energies, considerable both of them, to what's at best a pastime.'

'Would that apply to any job in football?'

'I've been thinking about that. If he got a job which meant I could stay on here, with my friends, with my job, I might agree to it, out of inertia mostly.'

Something she said made him glance sharply at her. 'If he knows, he couldn't possibly tolerate your continuing to work for me.'

'If that was the condition of taking a local job in football, he might. Of course, I'd have to tell him that you and I were finished. And I would have to mean it. Could you work with me under those arrangements?' She laughed without any trace of bitterness. 'I imagine you could, Derek. Self-preservation's an important part of your make-up. And you've made me, haven't you?'

He took her rebuke in good part. 'If I didn't know you were a virtuous wife, I'd swear you'd been doing this all your days. If that's the way it works out, I'll mean it too. You've got a real grasp of the retail side of the business. We could arrange it so that you didn't see me much on a day-to-day basis. You'd be ideal to run Crabble Park.'

She sighed. 'I'll have to talk it out, to get *him* to talk it out when he comes home.'

'Which is?'

'In about two months' time.' She looked at the darkening sky. 'I must get dressed now.'

'Not yet.'

Joan attempted to rise but he pressed her gently back on the pillows.

'Let me up, Derek.'

He bent to kiss her and his hand strayed to the inside of her thigh. There was an involuntary flicker of interest in the blue eyes beneath the auburn hair.

'Let me up, Derek,' with marginally less force.

He kissed her breasts with calm assurance. Joan, knowing he had done this self-same thing scores of times, stirred with delight as his lips brushed her nipples.

'Joan, when you have the chance with a woman, and you like her, and you're good with her, and it's your last chance . . .'

She drew him down to her quickly. Afterwards they dressed lingeringly, breaking off now and then to take leave of each other's body. Derek insisted on driving her all the way out to Tarkington, telling her that she could leave the Mini where it lay in the overnight car park. He came in with her while she checked out the house and then left without making any suggestion to stay. Already they were distancing themselves slightly. On the way out, he bent to hand her the morning's post which had fallen behind the storm door.

She did not watch him go but locked and bolted the heavy wooden doors and went into the kitchen to make herself a cup of coffee. She watched the saucepan of milk carefully then carried it to the table, poured it into the coffee cup, and looked listlessly at the mail. There were a couple of bills, three congratulations cards for Phyllis by the look of them, and a US airmail letter from Bob. She finished her coffee and went upstairs to the double bed, leaving Bob's news to await a morning reading.

23

It seemed to Joan that she had no sooner read Bob's letter than her husband was home. He looked tanned and relaxed, for he had broken his journey for a night in London on the way back. A duty-free plastic bag stood on the kitchen cupboard top, two large packages of cigarettes lay on the kitchen table. The clothes-basket was filled to overflowing with his shirts and underwear. It was late Sunday afternoon. Phyllis and Fraser, having greeted their returned parent, had gone out on their own social occasions, Fraser anxious to squeeze the last hours from his lease of the Toyota.

Joan and he had given each other the snippets of news they had — it was more a case of Bob catching up with what had been going on in his absence. He learned that the supermarket lobby had won the day over housing and a bus station for the Jubilee Park site. A bad decision for the town, he thought, short-term gain as against the lasting advantage which a housing development would have brought.

Phil Gifford, surprisingly, was on an extended trial with Crystal Palace. Calderwood promised himself he'd think seriously of abandoning managership if Gifford made it. He flicked through the mail which had gathered for him during his absence and which had been re-directed to his home from the ground. He opened a couple of letters and groaned. Each of the writers wanted him to supply a précis of the club's history, together with his own thoughts on its disappearance. From the look of the mail there would be about four or five similar requests lurking amid the heap. He resolved to send all such enquiries to the club secretary, Leonard Steele, who would have a few months' winding-up work in prospect anyway.

He had given Joan her major present, a rather expensive silver and turquoise brooch, which he had bought in San José. Her reception of it told him that she was genuinely pleased by his thoughtfulness, and that she didn't really like it. The book on American vintage cars for Fraser had been a more inspired choice.

He had looked quickly at the Sunday papers, adjusting to the staider prose of the sportswriter on this side of the Atlantic. He was interested to see that the new boys, Hereford, had won two and drawn one of their four games. A good start for them, he thought admiringly. When promoted from non-League Football, or even within the League for that matter, it was crucial for the promoted club to win an early match, to give the players the knowledge and the confidence that the bigger boys could be beaten.

Four hours had elapsed since his return to Barford. He was well and truly home, but all conversation between Joan and himself had been pleasantries and polite enquiries. Having satisfied herself that he was neither physically tired nor mentally jet-lagged, his wife decided that perhaps it was time to get down to cases.

She sat down at the unvarnished kitchen table and invited Bob to do the same, sweeping aside the cigarette cartons that reared like a rampart between them.

'I think it's high time we talked, Bob.'

'What about?'

'About us. About where you're going, where I'm going, whether it's the same road.'

'I see.' His tone was placid, unhelpful.

She pushed on. 'Let's try to talk it over calmly, try not to score points, just consider where we are in our marriage.'

'A marital balance-sheet?'

'No. But there's your job and mine. I want to make my feelings about your staying in football perfectly plain.'

'You've scarcely wrapped them up at any time.'

She shook her head doggedly. 'I want to try to convince you that I'm largely thinking of you in this. Suppose you got another job in management tomorrow. You'd be back immediately in the world of glib catch-phrases, treacherous directors, problem players, intrusive reporters. Wherever you go, you'll fail in the long term. You're bound to.'

He thought for a moment before replying. He would keep the exchanges low-key if he could.

'Everything you've said is true. What you can't know are the joys of the job. You practise a set-piece all week in training, a free-kick or a corner-kick. On the Saturday it works perfectly and you score. Or you win against great odds, or you spot a rare talent in some public parks match.'

'And that makes up for a bunch of foul-mouthed yobs shouting abuse at every home match?'

'It helps. If we say football's a business then perhaps the customer *is* always right.'

He fiddled with the cigarette cartons. 'I'll tell you something

184

else too. It's one of the last jobs in this country where you can actually control men, make them do as you see best.'

'Like Les Frith?'

'I greased the stairs for Leslie quickly enough.'

'We're not short of reasons for splitting up, Bob. There's the matter of Derek. I'm an unfaithful wife.'

There was a time when the melodramatic phrase would have made Bob laugh. Now he registered it as a slightly prim statement of fact. She looked directly at him, cheeks burning.

'While you were away we lovers again. Once. It's totally over now, and I don't expect you to believe me. Why should you?'

'Because we've been married twenty-two years and I find you basically an honest person.'

He was attempting, none too successfully, to build a pyramid with the cartons. Giving the project exaggerated attention, he said to the table: 'Since we're into honesty, I can't let you go on thinking that you're the only adulterer in the family.'

She looked at him in an intense silence. From the garden next door a lawn-mower rattled faintly.

He looked up from his fidgeting. 'It's true, I assure you. I'm not nobly inventing some mythical woman to make you feel easier.'

'Who is she? It would be in America?'

'No. Right here. Enid.'

There was no expression of opinion, just a one-syllable question.

'When?'

'On and off since February.'

'February?' Her face took on the shape it would have permanently in her fifties. 'You allowed me to tell you about Derek and me and all that time . . .'

'I found out about Derek and you,' he reminded her.

'How could you do that? How could you live with yourself?'

'I was on the point of telling you after you confessed about Derek. You needn't believe it, but it's true. There was one moment when it would have been very easy. That moment went, and I found it impossible afterwards.'

'I would have said you'd more courage than that.'

'So would I.'

185

They sat for several minutes, saying nothing. Joan at length broke the silence with a dry laugh.

'Derek suspected it, you and Enid, and I laughed it off.'

'What put that into his head? Did he see us? We were very careful.'

'Isn't the word discreet?' She caught herself. 'Good God, what right have I to talk? Is it over?'

'I'll tell you the absolute truth. It's weakening perhaps, not over. I saw Enid in London last night.'

'I see. Then how do you mean it's weakening?'

'There's another chap around. He's younger, he's there. He'll win.'

'Will you be sorry?'

'Yes. Being a bit ashamed doesn't stop me being sorry. I tell you this because I don't want to hold anything back from you. I had great pleasure in our lovemaking. She encouraged me to believe I was a good lover and perhaps because she gave me that belief, I was a little better than I have been before. I say that not to hurt, I'm very conscious that I've been clumsy with you.'

'That's not for you to say,' Joan said jerkily. 'Perhaps I wasn't so marvellous. And, curiously, I know what you mean about a change of bedmate. I came to enjoy the different body. Derek was good in areas where you've never chosen to compete — the dancing, the squiring, the off-colour jokes.'

He looked at her for opinion and guidance. 'Well, where do we go from here?'

'One answer would be that two negatives make a positive and we should just get on with it. We've lied to each other, although I'm bound to say you lied longer and better. And possibly laid longer and better.'

The unexpected flash from Joan struck home.

'If we write off Derek and Enid, can we go on? Should we go on?'

'I'm not sure, from what you say, that you've written Enid off. I think she could get you back into her bed if she wanted. Derek thought you'd taken up with her to get back at Schofield.'

He reacted furiously. 'We don't all see women as collectors' pieces or revenge symbols. Whatever else you choose to believe,

186

I swear that thought never entered my head. I liked Enid, I still like her.'

'I believe you,' Joan said. 'The date doesn't fit Derek's theory.'

'What the hell was he theorising for anyway?'

'I told him you'd found out about him and me. He was wondering why you hadn't reacted more violently.'

'I didn't know what I wanted to do. And I wasn't exactly Sir Galahad myself.'

With the suggestion of a smile Joan said, 'Well, I suppose I should be grateful it's one mistress and not the three you claimed at the time.' She looked quite fondly at him. 'Twenty-two years is a very large investment of one's life. Marriage is perhaps about the dull things, keeping the house repaired, seeing the children mature.'

'We've done that anyhow,' grunted Bob. 'They don't need us any more.'

'I doubt it. It's a phase. Fraser clearly respects you even at his stroppiest. Did you behave like a paragon to your father at that age? Besides, I'd like to see them through to the grandchildren stage. Any words I use sound trite and *Woman's Own* — maybe the great truths are *Woman's Own*. Marriage is the bread, Bob, the other is the cake.'

' "Let them eat cake." '

She looked at him levelly. 'That's for you to decide. Along with other things, like what then happens to the house, how much do we tell Fraser and Phyllis. If you believe it's worth making any attempt at all to save us, I have a proposal.'

'Let's hear it then.'

'It's a trade-off, really. I'm prepared to let you have another go at managership, and stay with you to see if things work out, on two conditions.'

'Those being?'

'That you get a job in football which allows you to stay here.'

'That rules out about two-thirds of the Football League.'

'That leaves thirty clubs within a thirty-mile radius. Coach, assistant manager, even general manager, you've a fair choice. You'd make a good general manager.'

'Sure I would, but you gravitate to that from team manager.

I've about three years left here when I'm credible as a track-suit manager, maybe twice that in the States. I'm not sure, Joan. I wouldn't reject it out of hand. I've got over a year's salary for the unexpired portion of my contract and I can almost certainly earn a few thousand pounds in the States again next summer. What's the other "condition"?'

'That I carry on working at Naughton's.'

He blew up. 'Why don't I just give up football altogether and become a professional pimp? It would give you more variety as well.'

'Derek and I are finished. I could work for him perfectly safely. And I wouldn't be working with him every day. He wants me to take over the Crabble Park shop.'

'For services rendered,' sneered her husband.

'I'll remind you that it's one-all in the Infidelity Cup. Derek's not that sentimental. He knows I'll run the shop well. If he didn't he'd fire me. I'll tell you again, he's a collector, you're quite right about that, and I've been collected. He also has a very strong streak of caution. He realises how lucky he has been not to have been splattered across the papers.'

She lit a cigarette and blew smoke out noisily. 'We've been lucky too, for that matter, Bob. We can pretend to be as hard-boiled as we like, but we'd have hated to have to explain *that* to the children. They think they're sophisticated to a degree, but they're not. For all Fraser's ruderies to me — and he's quite filthy sometimes — he and Phyllis can't really imagine you on top of me, and still less us doing it with other people.'

Joan shrugged. 'It's a decision for you to make, you could give London and Enid a go. She might not have you at all, you might move in with her and find you were back in a bread situation again. Or it might work, you're an attractive man.'

He had paid little attention to the Enid scenario. 'I can't possibly let you go back to Naughton's. He'd have you on your back and your legs in the air in five minutes.'

'We really are earning golden opinions today,' Joan said coldly. 'Derek's a persuader, not a rapist. He doesn't persevere in the face of determined opposition. He's not sufficiently involved.'

She stirred from the table. 'I'm thirsty with all that talking. Do you want a coffee?'

'No. I'll have tea if you don't mind. It's one of the few things they don't do too well over there.'

She brought the mugs to the table, plonked them down and sat opposite Bob, her blue eyes regarding him coolly.

'You needn't worry about Derek and me. Though I'd take the point that, having strayed once, you and I might find it enticing again. Was there a moment in which you were surprised you'd been faithful so long?'

He nodded, sipping his tea.

'Me too. We'll maybe have to work harder in bed together. Perhaps what has happened might help us. I don't know.'

He sought to press home an apparent advantage. 'Look, Joan, if marriage is the bread, as you say, shouldn't you follow the argument to its logical conclusion and follow me and the job?'

Her headshake was totally dismissive. 'Absolutely not. I'm a fool for even being prepared to go along with it as far as I am. I want my home, my job, my friends. Are you willing to try for the job you want to do, but in this area, and see if we can salvage anything? It's my best offer, Bob, I advise you to take it. It might not work, but it seems to me the best that's in prospect.'

The ringing of the phone seemed unusually disturbing and loud. Joan answered it and he saw her lips purse slightly. Wordlessly she handed the receiver to him.

It was the manager of a First Division London club. He had read in the morning papers that Bob had returned from Milwaukee. He had always regarded him as a good judge of a player, and had asked his own chairman for permission to approach Bob to act as scout in the Lancashire-West Yorkshire area. They'd want him to concentrate on promising players in the lower divisions of the Football League. They already had someone checking out schools and minor football.

Bob scribbled the salient facts on the message-pad for Joan while the far-off manager talked. The latter realised that Bob would want to return to managership some day, but meantime this would be a useful way of keeping in touch with the game. The retainer suggested was generous, and there would be help

189

with a car. His present house at Tarkington would make an admirable base for the post in question, but they would like him to come to London on Tuesday for a general discussion on club strategy.

Joan nodded, well content, and went back to the kitchen. Calderwood thought hard as he tied up travel arrangements and thanked the manager for his offer. From experience he knew that he could negotiate a short period of notice if a management job cropped up. It occurred to him that he would go to see Enid and tell her of developments. It would be less than honourable to drop the girl altogether at this stage.

And another managerial post would certainly crop up, perhaps even within Joan's stipulated radius. It was difficult to get a horse on the *Magic Roundabout*, and once astride it, you fell off quite frequently. With experience, however, you learned to stand at the side of the *Magic Roundabout*, and sooner or later a riderless horse would come along.